Skating Around
The Law

Skating Around The Law

Joelle Charbonneau

Minotaur Books

A Thomas Dunne Book · New York

This is a work of fiction. All of the characters, organizations, and events
portrayed in this novel are either products of the author's
imagination or are used fictitiously.

A THOMAS DUNNE BOOK FOR MINOTAUR BOOKS.
An imprint of St. Martin's Publishing Group.

www.thomasdunnebooks.com
www.minotaurbooks.com

Library of Congress Cataloging-in-Publication Data

Charbonneau, Joelle.
    Skating around the law : a mystery / Joelle Charbonneau.—1st ed.
    p. cm.
    ISBN 978-0-312-62980-9
    1. Roller-skating rinks—Fiction.   2. Murder—Investigation—
Fiction.   I. Title.
    PS3603.H3763S53 2010
    813'.6—dc22
                                                    2010027140

First Edition: October 2010

10 9 8 7 6 5 4 3 2 1

For *Andy*—my biggest cheerleader;
and for *Mom*—my biggest inspiration

Acknowledgments

Writing a book is like being in a play—a huge crew of people is required to help bring the book to life.

First, I have to thank my family. Especially my husband, Andy, who has read every word I've written and still encourages me to write more. My mother, Jaci, who taught me how to skate and has always cheered me on. My son, Max, who laughs at me even when I'm not trying to be funny, and my father, who taught me the importance of never taking no for an answer.

I owe countless thanks to my incomparable agent, Stacia Decker, for championing me and my work. You have no idea how grateful I am to be a member of Team Decker. Also, thank you to my wonderful editor, Toni Plummer, for making this book shine. Special thanks to my publisher and publishing team. You're all a class act.

Much thanks is owed to my writer colleagues. First, a huge thank you to Susan Elizabeth Phillips, who has always given me great career advice including "Join RWA." To the writers of

Chicago-North—you are an amazing group of teachers. To Maureen Lang, Deb Gross, and Nancy J. Parra—I don't know what I would do without you. To the members of Team Decker—you guys rock!

Last, to all the booksellers, librarians, and readers who pick up this book—thank you from the bottom of my heart.

Skating Around
The Law

One

Falling on my ass really hurts. My mother told me that after taking my first steps I fell smack on my butt. Well, I've been whacking my backside on the floor ever since, both figuratively and literally. Today, I did it surrounded by a bunch of five-year-olds.

A little girl with big brown eyes and a purple stain on her overalls leaned over me. She pulled her thumb out of her mouth. "Rebecca, you gonna be okay?"

Trying to maintain a little dignity, I struggled up to my elbows and smiled at the tiny faces peering down at me. The whole scene had me feeling a little like Gulliver surrounded by Lilliputians.

One Lilliputian's eyes filled with sympathetic tears. I plastered a fake smile on my face and said, "I'll be fine." Or I would be if no one started crying. I love kids, but my ability to console a hysterical child from the middle of the roller rink floor seemed chancy at best.

"That looked like it hurt *a lot*." This from an angelic-looking boy.

"It doesn't hurt at all," I lied, struggling back up onto my roller skates. Once all five foot six of me was right side up I gave a triumphant smile. I then looked down at my class of kids wondering what I was supposed to teach them next.

A masculine voice over the loudspeaker took pity on me. "All students come over to the blue wall. We're going to end today's classes with the Hokey Pokey."

The kids lost interest in my pratfall. They skated over to the far wall painted Crayola blue as music started blaring from the sound system. Once their happy faces were gone, I rubbed my stinging backside and rolled across the floor to the sidelines.

"You should probably brush up on your skating before teaching the next class." My grandfather's voice reached over my shoulder. I turned, and he smiled at me. The smile was kind even if it was a little scary. Pop had forgotten to put in his partial. "The kids lose respect for a teacher who spends more time on the ground than on her feet."

"It's a good thing I'm not their teacher," I replied. "I was just filling in while George took a phone call."

Pop gave me a stern look. "Rebecca Robbins, your mother taught classes every Saturday until she died. It wouldn't hurt for you to follow in her footsteps."

My mother was one of the most graceful people I ever met in my thirty years on this earth. She successfully taught hundreds of kids how to spin, jump, and roll. I was her one colossal failure.

"She was a professional roller skater, Pop. I'm not."

He wagged his finger at me. "Your mother said you would

have been great if you had applied yourself. Instead you ran off to the city to do God-knows-what at that office."

"I'm a mortgage broker, not a prostitute," I said. Although some days the idea of streetwalking seemed preferable. Xeroxing documents and having people sign on the dotted line didn't put me in the fast lane to success. Besides which, my boss had recently started showing a personal interest in me. An interest I didn't share. Still, the job paid well enough, and it wasn't Indian Falls. The last part mattered most.

"You're a roller rink owner now. It's time you took some pride in this place. Your mother dedicated her life to making the Toe Stop an important part of the community. People around here count on this rink."

"I know, Pop." His words made my stomach go squishy with guilt. "But I have a job and a life in Chicago. I can't keep the roller rink running from a hundred and seventy miles away."

This earned me a harrumph. My grandfather hitched up his bright red pants. "You could run this place if you wanted to. I did it out of love for your mother after she died, but my doctor says I can't anymore. A year was my limit. Besides, I'm too old to be running a business. Think of my blood pressure."

As far as I knew, Pop's blood pressure readings were better than mine. Still, hearing him talk about his health scared me, so I changed the subject. "You're not too old to have several different 'lady friends,'" I teased. "At least three different women introduced themselves to me as your significant other." I wondered what the doctor would say about that.

Pop shrugged. "I've been taking a few out for a test drive." Pop shook his head and scolded, "Don't look at me like that. Your grandmother passed years ago. I'd say it's about time I started dating again. You don't want me to live the rest of my life alone, do you?"

"Of course not, Pop," I said. My grandfather deserved to be happy. Problem was, I found it embarrassing to have a grandfather with a more active social life than mine.

"Rebecca, I want you to think about what you're doing here." Pop gave the rink a wistful look and ran his hand through his bushy white hair. "This place is special. Once you get rid of it you'll never get it back."

Pop shuffled toward the door and into the May sunshine, leaving me on the sidelines alone. I listened to the song as it asked people to "put your whole self in." As far as I was concerned, my whole body was already in, and I really wanted out. Since my dad ditched us two decades ago, my only dream was to get away from Indian Falls, Illinois.

And I had.

I headed for the office and closed the door. My mother's face smiled at me from a frame on the scarred wooden desk. The picture had been taken about twenty-five years ago. Mom's brown hair was pulled into a ponytail. She wore a short blue skating skirt, and her fingers were holding a wide-eyed little girl's hand. The little girl had red corkscrew curls and freckles and was wearing skates and a big smile.

The little girl was me. Since I was nine, life had been just like that picture—Mom and me—with Pop and Grandma looking on with a smile. Last year I was shocked when a heart attack took Mom. Now, as much as it hurt, I was skating solo.

Sighing, I sank into the rickety chair and flipped on the computer. There were bills to pay, receipts to keep track of, and pay-

4

checks to write. Those things I understood. It was the blaring music coming under my door, the pull of Indian Falls and this roller rink, that I didn't get.

Kids got it.

My grandfather preached about it.

My mother loved it.

I looked down at the desk calendar with today's date circled in red. "Meet Doreen the Realtor at two."

I was going to sell it.

"I know it's my job, but I just hate the thought of selling this place." Doreen's eyes blinked at me from behind her rhinestone-encrusted black-framed glasses. "My kids loved learning to skate here. My granddaughter, Brittany, skates here now. She's right over there."

My eyes followed Doreen's red-tipped finger to where it pointed out a teenaged girl dressed in low-rider black jeans, a very tight black shirt, and heavy black eyeliner. Too bad the tan rental skates kind of ruined the great goth look Brittany had going.

Doreen gave a little finger wave. The girl glared back, eliciting a small "tsk" from her grandmother. "I can't imagine what'll happen to the kids in this town if this place closes. Where will they go? Your mother understood how important the Toe Stop was to the community."

Translation: I was a complete schmuck for not caring. I did, but I wasn't about to stay here.

"You know what the rink looks like," I said. I gestured to the side door. "Why don't we start the tour upstairs in the apartment?"

Doreen nodded her permed, champagne-colored head. She

trailed behind me, chattering all the way. "The rink is in great shape—new floors, new carpet, fresh paint. Anyone can see that. My granddaughter raves about the new sound system. All those renovations must have cost your mother a fortune."

Yep. The checks I'd been writing to cover the loan she'd taken out proved it.

We reached the top of the stairs, and I fiddled with my key ring, trying to find the right key.

"It's too bad your mother didn't live long enough to enjoy the benefits of that investment. I don't think her death will hurt the sale of this place, but you never know. Once we hold the open house, we'll get a better handle on how quickly we can get a sale."

The keys fell from my fingers. Doreen adjusted her sparkly glasses and peered at me. "Are you okay, dear?"

"I'm fine." Maybe. I grabbed the keys. Quickly, I flipped through to find the one for this door. "What did you mean when you said my mom's death could hurt the sale of the rink?"

Doreen twittered. "Sometimes people feel a little squeamish investing money in a place where someone died. You know"— her voice got low and whispery—"because it could be haunted or cursed."

Cursed? My body shivered as one of the keys slid into the lock. A turn of the handle and the door swung open.

Any ghost in here? I thought. Mom?

I flipped on the light. Nope, no ghosts. Just some furniture and a lot of dust. Otherwise everything was the same.

That fact shouldn't have surprised me. I hadn't stepped foot in the apartment since Mom died. Pop took care of packing up designated items in the will and stuff for charity. I just couldn't do it.

Doreen wandered around the expansive combination living and dining room, nodding with approval. The room ran the width of the roller rink. A large, recently updated kitchen was to our right. Bedrooms were down on the other end. The apartment even had a window that overlooked the rink floor. When I was a kid, my mother used to shout instructions to me as I stumbled around on my skates.

"How many bedrooms did you say there were?"

I wrung my hands together and shot a look toward the stairs. I couldn't stay here much longer. Not without losing it.

"Three," I answered. Mine, Mom's, and the obligatory guest room. I hadn't used my bedroom much since I'd left for the city eight years ago.

"And only one bathroom?"

If you didn't count the ten stalls just down the stairs.

"Is that a problem?" I asked.

Doreen shrugged. "You never know about these things. You should probably have someone come fix things up a bit before we start showing the property. I noticed a couple of places where the paint was chipped, and a new knob and lock on the front door would be a good idea. I thought I saw Mack Murphy downstairs with his tools. He could do it for you. Just make sure you don't pay him until he's finished."

"Mack always did good work for Mom." He had been nice to me while I was growing up, too. That combination made me leap to his defense.

Doreen gave a fierce frown. "Mack's changed. You'll have to take my word on it, and I'll leave it at that."

I let Doreen wander around the apartment alone. Ten minutes later, I was relieved to head back downstairs.

Hip-hop music assaulted us the minute we stepped back into the rink. A couple of dozen kids were racing around the wooden floor in a circle while strobe lights flashed from the ceiling. It was just one big dance party hosted by yours truly.

I took a step toward the refreshment stand and felt a tug on my arm. It was Doreen's granddaughter. She wasn't wearing the angry scowl. In fact, she looked kind of freaked.

"Is something wrong, Brittany?"

Brittany's black-lined eyes shifted toward the bathrooms behind us. "I think someone is sick or something in the girls' bathroom."

I rolled my eyes. Of course someone was sick. Eating junk food and then racing around in a circle was enough to make any hyperactive kid puke.

"Okay." I gave the girl a smile. "I'll go take a look."

I dodged a few kids zooming toward the refreshment area and pushed the girls' bathroom door open. Except for the music, everything seemed quiet.

The bathroom smelled of Pine-Sol and hand soap. My nose didn't detect any vomit. Hopeful that Brittany was mistaken, I braced myself for previously chewed pizza and began pushing open the stall doors. Nothing. Next one. Nothing. I reached the handicapped stall. Four down. So far so good.

I gave the door a nudge, peered in, and almost passed out. My knees trembled. My stomach did a triple gainer, and I leaned against the stall door for support. On the stall floor, not moving, was handy Mack. His arms were wrapped around the toilet tank. His head . . . well, I think he put his head in and shook it all about. His face was

8

somewhere below the water level, and he wasn't moving. Both were very bad.

I heard the door swing open behind me. The click of heels was followed by a loud "tsk." Doreen's voice chirped, "Damn, Rebecca. This is going to kill the rink's market value for sure."

Two

"*Oh my God.*" Mack must have slipped and hit his head or something.

Swallowing down my panic, I approached the toilet. With a yank, I pulled Mack's head from the water. His lifeless eyes stared into mine, and I dropped him with a shriek.

Sploosh.

Damn. I couldn't leave him like that. I took a step back toward the body.

"Is he okay?"

I turned toward Brittany's frightened voice. I was surprised to find she'd come into the bathroom.

Swallowing hard, I shook my head. "He's not breathing."

"Maybe you should give him mouth-to-mouth," Doreen suggested.

Brittany's white face looked at me with hope. The three of us turned to look down at Mack.

Okay, I wanted to be heroic. Reviving Mack and saving his

life would be a great thing for me to do. Only I couldn't. He was dead. I was certain of it. Besides, the man had his head in a toilet. That alone sucked all the heroic right out of me. Still, I did what I could and pulled his head back out of the water and rested it gently on the toilet seat. Now he looked more like a man who was paying for a heavy night of drinking than someone who had just gone bobbing for apples and lost.

I stepped in front of the stall door, blocking Brittany's view of Mack's plumber's crack. "I'm sorry," I said to both Brittany and Mack's ghost, just in case he was floating nearby. "There's nothing I can do."

Brittany's lip quivered as tears streaked down her face. That's when her entire body started to shake.

I pulled Brittany and Doreen toward the entrance of the bathroom. "I think the best thing to do is call the sheriff's office. They'll know how to handle this."

Brittany held up her cell phone. "I'll call them." The kid's trembling fingers dialed before I gave the go-ahead. Her voice was firm as she related the problem.

I was impressed. There was more to Brittany than teenaged angst. In fact, her current calm put me to shame. All I'd wanted to do since finding Mack was to throw up and run screaming from the bathroom. Of course, I couldn't. Mack had died in my rink. On my watch. With kids present.

Oh God, I thought. My eyes shifted to the bathroom door. What if the little kids from my class came in here?

Grabbing Doreen's arm, I said, "I need to ask everyone to leave the rink. Could you guard the bathroom door? Make sure no one else wanders in here. I don't want kids to see this."

"You're right," she said with a frown. "Mack's caused

enough trouble in this town. Don't want him to hurt our children, too."

I blinked. Mack was dead. He deserved a little sympathy if not respect. Then again, maybe Doreen was just in shock from seeing a dead body. I knew I was.

Doreen's agreement to play bouncer outside the bathroom door sent me racing into the rink. "Wipe Out" was being pumped through the speakers as I made my way to the sound booth.

Hauling myself into the cramped space, I hit the ON button for the mike and announced that the rink was closed due to "plumbing problems." A couple of kids shot me dirty looks. Otherwise, the mass exodus went smoothly. By the time the ancient Indian Falls sheriff waddled through the door, the rink was almost empty.

Donald Jackson had held the post of sheriff since my mother was a little girl. A favorite town game was "Guess Don's Age." By the leathery quality of his bald head and his steel gray party-favor mustache, I would guess one hundred and four. The correct answer was probably closer to seventy.

Right now he looked bored and annoyed. Probably because I'd interrupted his afternoon nap. I hurried across the rink to meet him.

"Rebecca, some teenager called. She claimed there was a dead body here." He snorted and started coughing.

I resisted the urge to slap him hard on the back. Instead, I pointed toward the girls' bathroom. "He's in there."

"You mean there really is a dead body?"

The sheriff's words echoed through the almost deserted rink. The few kids remaining at the skate rental counter turned to look at us. So much for keeping the situation from them.

"Follow me." I snagged the sheriff's arm and pulled him toward the bathroom.

Brittany and her grandmother hadn't moved from their guard post outside the bathroom door. The sheriff nodded at them as he went in, and Doreen and Brittany followed behind me. I gave Sheriff Jackson a tiny shove toward the back stall and stayed behind. Seeing the body again wasn't necessary for me. The terrible image was already etched firmly into my memory.

"Holy crap! It's Mack!"

Sheriff Jackson had summed up my exact feelings.

"I gotta ring the medical examiner," he muttered as he pulled out his cell phone and dialed.

While the sheriff was occupied, I turned toward Doreen and her granddaughter. Doreen looked fine, but Brittany's face was a strange ashen green color. Brittany needed to get out of here. Now.

"Doreen," I said, "I appreciate your help today. The sheriff is handling things now. Maybe you should take Brittany out of here. Neither one of you needs to see any more of this."

Doreen looked liked she wanted to protest, but my meaningful glance at Brittany followed by a firm glare seemed to settle the issue. With a "tsk," Doreen herded the frightened teen out the door. That left Sheriff Don and me alone to deal with Mack.

The sheriff hung his phone back on his belt. He gave a sad shake of his head. "Doc will be here in a minute. He should look at Mack before we move him."

Then the two of us stood staring at each other. I had no idea what to say, so I waited for the sheriff to start asking questions. Only he didn't. He just stared at me while the faucet went drip, drip, drip in the background. At least I think he was staring at me.

His eyes had a familiar glazed look. It reminded me of the one Mack was wearing when I fished him out of the toilet bowl.

I asked, "Sheriff, do I need to fill out a report or something?"

"Huh?" The sheriff noisily sucked in some air. He blinked and scratched his stomach. "Oh. Oh, sure. I guess we should go over everything before Doc gets here." He pulled a pad of paper out of his back pocket and flipped to the first page. "Tell me what happened."

I walked the sheriff though the events leading to my discovery of Mack's body. Talking about it made my knees weak. When I was done, the sheriff snorted and walked back to look at Mack.

"Rebecca, when you touched the body, did you move anything besides Mack's head?"

"I don't think so." I couldn't say for certain. Not without looking again. Taking a deep breath, I joined the sheriff in the death stall.

I scanned the space, trying to ignore Mack's unblinking eyes. Mack's toolbox was against the side wall, and a plunger was to the right of the toilet. My eyes shifted to the left.

"What's that?" I asked with a frown.

Sheriff Jackson blinked. "What's what?"

"That," I asked, pointing to the farthest corner of the stall. There, half hidden from view by Mack's inert body, was a bottle of prescription pills. "There's a pill bottle back there."

"Sure enough." The sheriff scratched his chin. He leaned closer. "Mack's name's on the bottle. Huh. Maybe this wasn't an accident after all. Tell you what, I think Mack committed suicide."

Sheriff Jackson turned, his chest puffed out, proud of his deductive skills. Call me crazy, but I didn't feel excited. Mack was still dead.

I looked down at my feet, trying to pretend I was somewhere else. Anywhere else. My eyes shifted again to Mack's toolbox, and a stack of stamped envelopes caught my eye. I raised my gaze back to the sheriff's and shook my head. "I don't think so."

His face fell. "Why not?"

"Do suicidal people pay their bills before killing themselves?" I pointed toward the stack of envelopes. The top one was addressed to the cable company. If I were going to kill myself, the cable company was the last place I'd send money to.

The sheriff shrugged. "Could be he was getting his affairs in order. Doesn't mean he didn't commit suicide."

"But why here?" I wondered aloud. "I'd want to do it somewhere a little more private than a roller rink. Wouldn't you?"

Sheriff Jackson straightened his shoulders. His eyes narrowed. "I wouldn't commit suicide at all. I don't appreciate you saying I might or questioning my professional judgment."

"I didn't—" The bathroom door swung open, cutting off my halfhearted attempt at an apology. A robust, familiar-looking gray-haired gentleman strode in.

The sheriff's face broke into a smile. "Glad you're here, Doc. Would you come take a look at this? Maybe you can convince Rebecca here that this is a cut-and-dried suicide. Poor Mack didn't deserve to die this way, but it's as simple as that."

The doctor nodded to me as I backed out of the stall to give him room. That's when it hit me. The Indian Falls medical examiner was none other than Doc Truman. The man had patched me up during my active childhood and always gave me a lollipop afterward. I remembered the doctor as being kind, gentle, and a whole lot younger. Now Doc's forehead looked like it was sliding onto his eyebrows.

"So, Doc." The sheriff's voice echoed against the pale pink bathroom tiles. "Am I right? Did Mack commit suicide?"

The two men came out of the stall. Doc Truman was holding the bottle of pills. He flipped the bottle open and peered inside. "The bottle's almost full. That means Mack didn't take enough pills to commit suicide." He emptied some of the round white pills into his hand and squinted at them. Frowning, he looked at the sheriff. "This isn't right."

"What?" Sheriff Don peered down at the pills. "What's wrong?"

The doctor's eyes narrowed. "Half of these aren't Mack's pills."

"What do you mean?" The sheriff's voice was gruff. "Those pills all look the same to me."

"Mack's pills were for his thyroid," Doc Truman explained. "Prescribed them myself. Half of these pills have a *C* stamped on them. The thyroid pills don't."

The sheriff's expression turned stony. "That just means Mack was taking some other kind of drug you didn't know about. Doesn't surprise me."

Doc Truman raised an eyebrow. "Well, it would surprise the hell out of me. Mack was allergic to a lot of medications, and he hated taking pills. It took me almost two years to convince him to take something for his thyroid problem." Doc shook his head. "No, Mack would never have taken another pill. Not without talking to me first. I'm guessing he didn't know there were two kinds of pills in this bottle."

"What does that mean for my case?" The sheriff blustered. "Is Mack's death a suicide or an accident?"

I held my breath as the doctor put the pills back in the bottle. He handed them to the sheriff and let out a sigh. "Can't say for sure. Still, if I were to guess, I'd say the pills contributed to Mack's death."

The sheriff grinned at me. "So suicide, then."

Doc shook his head. "I don't think so, Don. The two kinds of pills make me think Mack was murdered."

By the time Mack's body was taken away, it was after eight o'clock. Locking up the rink, I looked around the parking lot for my car. It wasn't there. I was about to panic, then remembered that I'd walked this morning. It had seemed like a good idea at the time. The sky had been blue, the weather was mild, and I needed the exercise.

Now it was dark, and a possible murderer was on the loose. That was often the case in Chicago, but here it felt different.

I was bunking with my grandfather while trying to sell the rink, and I thought about calling him for a ride. Asking for help seemed wimpy, though, and I immediately chucked the idea. While I walked the four blocks to Pop's house, I contemplated how to break the news about Mack. Inspiration hadn't struck by the time I let myself in through the side door and walked into the kitchen.

Pop hadn't changed a thing in the house since Grandma passed fifteen years ago—same avocado-colored appliances, worn rugs, and scratched pots and pans. Pop and my grandma proved to me that occasionally love could last.

"Rebecca, is that you?"

Pop shuffled into the kitchen, bringing with him the strong smell of cologne. I blinked. Pop was still wearing his red pants, but he'd changed his top. Now he was sporting a silver shirt with the top three buttons left undone, which allowed several tufts of gray chest hair to peep out. Dangling from his neck were two very large, very shiny gold chains. Pop had even gelled his hair. One lock curled perfectly against his forehead, while the rest looked like it had been molded in plastic.

Maybe the furniture hadn't changed, but my grandfather had. Someone had morphed him into a geriatric pimp.

"Pop, what happened to you?"

My grandfather adjusted his teeth. "I got a hot date tonight. Marjorie Buckingham has been making eyes at me for weeks at bingo. So I asked her to a movie."

I glanced at the clock over the sink. Quarter to nine. "It's a little late to go to a movie, don't you think?" Wasn't it a law that old people had to go to bed early?

"Nah." He shuffled over to the fridge and popped open a beer. "We're going to see the late show. Nobody cares if you neck during the late show."

For the second time today I felt like throwing up.

Pop sat down at the table and took a swig from his beer. "So I heard you found Mack in the girls' bathroom."

My hand paused in the middle of reaching into the fridge for a drink. "How did you hear about that?"

"My phone didn't stop ringing all afternoon. This ain't the city, you know. When a guy's head is found floating in a toilet, that's big news here."

My hand swept past the sodas and latched onto a beer. I joined my grandfather at the kitchen table and gave him a weak smile. "It was pretty big news to me, too."

Pop frowned over his beer. "You holding up okay?"

No. "I'm trying."

"Good. Mack screwed up this town enough. I'd hate to think he hurt you, too."

I set my beer on the table with a clunk. "What did Mack do? You and the rest of this town used to like him. What happened?"

"Mack started taking people's money without doing the work they paid for. That kind of thing doesn't go over well here."

As if city folk didn't mind getting ripped off.

"I guess that explains why Doreen wasn't upset to find Mack dead."

Pop shrugged. "A lot of folks won't be unhappy hearing the news. Mack wasn't too popular."

My grandfather took a swig of his beer and leaned back in his chair. "Most folks will be more concerned someone decided to off Mack in a family place like the Toe Stop. Murder is the kind of thing that gets people scared, angry, or both. I know I had to do some fast talking to get Marjorie to come out with me tonight. She was worried someone was going to attack us in the dark."

"And you're not?"

"Nope." Pop grinned and flexed his biceps. "Ain't nobody gonna hurt Marjorie with me around."

I didn't think a bad guy would be intimidated by the muscles under my grandfather's sagging skin. Still, I wasn't about to hurt his feelings by telling him so. Instead I asked, "So you're not worried about a killer walking around Indian Falls?"

"Mack upset someone enough to get himself killed. End of story. Ain't like we got a serial killer or something. Although that might spice things up around here. This town's been awful dull lately."

Dull? I took another long sip of beer. This conversation was getting weird, fast.

I said, "The sheriff hasn't said this is a murder. He believes Mack killed himself."

"Doc says otherwise."

I gaped at Pop. "How do you know all of this?"

"The senior center. There was a card party going on today. They heard the sirens from the ambulance going by. The center's women have been on the phone ever since, getting the gossip."

I had to ask, "Like what?"

Pop leaned back in his chair. "Mack stuff. Guess he was seen arguing with Annette Zukowski at the bakery last week. Stiffed her on the work he was supposed to do; least that's what the bingo crowd was saying. Although he did a good job on Lionel Franklin's barn."

"Lionel Franklin? Should I know him?" Annette I knew. She and my mother had been best friends.

Pop shrugged. "You don't have any cows, so probably not. He took over Doc Johnson's vet practice a while back. Everyone likes him, especially the women. He has nearly as many dates as I do."

I blinked and steered the conversation back to the murder. "Did your spy network have any gossip on who the sheriff thinks might have murdered Mack?"

"Nope, but Doreen stopped by the center. She said an unsolved murder might slow down interest in the rink—was worried about the open house not drawing a crowd." Pop leaned forward. There was a gleam in his eye. "You're welcome to stay with me as long as you need. Could be a while."

Oh God, I thought. He was right. My life as I knew it had come to an end the minute poor Mack's did.

"The sheriff could make a quick arrest." My protest sounded weak, even to me.

Pop stood up with a shake of his head. "I wouldn't count on it. The sheriff is a good man, but word around the center is he spends most of his days pretending he didn't forget what happened the day before. Funny, but we elected him anyway. Guess it's because the job isn't normally that demanding. Riding on a float for parades doesn't require a whole lot of effort. Besides, what else would he do with his time?"

Pop adjusted his pants. "Don't worry, Rebecca. Don still has his good days. He'll get Mack's murder solved even if it takes him years. Don't wait up."

With a smile, Pop patted my cheek and ambled out the door for his date, leaving the strong antiseptic smell of his cologne to keep me company. Depressed, I grabbed a bag of chips and trudged upstairs to my room.

Needing a distraction from how bad my life sucked right now, I turned on the television. A cop drama was on. Normally I skipped those shows in favor of silly sitcoms. Tonight, though, I was morbidly fascinated. I watched with interest as the TV cops talked to suspects. They sifted through the evidence. They even got help from a civilian to get the bad guy to confess. These cops were smart. They were witty. Best of all, they didn't have a mild case of Alzheimer's. Too bad they weren't employed by the Indian Falls Sheriff's Department.

By the time the show ended, I'd finished the chips and another beer. I also knew there was only one way I could prove the roller rink wasn't cursed and sell it.

I either had to pray the *Law & Order* gang would come to Illinois, or I had to solve Mack's murder myself.

Three

I padded to the bathroom the next morning with a blinding headache, no doubt caused by the beer I'd consumed. The alcohol was probably also to blame for the strange dreams I remembered having. Or maybe it was the memory of finding Mack's body that had me hearing sounds in the dark. I'd found myself jumping at creaking and banging sounds all night long.

Pop's medicine cabinet was a mini pharmacy. I popped the lid on a bottle of aspirin and downed four of them. Looking down at the counter, I noticed two glasses sitting on the counter. They both contained a set of teeth. In the week I'd been staying with Pop, I'd almost become accustomed to seeing soaking dentures. Still, the extra glass confused me. Why would Pop . . .

Oh God! I winced as the source of the middle-of-the-night creaking made sense. I hadn't been listening to Mack's ghost. My grandfather had gotten lucky.

Opening the door, I peeked down the hall and hurried back to my room. I didn't want to run into my grandfather or his date outside his bedroom.

I got dressed and sprinted down the stairs just as my grandfather was coming up, wearing his bathrobe and balancing two steaming mugs.

"Coffee's ready in the kitchen. I made a full pot seeing as how I was up so late last night." My grandfather gave me a toothless grin. "Good luck on the open house today. Let me know how it goes."

Seeing him toothless always made my stomach feel a little squishy, but knowing a second dentureless person was upstairs sitting in bed made me want to faint. I choked out a "Thanks, Pop" and flew into the kitchen, grabbed my purse, and bolted out the door. It's not like I begrudged my grandfather some action. I just didn't want to be under the same roof where it was happening. Some things were not meant to be shared.

Now that I'd gotten out of the house, I had no idea what to do with myself. The rink wouldn't open for three hours. The sheriff didn't think closing down the place was necessary. He didn't want to scare the citizens by taking away their favorite pastime. Last I heard, the back stall of the girls' bathroom was off-limits, but other than that the Toe Stop would be ready for business as usual, and the open house would go on as planned. Technically, I wasn't needed for either. George had a key and was used to teaching lessons without supervision. Plus, the rink would probably sell best without me there worrying about a dead body's effect on the real estate market.

Suddenly I was reminded of my pledge while watching television. Solving Mack's murder sounded less plausible in the light of

WITHDRAWN

day than it had with a Budweiser in my hand. I had no investigatory skills and no idea how to even get started.

Still, a guy was dead, and he had died in my mother's roller rink. I figured I should run by the sheriff's office and see what progress Sheriff Jackson had made on the case. Maybe Pop had turned off the ringer on the phone. Then he would have missed the call from the old people spy network telling him the killer had been captured. I hopped in my bright yellow Honda Civic and motored off to the north side of town, half convinced the whole thing was already solved and my real estate troubles were over.

Indian Falls is a small town in west central Illinois near the Mississippi River. Not the greatest place to grow up, but I'm sure there are worse. Not much had changed about the downtown area since I was a kid. The sheriff's office was on Main Street in the heart of downtown and right next to the DiBelka Bakery. Convenient for all parties involved, I thought.

No one was manning the front desk at the sheriff's office. I noticed a silver bell sitting on the counter and gave it a whack.

A vaguely familiar petite woman with very big, very platinum hair teetered to the front. "Can I help you?" Her voice sounded like a rusty hinge. My body stilled as recognition set in. This was Roxy Moore.

"Is Sheriff Jackson around?" I asked, forcing myself to smile.

"Sorry, Rebecca." Roxy sat down behind the counter and picked up a nail file. "The sheriff doesn't come in until late on Saturdays. He likes to sleep in and putter around his garden. You know the St. Mark's Ladies Guild is having their annual Beautiful Garden Contest in June. The sheriff's won three years straight, and he's trying his best to win again."

Impressive, but not exactly the credentials I was looking for in my law enforcement team. The fact that their secretary had once berated my mother about not knowing how to handle her man didn't help.

The marital counselor looked up from whittling her thumbnail and said, "I wasn't surprised to hear Mack turned up dead. He'd upset a lot of people recently."

"What was he doing?" Maybe Roxy had some info Pop didn't.

Roxy put down the file and pulled out a bottle of Passionate Pink nail polish. "It's what he wasn't doing that caused all the problems. We got a bunch of complaints about Mack taking money and not finishing jobs. Then there's the business with Agnes Piraino. She's filed three reports against him for harassment."

I remembered Agnes. She had retired from her position as town librarian my last year of high school. When I was a child, she rapped me on my knuckles with a ruler for having sticky fingers. Needless to say, I didn't go to the library much after that. "Mack harassed Agnes Piraino?"

"No. He harassed her cats."

"Is that a crime?"

Roxy giggled, which to me sounded a lot like nails on a chalkboard. "Not that we know of, but the sheriff took the reports anyway just to make Agnes happy. Apparently, Mack was doing some work for Agnes's neighbors. Her cats kept getting in Mack's way. He finally threatened to poison the things if Agnes didn't keep them in the house."

"Did she?"

"Nope. One of the cats bit him, and he drop-kicked it across the yard. Agnes wanted Mack arrested for assault, but as far as Sheriff Don was concerned Mack was acting in self-defense."

"Do you think the sheriff is going to make an arrest soon?"

I leaned on the counter. "I mean, I'd feel safer knowing the murderer is off the street."

Roxy looked at me through her mascara-laden lashes. "Our department will catch the person who slipped Mack those pills. In the meantime, Indian Falls is safer than living in the city. Since you plan on selling the rink and going back, I don't see a problem for you."

Her attention drifted back to painting her nails, and I scooted out the door feeling less optimistic than when I went in. Although maybe I was tying myself up into knots for no reason. Maybe the right buyer was at the rink right now.

My jaw dropped as I pulled into the rink's almost full parking lot. I steered around a couple walking through the lot carrying camera equipment and parked in a spot near the back.

A Mozart piece was playing over the loudspeaker as I walked into the rink. George and one of his students were circling the floor. The rest of the rink was chaos.

People filled the sidelines. Walking farther into the rink, I spotted several teenagers who frequented the Toe Stop and a couple of their parents. Curiosity over the sale of the rink and Mack's death probably brought them out. I waved at the teenagers and did a double take. Behind them, at a table across from the bathrooms, was a group of unfamiliar adults swathed in black and deep purple. Perhaps more distinctive than their color palette was the fact that they were all chanting and holding hands.

This was an open house? It looked more like a séance.

Oh God!

My eyes darted to the bathroom. The yellow crime-scene tape barring entrance was still intact, but clusters of people were posing in front of the door while their friends took pictures.

I peered into the snack area and groaned. A group of white-haired seniors huddled around a Ouija board, sporting expressions of equal parts amusement and fear. In the middle of the group was my grandfather. He spotted me after the woman on his left elbowed him. Pop gave me a shrug and put his hand back on the planchette in the middle of the board. Apparently, Pop's group had expanded its gossip vine to the great beyond. This was just perfect.

"Rebecca. I'm so glad you made it."

I turned, and Doreen gave me a tight, overly bright smile.

"Is anyone here for the open house actually interested in buying the rink?" I asked.

"Well . . ." Doreen glanced around the place and pointed to a man in a suit who was currently crawling around the edge of the rink on all fours. "That individual might be interested in opening a museum on the premises, but I think he's only looking to rent."

"A museum?" No one came to Indian Falls unless they had to. "What kind of museum?"

"A paranormal one. If he makes an offer, he plans on having psychic readings and séances."

I blinked. To Doreen's credit, she had managed to break the news with a straight face. If nothing else, she was professional.

I swallowed hard. "Are you kidding?"

She shook her champagne-colored coif.

"Is there anyone interested in actually owning a roller rink?"

Her lips pursed, she scoped out the room. "Not today. I figured it would be a hard sell considering the specialty nature of the business, but I thought I had one or two potential buyers lined up. Both of them called this morning to say they weren't interested. At least not until some time passes. They don't want to be associated with death or, worse yet, murder."

Death and murder weren't on the top of my list either. Unfortunately, I was stuck with them until the sheriff solved the crime and I sold the rink.

"What do you think I should do?" I asked.

"I hate to think of this place turning into a museum for the dead, but that's the only offer I see us getting for a while. It's not my place to tell you whether to turn it down."

Maybe not, but I could see she wanted to—and to be honest, while the rent on my apartment was almost due, that wasn't as important to me as the fact that Mom loved her roller rink. While I didn't want to run the rink myself, I wanted to find a buyer who would keep Mom's dream alive.

"Turn him down." I sighed as a flashbulb went off in my face to commemorate the moment. "And anyone else not interested in owning a roller rink."

Doreen's eyes twinkled behind her rhinestone rims. "It could take a long time for the sheriff to put Mack's death to rest. Things don't move as quick around here as they do in the city."

"I know," I assured her. "Just do the best you can, and could you get these people out of here? George looks like he is about to go into cardiac arrest."

Leaving Doreen to deal with the fallout, I slid into my stifling car and cranked the air to arctic. Now what? A frightening vision of the rest of my life trapped in this town flashed before me. I didn't relish the idea of handing out skate rentals and dodging Pop's dates for the next decade.

Laying my head against the steering wheel, I considered my options. There was only one. The case needed to be closed and fast; otherwise my life was going to resemble a country-western song.

Too bad the sheriff's department didn't seem to function at a speed above mosey.

But I did. Between Pop's information network and visiting Roxy's House of Nails, I now had a list of potential suspects—Agnes Piraino, Lionel Franklin, and Annette Zukowski. Since Sheriff Jackson was busy pruning his daisies, paying them a visit probably wouldn't hurt.

Someone should, right?

As my car chugged through the downtown area, I spotted several familiar faces. A woman coming out of the Lutheran church looked familiar, and I waved as I sat at a stoplight. Instead of giving a typical Indian Falls smile, though, the woman hurried around the corner, her eyes filled with fear. The light changed, and I continued down the street with the weird feeling that the woman thought I had something to do with Mack's death. Just one more fun problem to deal with, I thought as I parallel parked my car down the block. Getting out, I prepared myself to interview my first potential murder suspect and my godmother—Annette Zukowski.

Annette ran the town's only beauty salon, Shear Highlights. She'd opened it when I was in high school. Today the salon was filled with women getting their hair set and colored in time for Sunday morning services. Several of them jumped as I opened the door. Clearly they were spooked about a murder taking place in Indian Falls. Still, that wasn't enough to keep them from their weekly beauty ritual.

I spotted Annette in the back clipping a little girl's blond hair. Annette and I were a lot alike physically. She was thin, about average height, and had large quantities of hair, which today she wore pulled back at the nape of her neck. Hers was dark brown where mine was red. Annette's bright blue eyes were crinkled in perpetual laughter, and her smile never failed to lift everyone's spirits. The minute she looked up from her work, she smiled and waved me forward.

I strolled down the aisle, trying to ignore several sets of eyes widening as I passed. My shoulders tensed, and I took a deep breath. Being stared at by gossips in this town hadn't gotten any easier in the past decade.

Annette's scissors didn't stop snipping as she shot me a large smile. "How are you doing, Rebecca? Did you come by for the haircut I promised you?"

A year ago, after my mom's funeral, Annette suggested I get a makeover to assist me through the sadness. When I turned her down, she helped me consume the better part of three bottles of wine and tucked me in when I passed out.

I shook my head. "Next time. I kind of wanted to talk to you about Mack."

Blow-dryers all around me went silent.

Annette just raised a perfectly plucked eyebrow. "I heard about what happened to him yesterday. It's awful."

I leaned forward and lowered my voice. "Pop said the two of you had an argument. What was it about?"

She sighed. "Two months back I hired him to install some new lights and mirrors and gave him a deposit for the job. He took the money and then proceeded to avoid my calls. When I saw Mack in the bakery last week, I asked him for my money back."

"That's it?"

Annette picked up a blow-dryer and a brush. "Sorry it wasn't more exciting. Are you asking because you're curious or is there something more to it?"

I could feel ears straining across the room, so I chose my words carefully. "I was just wondering. He died in Mom's rink, and I didn't really know him well."

She turned the blow-dryer on and attacked the little girl's hair. "Sure. Well, if you need to talk some more, come by the house." Glancing at me, she winked. "I'll open a bottle of wine, and you can tell me everything."

I winked back. Leave it to Annette to understand the unspoken. Moments later, I was in my car and driving to our former librarian's house. I knew I was at the right house when I spotted four cats sunning themselves on the front porch.

Careful not to step on any tails, I made it to the front door and rang the bell. A minute later, I heard a timid voice ask, "Who is it?"

Using my most cheerful tone, I said, "Hi, Mrs. Piraino. I don't know if you remember me, but I'm Rebecca, Kay Robbins's daughter."

The door opened as far as the security chain would allow, and a set of fearful eyes peered out at me. "Rebecca Robbins? Is that really you?"

Before I could nod, the door closed. I could hear the distinctive sound of the security chain being undone, and then the door flew open again. The diminutive Agnes Piraino appeared behind the screen door. With her white hair and sweet smile, she looked like everyone's idea of the perfect grandmother. "How are you, dear? Your grandfather told me you were coming into town."

I gave a tiny prayer that Agnes's teeth hadn't been soaking in my bathroom before getting to the crux of my visit. "I'm guessing you might have heard that Mack died yesterday at the rink."

"I did, dear. It's a shame when a person dies so young. At my age you expect to go any day, but Mack was a real shock. To think that someone in our town might have killed him . . ." Her eyes misted over, and she clutched her hands together.

I put a reassuring hand on her shoulder and gave it a tiny squeeze. "I know. I feel bad since I don't know a lot about Mack and he died at the rink. So I thought I would talk to people who knew him. I heard he did some work for you?"

"Oh, not me. He did odd jobs for my neighbor." Agnes swung open the screen door and stepped onto the porch. Immediately, two cats rose and began rubbing against her legs. "I don't like to speak ill of the dead, but Mack wasn't very nice. He hated my babies for no reason. He was working next door on the fence, and my babies love people, so naturally they went to say hello. Well, Mack threw a fit like you've never seen. He started hollering and throwing things. He even painted poor little Hemingway's tail. I made a report to the sheriff's office, but they just told me to keep my babies inside."

Agnes settled into an old rocking chair, and one of her babies jumped into her lap and began to purr. She pointed to the chair next to her, and I settled in.

"Did you follow their advice?" I asked, even though I knew the answer.

Agnes shook her head. "I couldn't. My babies weren't meant to be cooped up inside. But I wished I had. Then Mack wouldn't have kicked Precious."

She pointed to a fluffy yellow cat that was coming up the steps. The minute the cat spotted me, its ears flattened and the hair on its tail stood on end. Seconds later, Precious's lips curled back to reveal a set of very sharp teeth. For a moment I wondered what Mrs. Piraino needed with the security chain. Cujo didn't have a thing on Precious.

"Was that the last time you saw Mack?"

Agnes stroked a cat's back and tilted her head to the side. "I think so. Mack avoided me after that. I'm guessing the sheriff finally told him to leave me and my babies alone." She leaned forward and gave me a sly look. "Sheriff Jackson and I dated when we were younger."

I thanked Agnes for her information and got up to leave. Precious hissed and pulled back into a crouch, making me take a step backward.

"Stop that, Precious." Agnes's voice took on the authoritative tone I remembered from my library days. "Don't mind Precious. She gets a little cranky if she doesn't get her medication on schedule."

Precious stopped hissing and gave me a flat stare. "If it makes her happy, you should probably give it to her," I said. It would probably make the rest of the neighborhood happy as well. Who knows how many children Precious might eat without drugs?

"I will, dear." She assured me. "Thank you for stopping by. I like having visitors."

I said good-bye to Agnes and Precious. Hurrying to my car, I scratched Agnes off my list of suspects. The woman might be a little batty about her cats, but she was harmless. Turning the key, I headed off for the next potential murdering maniac on my list.

Dr. Lionel Franklin's veterinary clinic and farm was located about fifteen miles north of town. When I reached a green and white farmhouse with a sign reading LARGE ANIMAL VETERINARY CLINIC outside, I parked next to an enormous black pickup truck and hopped out of my car. A placard on the door said the doctor was in, so I rang the bell. When no one answered, I tried the handle.

Locked.

I decided since I'd driven all the way here I might as well look around. The sign did say the doctor was here somewhere. I wandered around the side of the house and followed the dirt path, poking my head into a few small sheds on the way. In one were some gardening tools; in the other, a couple of large pieces of farming equipment. No Dr. Franklin. I continued toward the large white barn at the end of the path.

The light was dim as I walked into the enormous barn and stopped. The smell of horses and hay wasn't unpleasant.

"Dr. Franklin?" I called. My voice echoed in the barn, and several horses poked their heads over stall doors on either side of the wide center aisle to look at me.

When no human answer came, I took a few steps down the center aisle. A noise from the left stall made me jump. Curious, I poked my head in. Standing in the stall was a camel—and he was wearing a hat.

Four

I squeezed my eyes shut tight, shook my head, and opened my eyes again. The camel was still there, and he was sporting a black fedora.

I blinked.

The camel blinked back.

Then the camel poked his head over the chest-high door to get a closer look at me. Certain this was a hallucination, I reached toward the animal with my hand. The camel sniffed at me, and I petted its nose. The camel gave a funny little snort and rolled its eyes.

I scratched the side of his face. That got me another eye roll and a throaty kind of grunt. I smiled. Not only was the camel real, but he liked me.

"I see you've met Elwood."

I spun around and came face-to-face with over six feet of intense maleness. If this was the doctor, I could see why the women in town were in hot pursuit. He looked to be in his midthirties with tanned skin and a chiseled jaw. His thick brown hair that had probably needed a haircut three weeks ago now looked just plain sexy. In the barn's dim light I couldn't tell if his eyes were hazel or green, but either way, this man was perfection. Of course, there was one major drawback—he was covered in blood.

I took a step back and found myself wedged up against the camel's stall praying this guy wasn't the killer.

"Elwood? Oh. Sure. Elwood," I rambled as the smell of the guy's shirt turned my stomach. "I was looking for Dr. Franklin. The office was locked."

"Sorry about that," he said in a deep voice that almost made me forget the blood. "I had an emergency and forgot to change the sign. I'm Dr. Franklin, but folks around here call me Lionel."

He held out a hand to shake mine, but I couldn't do it. His hands were clean, but his long-sleeved shirt was caked with goo, and the smell was growing stronger.

He looked down at his clothes and grinned. "Excuse my clothes, but Doc Truman's horse was giving birth and required my assistance. Birthing of any kind can be a little messy."

"I can see that." I let out a sigh of relief that the blood wasn't human. I didn't want this guy to be the killer. He was too good-looking for that kind of disappointment.

We stared at each other for a minute, not sure what to say. I felt a wet camel nose against my cheek and flinched, making Lionel laugh. It was a deep, rich sound that made my body hum.

"I see Elwood likes you. He doesn't normally take to people so fast."

I smiled and gave Elwood a pat, careful not to dislodge his fedora. "Elwood is a strange name for a camel." Then again, I'd never met a camel, so what did I know?

Lionel scratched Elwood's side and nodded. "I thought so,

too, but it suits him. Elwood was a circus performer before he was sent to me. Strangely enough, he used to do a Blues Brothers act with a clown. They tell me it took the clown a year to train Elwood to wear a hat, and now he won't go without one for more than a couple of minutes."

"I'm surprised the clown gave Elwood up. I'd think a hat-wearing camel would be big a box-office draw." I know I'd buy a ticket. Right now I was trying to decide how well a camel would fit in my Wicker Park apartment.

Lionel put his forehead against Elwood's, and the camel made another throaty noise. "The clown died, and Elwood became so depressed he wouldn't eat. That's why six months ago the circus manager brought Elwood to me. Turns out he liked it here, and he's been with me ever since." Lionel took a step back from the camel and let his eyes roam from my feet up to my hair, finally stopping to look me right in the eyes. "Now that you know me and Elwood, would you mind telling me who you are?"

"Oh, sorry." I straightened my shoulders and gave him my perkiest smile. "My name is Rebecca Robbins. My mom owned the Toe Stop."

"I'm sorry about your mother," Lionel said, his eyes darkening with compassion. "She was a real nice lady."

"Thanks." My own eyes started to tear up, and I clenched my fist. I wasn't going to get all weepy.

"So," Lionel asked, scratching the camel's side, "did you come by for a reason?"

My eyes widened. I had no idea what to say. A real investigator would have thought of a cover story, but I wasn't a real investigator, so I hadn't. And while honesty was normally the best policy, asking straight out if he killed Mack seemed like a bad idea.

I looked around for inspiration. The guy was a vet. Talking about animals seemed like the most logical option, so I said, "I was thinking about getting my grandfather a pet and thought you might be able to recommend one."

Lionel's lips quivered. "Really?"

I nodded and expanded on my lie. "I hate the idea of Pop living alone and thought a pet would be good company."

"From what I hear, he has plenty of company."

My cheeks heated. Apparently, the whole town knew about Pop's indiscreet sex life. Well, I couldn't worry about that now. I had to focus on the problem in front of me—getting information and getting the hell out of here.

Cocking my head to one side, I said, "Maybe I came to the wrong place for advice."

"Maybe you did." Lionel took a step closer. "Unless you want to get your grandfather a cow. I'm a large animal veterinarian. Guess you didn't read the sign when you drove up."

"Guess not. Since you can't help me, I should probably get out of your way." I took two steps toward the door and turned. Doing my best casual voice, I asked, "Did you know Mack Murphy well? I heard he did some work for you."

Lionel stared at me for a second, then grinned. "I was wondering when you were going to get around to that."

My mouth dropped open, and Lionel started to laugh. The sound made me cringe from embarrassment and want to jump him at the same time. For a moment, I thought about coming clean about my investigation, but I decided against it. Just because Lionel was hot didn't mean he was trustworthy. "I really am worried about Pop living alone," I explained.

Lionel leaned against Elwood's stall door and crossed his arms. "You also stopped by the sheriff's office and Annette's beauty parlor this morning and asked a lot of questions about Mack's murder investigation."

The yenta phone tree in Indian Falls was more efficient than the CIA. I had just been caught red-handed.

"Okay. I feel guilty Mack died in my rink, and Pop mentioned to me that Mack did some work for you. Since you knew Mack, I thought I'd ask you about him." Okay, that was only part of the truth. Sue me.

"You forget to mention the fact that Doreen can't sell a place with an unsolved murder looming over it."

Busted again. "I liked my explanation better. Yours makes me sound self-centered."

"Honey, you're the one who used your widowed grandfather as an excuse to question me. What would you call that?" Lionel walked toward me, his body stopping only inches from mine. He was close enough that I could feel the heat coming off him. "Since you're Kay's daughter, I'll tell you what you want to know. I hired Mack to do some roofing work. It took him a lot longer than it should have to get it finished, but he and I had a conversation about it over poker, and two days later it was done."

Lionel's head bent down. His lips were now within an inch of my face. Suddenly, the bloody clothes and the smell faded from my mind. "I didn't kill Mack," he said firmly, his green eyes staring into mine. "Isn't that what you're really here to ask?"

"No." Yes. I took a step back, tripped over my own feet, and fell against the barn's door frame. Lucky for me it was there; otherwise I would have ended up on my butt. Again.

Lionel pulled me fully upright and grinned. "Well, you let me know if you think I did it. I deserve a chance to try to change your mind."

His hands on my shoulders sent little tingles down my spine. I licked my lips and couldn't help asking, "How would you do that?"

He looked down at me. His smile told me that my attraction to him was obvious and that he was enjoying it. "I think we could figure something out. Right now I have to take a shower and get back to work." He took a step toward the back of the barn and added, "I'll let you know if I come up with a good pet for your grandfather."

Lionel walked away from me down the center aisle of the barn. For a moment I enjoyed watching him go. Coming or going, Dr. Franklin looked good. Then, shaking my head, I scooted out to my car.

Minutes later, I was cruising the streets toward downtown feeling a little dejected about my PI abilities. In the last two and a half hours I'd discovered that Annette had purchased new mirrors and lights, Precious suffered from a personality disorder, and Lionel owned a camel that wore hats. While the information might make for interesting party conversation, none of it got me any closer to solving Mack's murder or selling the rink. Hopefully Sheriff Jackson had finished pruning his daisies. Alzheimer's or no, he'd be making better progress than I.

I drove to the rink and arrived with twenty minutes to spare. Walking toward the front door, I stopped dead in my tracks. My eyes were riveted on my mother's newly refinished double doors. Yesterday when I left, the glass was sparkling clean. Today it had a bright red message scrawled across it.

GO HOME. MIND YOUR OWN BUSINESS. OR ELSE.

Five

My first thought was "Okay." I could hit the road tonight and be back in Chicago in time to meet some of my friends at the bar. Saturday was half-price margarita day at Uncle Hector's Hacienda. The way my life was going, I needed at least a dozen.

Still, as much as I wanted to get out of this town and back to my real life, I wasn't about to let a little graffiti chase me away. I was made of stronger stuff than that . . . I thought. Besides, my questions seemed to have actually hit a nerve. Despite my inexperience, my investigation might be getting somewhere after all.

Grabbing my cell phone, I dialed Roxy at the sheriff's department. My voice only quavered once as I filled her in on my situation. She informed me that the sheriff was still busy at home but a deputy would be by soon. Then she hung up. No doubt Roxy wanted to get back to her personal grooming.

I turned my back on the threatening message, just as George's beat-up Ford Escort pulled into the lot. George barely gave the car a chance to stop before he bounded out and came to stand in front of the door with his mouth slack and his eyes glazed.

Finally he spoke. "Who would do this? Your mother spent a fortune on these doors."

Hmm . . . not my first or even second reaction.

I resisted the urge to yell at George because I liked him. His whole name was George Szczypiorski, but no one could pronounce it. I knew I couldn't, but I could spell it since I was currently writing out his checks.

George was about ten years older than me with white-blond hair and a tall, lanky frame. Growing up, I was always hearing how beautiful George's skating was and how I should try to be more like him. Well, now he was the rink's only full-time teacher and the person I relied on to keep things limping along. This was scary because, though I liked him, George reminded me of the Misfit Elf who wanted to be a dentist. I was certain that if someone offered George a sequined turnip costume and a ten-dollar-a-week job in the Ice Capades, he'd leap at it. George liked shiny things and applause.

A squad car swung into the lot, and a sheriff's deputy climbed out. "Well, what do we have here?"

He sauntered up next to George, and I groaned. The deputy was none other than Sean Holmes—three years older than me, perfection on the high school football field, and the biggest horse's ass I'd ever had the privilege to meet. My day was just getting better and better.

"Hi, Sean. Thanks for getting here so fast." I smiled, hoping he'd matured in the twelve years since high school.

He grinned back. "I'm pretty fast at everything."

So much for maturity.

"So I guess you want me to take your statement?"

I did a mental eye roll. "Well, since you came all the way here, I guess we should."

Sean walked back to his squad car just as George's first student arrived. I let them in through the side door, then walked back to where Sean was standing with a clipboard.

Sean uncapped his pen. "Name."

I gave him my best "you're such a schmuck" look. "Oprah Winfrey."

Sean wrote it down without blinking. "Address."

It went on like that until he finally walked over to the door for a closer look. He snapped a couple of pictures with his camera phone and walked back toward me. Sean gave me the clipboard and asked me to sign the sheriff's report, which I did.

"Don't you think we should test the paint or something? You know, collect evidence of the crime." My late-night television watching reared its head.

"No point." Sean gave me a superior look. "My guess is all your poking around today asking questions pissed somebody off. If you'd let the sheriff's department do their job, you wouldn't have any problems. Keep your nose out of other people's business and let trained professionals handle Mack's murder. I'd hate to see anything happen to that pretty neck of yours."

I took my copy of the official report, thanked Sean, and watched as he headed out of the parking lot—Indian Falls' finest on his way to save the world. Too bad he didn't seem all that interested in solving my graffiti problem.

Walking back to the doors, I took a closer look at the scrawled message. Huh. The words didn't look like they were written in paint. I ran my finger along one of the letters, something Sean didn't think of, and the writing smeared.

43

Lipstick?

I rummaged through my purse until I came up with a Dairy Queen napkin. Then I rubbed some of the graffiti onto it. With the sample safely stored in my purse, I proceeded inside to get a bucket of water and a sponge.

Mom had been very proud of those new doors. Cleaning them was the least I could do.

I spent the rest of the afternoon behind the rental counter giving out skates in exchange for my customers' smelly shoes. The task required only two of my brain cells, which allowed the rest to think about Mack.

Mack taking money from people and not finishing the jobs they paid for didn't sound right to me. My mother always said Mack was a stand-up guy who did good work. I remembered her mentioning that she'd hired him to do a bunch of the rink renovation.

I zipped back to the front office and checked the books. Sure enough. Mack had painted the rink walls and hung the new lights. Ironically, he'd even laid the bathroom tile. After each job my mom had drawn a smiley face—her bookkeeping technique for signaling a job well done. Several entries for other workers had frowny faces, but not Mack. A year ago Mack was still doing his job well, so what happened?

Around six o'clock, George popped his head into the office. He told me he was going to stay till close and could lock up. The rink wasn't all that busy. Not surprising considering a murder had taken place here. Parents were going to be careful about letting their kids go out at all, let alone come here to skate. That meant the rink's bottom line was going to take a hit. One more reason to solve the murder, I thought, as I grabbed my purse and headed home for the night.

Walking into Pop's house, I could hear the television blaring from the living room. Peeking in, I saw Pop watching TV with a date. Terrified about what else I might see, I tiptoed past the doorway and headed up the stairs.

"Rebecca, is that you?"

Caught. I backed down the stairs. "Yeah, Pop. It's me."

"Well, come on in here. I have someone I want you to meet."

My stomach clenched in protest as I walked into the living room. My grandfather had his arm draped around a robust, champagne-haired lady with apple cheeks. They were seated on the living room love seat facing the television. Both turned to flash their convertible teeth in my direction.

I forced a cheerful smile and waved. "Hi. I'm Rebecca."

My grandfather gave the lady's shoulders a squeeze. "This here is my date, Louise Lagotti. She's one of Indian Falls' artists. Runs a craft business out of her house."

Louise? I could have sworn last night Pop said his date's name was Marjorie. I stood there awkwardly for a moment as they looked at me with expectant expressions. I asked, "What kind of crafts do you make?"

Louise's face turned red with pleasure. She gave a cloying little giggle and smiled at Pop. I waited for her to tell me she strung beads for jewelry or crocheted doilies—the usual Indian Falls Senior Center craft projects. Instead she answered, "I make scarecrows."

Maybe the rink music had affected my hearing. "Did you say scarecrows?"

Louise nodded. "I started making them for Halloween, but I liked mine too much to put it away. So I made it an outfit for Christmas. My friends all loved it. They even said I should go into business. So I did, and it's been wonderful." Louise gave another giggle, which turned into a loud snort.

Pop patted Louise's hand. "Isn't she something, Rebecca?"

She was something, all right. I just wasn't sure what.

"I'm going to the kitchen to get a drink. Would the two of you like anything?"

Pop and Louise declined, so I left them watching TV and made a beeline for the fridge. I grabbed a soda and a pad of paper and a pen. Balancing everything, I took a seat at the kitchen table and wrote down what I knew about Mack thus far.

Gnawing on the pen, I studied my efforts. There was a picture of a demented cat, a sketch of a smiling camel, and a stick figure of Lionel that didn't do his body justice. All this told me was that I needed art lessons, not to mention someone who knew Mack and could tell me what he needed all the money for. Drugs? Women? Gambling? In the mortgage world, I'd seen any one of the three doom someone's credit. One of them could have gotten Mack killed. All I needed was someone to tell me which one it was.

I grabbed my soda and walked back toward the living room. "Hey Pop, do you know—"

My grandfather and Louise stood up from the love seat with guilty expressions and disheveled clothes. Louise's face was almost purple as she tucked her blouse into her hiked-up skirt.

"Did you want something, Rebecca?" My grandfather sat back down on the couch and patted the seat next to him for Louise, who smoothed her skirt and sank down next to him.

I squelched my scream and squeaked out, "Did Mack have any close friends?"

My grandfather shrugged. "Mack pretty much kept to himself, but he did go to a weekly poker game at Doc Franklin's house. You should ask him."

"Oh, I will, Pop," I said as I felt my blood pressure rise. You bet your ass I will, I thought.

I turned to go up the stairs as the sound of an opening zipper rang throughout the house. I took the stairs two at a time and ran into my room. An hour later, showered and changed, I checked to make sure the living room was empty before walking past it toward the door.

During the drive to Lionel Franklin's house, my irritation began to smolder into full-fledged anger. Lionel was friends with Mack Murphy and didn't tell me. He had let me believe that Mack was his handyman, period. Could it be the handsome Dr. Franklin had something to hide? I didn't know, but I was determined to find out.

I pulled up in front of the vet clinic and poured myself out of my car. While getting dressed, I'd decided I needed an edge when talking to Lionel. That's why I was now sporting a skintight denim skirt that showed a lot of leg and a shiny green blouse that showed a hint of cleavage. Problem was, I hadn't counted on my three-inch heels making it difficult to navigate the gravel sidewalk. Sidewalks were made of cement in the city where I'd bought the shoes.

I teetered precariously to the front door and turned the handle. Locked again, and this time a sign wasn't posted telling me he was here. Damn! I peered around the corner of the house. Lights were on in the barn. Maybe Elwood the camel was throwing a party?

47

I decided to risk possible maniacs hiding in the dark and a sprained my ankle to find out.

The sound of laughter hit me the minute I walked into the barn. Elwood trotted down the center aisle to greet me. Tonight he was wearing a card dealer's visor.

After giving him a pat, I teetered to the back of the building toward the source of the laughter as Elwood cantered beside me. We passed stalls occupied by horses, cows, a donkey, a couple of goats, and a llama. From the number of animals, it looked like Lionel had a successful veterinary practice going. The Indian Falls 4-H Club would probably bail him out if he got busted for murder.

Elwood stopped to commune with the llama, and I followed the murmur of voices through the far door. I turned the corner into a comfortable-looking den with an overstuffed couch, a small refrigerator, and a large round table that was situated on a faded area rug in the middle of the room. Four men were seated around the table with poker chips stacked in front of them. Every pair of eyes was focused on me.

Wow, was this lucky, I thought. The poker game Pop told me about was going on right now.

I didn't recognize the two men who were staring at my high heels and short skirt. The other two I did know had different expressions. Lionel wore a frown. Dr. Truman, town physician and medical examiner, was smiling. Maybe bumping into him tonight was a sign my luck was improving.

Lionel gave my outfit a dismissive look. "What are you doing here, Rebecca?"

I ignored him and gave the other men my best flirty smile. "Pop said you had a poker game going. I love poker. Do you mind if I play?"

"Yes. As a matter of fact I do." Lionel stood up and crossed to me. "We have plenty of players, so I'll just show you out."

He took my arm to guide me toward the door. I tried to turn around, but my left heel caught on the edge of the area rug. That sent me toppling straight into Lionel's back. Caught off guard, Lionel went careening to the floor.

I, however, remained standing.

"Lionel." Dr. Truman wagged his finger at Lionel's sprawled body. "That's no way to treat a lady."

"Apologize to the lady. She was just trying to be friendly." This from an attractive blond guy wearing jeans and a polo shirt. The dark-haired man wearing jeans and a Chicago Cubs jersey nodded his agreement.

Lionel brushed off his pants and returned to his seat at the table. I gave him an innocent smile, and his eyes narrowed.

I swallowed hard. This was not a man who wanted to apologize, I thought. This was a man contemplating how his hands would fit around my throat.

The image of Mack's head encased in porcelain danced through my mind. Maybe coming here had been a miscalculation. I took a step toward the exit and stammered, "Lionel doesn't have to apologize. I'll just leave you guys to your game and see myself out."

I could question Dr. Truman at his office, and Lionel I'd talk to when it was daylight. And when I was wearing tennis shoes. High heels were useless when outrunning a potential murderer.

"No. You should stay, Rebecca." Lionel's voice was soft. I wasn't fooled by his calm tone. Behind the quiet exterior a storm was brewing. "It might be interesting to play poker with a woman."

Right, I mused. Kind of like the lion finds it interesting to play with a rabbit just before he eats it.

Dr. Truman pulled out a chair before I could come up with a good exit strategy. That's how I found myself sitting between him and the Cubs fan. A moment later, I was equipped with a beer and a stack of chips that I had to pay twenty-five bucks for. The beer was free.

Lionel shook his head at me and shrugged. "I guess since you're staying you should meet everyone. You know Dr. Truman?"

I nodded.

"I'm Tom Owens," said the man in the jersey. "I teach physical education at the high school and coach the varsity football team."

I turned toward the last man, who was seated across the table from me. "And you are?"

"You probably don't remember, but we went to high school together." He leaned back in his chair. "Zach Zettel."

I bit my lip and let my mind do a mental flip through the yearbook. "You were really into cars, right?" If I remembered right, he also hung with the crowd that thought it was cool to drink their sodas with nose straws.

He grinned. "Still am. I own the auto body shop outside of town on Magnolia. If you ever have any car problems, make sure to give me a call."

Lionel grabbed the cards from the center of the table. "Can we play poker now?"

I turned to Doc and whispered, "What are we playing?"

"What we always play." Doc flashed another smile. "Texas Hold 'Em."

My game. I did my best to look confused while doing an internal dance of glee.

Lionel shuffled the deck, and the cards were dealt. Tom leaned over to ask if I needed the game explained to me. The way he looked down my blouse, I was pretty sure he was more interested in playing doctor than teacher. "Thanks," I said, "but I know how to play."

My comment drew condescending smiles from everyone but Doc, who gave me a considering glance. Obviously Doc wouldn't fall for the dumb woman routine. I filed that information away for the future, and the game began.

I folded the first three hands immediately in order to get a feel for the way everyone at the table played. Besides, I needed time to come up with a strategy. In the city I played Texas Hold 'Em tournaments in bars and won more than I lost, but tonight I really didn't care if I raked in the chips. I wasn't here to take these guys' money. I was here to get information on Mack Murphy. The real question was: Would throwing the game make the men feel sorry enough for me to give me the information I wanted or would I just lose my money?

The room was deadly quiet as I peeked at my next hand.

Two aces. My conscience wouldn't let me fold. It was time to play.

Six hands later, Tom was out of chips. Most of them sat in front of me. Five hands after that, Zach went out in a blaze of glory, quickly followed by Doc, who volunteered to deal until the end of the game.

Now it was just me and Lionel. Since Tom and Zach looked bored, I decided to chat them up while playing my cards. "I guess you were all good friends with Mack."

Lionel frowned at my obvious fishing, but Doc took the bait, saying, "Mack and I played cards for fifteen years. He built my wife's porch swing for our anniversary last year and wouldn't even let me pay for it. Insisted he couldn't take money from a friend."

Lionel grunted and threw some chips in the pot. "He never had a problem taking my money."

Interesting.

I raised my eyebrows, but Lionel didn't look up from his cards. Peeking at my hand, I added some chips to the pot and said, "I didn't know Mack well, but it was a big shock to find him in the girls' bathroom like that. I'm finding it hard to believe someone got murdered in Indian Falls."

"It could have been an accident."

We all turned to look at Tom, who was now seated on the couch looking miserable while drinking what had to be his eighth beer.

"What do you mean?" I asked, wondering what he knew that I didn't.

"Mack wasn't the healthiest eater. I should know. He was my best friend." Tom sniffled. "I tried to get him to eat anything besides take-out food, but he wouldn't. Mack liked pizza and french fries. He wouldn't exercise, either. Maybe all that saturated fat caught up with him and he had a heart attack. Makes more sense than someone murdering him." Tom teetered to the fridge and grabbed another bottle. He popped the top and staggered back to the couch with a shake of his head. I made a mental note to feed his keys to one of the goats.

"Hate to say, but it wasn't a heart attack. Did the autopsy myself. Mack's heart was fine." Doc's face turned gray. All of a sudden he looked like he'd aged ten years. "Nothing sadder than to be forced to cut open a friend."

I really wanted to change the subject and get Doc to smile. Only I couldn't—not if I wanted to get the case solved and the rink sold. I asked, "What do you think killed him?"

Doc made eye contact with everyone in the room, then slammed his hand on the table in frustration. "Damn it to hell. I might as well tell you. You're all going to find out anyway. Ever since the sheriff hired Roxy there aren't any secrets in this town." Doc looked down at the table and lowered his voice. "Mack drowned."

I blinked, then looked around the room. Everyone looked stunned, except Tom. He just looked drunk. "Drowned?"

"Yes. He blacked out and fell headfirst into the water and drowned."

Now I was confused. "That sounds like an accident to me."

"Would be except for those pills." Doc took a sip of his barely touched beer. "I spent my whole day in Rockford having tests run on them. They weren't the kind of pill Mack would take for recreation. I won't tell you what they were, but I will tell you they caused Mack's blackout. In my opinion, Mack was murdered."

Zach looked green, Lionel clenched a fist, and a choked sobbing sound came from Tom. I didn't think any of Mack's poker player friends had anything to do with his death, Lionel included. Maybe drawing conclusions from their reactions was a naive way to go about investigating a crime, but I couldn't change how I felt.

I threw some chips in the pot to nudge the subject back to poker and to taunt Lionel with a raise. Lionel gave me the first smile I'd seen from him all evening and called me. Doc dealt some cards, Zach offered me another beer, and the game was back on with Mack's ghost seemingly banished for the night. But I couldn't stop pondering those pills. Where did they come from, and who had given them to Mack?

Six

"You play a good game of poker." Lionel grabbed two empty bottles off the table and pitched them into the trash. Elwood was standing in the doorway. I fed the camel a pretzel, and he happily munched. Meanwhile, Tom performed a great buzz saw impression while passed out on the couch. Doc and Zach had left about fifteen minutes ago, leaving me to help Lionel clean up the mess. I didn't mind, since I'd come to the conclusion that Lionel hadn't killed Mack. If I was wrong, Elwood would probably protect me.

"I mean it," Lionel said, tossing an empty chip bag into the garbage can. "You bluff like a champ."

I grinned, but I was distracted. This morning I had been intimidated by Lionel's body and the gore covering it. Now that he was showered and in a change of clothes, I could see the man cleaned up well. The room's temperature rose ten degrees and the back of my neck started to sweat as I contemplated just how well.

"Becky, if you don't stop looking at me like that, you're going to get more tonight than just my money."

Oops. I realized I was sucking on my bottom lip and stopped. Unlike my grandfather, I wasn't looking for some quick action. Come to think of it, when it came to the men in Indian Falls, I wasn't looking for any action at all. I had men problems enough back in the city.

I turned away from Lionel and stacked the multicolored poker chips in their case. "Sorry, I must be tired."

Out of the corner of my eye I could see Lionel smirk as he said, "You're something, all right, especially in that getup. I thought Tom was going to bust a gut when you walked in the door."

I shrugged. "I thought the clothes might be a good distraction while trying to get information about your friendship with Mack."

"You could have just asked."

"I didn't think that would work or I would have. You weren't too forthcoming this morning when you acted like Mack was just your handyman. How about I ask you now? What else can you tell me about Mack?"

Lionel sat down. He put his hands behind his head, swung his feet up on the table, and gave me a quizzical look. "I thought you worked with mortgages. Your mother never mentioned you were a private investigator, too. Did I miss that part?"

I sat down hard on a folding chair. "You talked about me with my mother?"

His smile disappeared. "A couple of years ago, your mother found a stray dog that had been hit by a car. She brought him to me. Every day she came to visit that dog while he was recuperating. After the dog was taken in by a family, she still kept coming once a week. Kay talked about you all the time. I felt like I knew you after all the stories I heard." He flashed his pearly whites. "Boy, was I wrong."

56

I didn't know whether to be flattered or offended. Actually, I was more than a little surprised he had been such good friends with my mother. She'd never mentioned him. Or had she and I hadn't paid attention? The latter possibility made my stomach ache.

Lionel put his feet flat on the floor. Raking a hand through his hair, he looked me square in the eyes. "So what do you want to know about Mack?"

I raised an eyebrow. "I heard that a couple of months ago Mack started taking money without finishing the jobs people paid him for."

Lionel's forehead crinkled. "Mack used to be quick at completing jobs. He started dragging his feet recently. The change confused the whole town. He had a lot of run-ins with customers over their deposits, and more than one got heated."

"Like who?"

"Well, Sheriff Jackson hired him to make some flower boxes. He pulled Mack over several times to remind him about the work. Your mom's friend Annette threatened to stick a curling iron up his ass if he didn't finish hanging her lights. Even Tom here got into it with Mack at last week's game. Claimed Mack was backing out of an agreement they had. I don't know what Mack said in return, but Tom jumped him. If Doc hadn't stepped in, Tom might have taken Mack's head off."

I looked over at Tom, who was snoring peacefully with drool running down his chin. Didn't look all that dangerous to me. "Did you ever ask Mack why he was taking cash without doing the work?"

"Once. When he kept stalling work on my roof. I said I thought he was in trouble. He denied it."

"Did you believe him?"

Lionel leaned back in his chair. "At the time I did. Mack finished the roof, and I forgot about the whole thing. Looking back, I'm not so sure. The last couple of weeks Mack looked nervous. During a poker game he mentioned having some project he was working on. Said it was going to bring in big money. I asked what the project was, but Mack wouldn't say. Claimed he didn't want to jinx it. I'm guessing he was using the extra cash to finance this scheme of his."

"And whatever that was might have gotten him killed."

Lionel shrugged. "I don't know. Mack liked talking big, so it could have just been him blowing smoke. You never knew with Mack. Still, he was one hell of a poker player."

Men. A guy could be a lying, cheating swindler, but as long as he could play cards, men would think the jerk was worth his weight in gold. Funny, but what I'd learned so far made me wonder who, if anyone, really knew Mack. Lionel was Mack's friend, but he didn't seem to know anything personal about him. Maybe nobody did.

I asked, "Do you know where Mack lived?" Couldn't hurt to check out the place, right? Maybe I would find something there to explain the need for all that cash.

I thought Lionel wasn't going to answer. He stared at me for a moment with a strange look on his face. Then he gave me directions to Mack's place.

"You should be careful nosing around in other people's lives," Lionel added. "Small towns don't like when strangers start meddling in their affairs."

"I know," I said. "I grew up here."

"You've been gone a long time, Becky. You've made it clear you don't want to belong here."

This was the second time he'd called me Becky. No one called me Becky, at least not since I was seven. Speaking of which, I was the one who was from this particular small town, not him.

Turning, I headed toward the door. "I should go. See you around, Lionel."

From behind me I could hear Lionel's deep voice saying, "God help me."

Pop had already left for church when I got up the next morning, which meant I could walk to the bathroom without fear of running into one of his girlfriends or her teeth. That was something I should probably have gone to church and thanked God for, but I chose to say my thanks in the kitchen with a strong cup of coffee.

I made myself some scrambled eggs, drank two cups of coffee, and read the paper while waiting for church services to end. Once the clock hit noon, I hopped in my yellow Civic and took off for the rink.

I turned my key in the lock, hit the light switch, and watched as the fluorescent lights flickered to life. I had to admit the rink really did look good. Before she died, Mom had the rink floor sanded and refinished. Now, instead of the scarred, bumpy wood of my youth, the floor was gleaming and smooth. A definite improvement.

Lacing up my white skates, I glided onto the floor and did a few laps. Scary, but it felt good to stretch my muscles and have the wind racing against my face. I wasn't the biggest fan of working out, but skating was different. Mom had laced me into skates after I'd taken my first steps, and as much as I fought against it, skating was a part of who I was.

59

Enjoying myself, I did another couple of laps, this time backward. When I didn't fall on my face, I was inspired to try a spin.

Bad idea. I teetered off balance and landed flat on my backside. Again.

I struggled to my feet, rolled off the floor, and kicked my skates into the far corner of the office. Now I remembered why skating wasn't fun for me. I had to face the reality that no matter how I tried, things weren't going to be much different for me here at the age of thirty.

I sat down at the desk and typed up employee schedules and a summer class list while trying to ignore the icky feeling growing in my chest. When the rink opened and laughing kids filtered in, I couldn't ignore it any longer. Leaving George in charge, I strolled out to my car. Time to head over to the sheriff's office for a progress report.

A sign on the sheriff's door said the office was out to lunch, so I pointed my car toward the outskirts of town and followed Lionel's directions to Mack's house. Maybe, if I was lucky, the key to unlocking his death was there. I'd find it, and then the townsfolk could put the murder behind them and I could sell the rink. Everyone would be happy.

Mack Murphy lived about three miles outside the Indian Falls city limits. The house was a large, bright red and white ramshackle structure surrounded by a tall wooden fence. I pulled into the driveway next to a blue Ford pickup.

I walked to the truck and tried a door handle. The door opened. Whoever towed it back from the rink parking lot hadn't bothered to secure the vehicle. My luck was looking up.

I climbed inside. One thing was certain—Mack Murphy was a big slob. There were candy wrappers, petrified french fries, and a variety of fast-food bags scattered throughout the cab.

Yuck. A half-eaten Mars bar was stuck to several receipts in the center console. I pried the paper away from the gooey candy and read between the stains. Several receipts were for gas stations in Indian Falls, and two were from towns about twenty minutes to the west. Pocketing the receipts, I jumped out of the cab and walked around the back of the truck. Heaving myself up, I climbed into the truck bed.

The back of the truck didn't yield any information, either. I found some tools, a few boards, some nails, and—wait, tucked inside the toolbox was a note to Mack from Annette. She was threatening legal action if her deposit money was not returned and warning him not to tell anyone about their other arrangement—or else.

I couldn't help wondering, or else what? Annette wasn't the type to go around threatening people. At least I hadn't thought she was. Suddenly I wasn't so sure, and that made me feel queasy.

I started to pocket the note, then thought better of it. When the sheriff finally left his petunias, he would start looking for evidence. The chocolate-covered receipts didn't look all that important, but this did, and obstructing justice wasn't on my to-do list. Paying Annette another visit was. There were a few blanks she needed to fill in. I put the note back where I found it and hopped down from the truck.

Back on the ground, I followed a graveled path to the porch and tried the front door handle.

Locked. No surprise there. I peered through the front windows and wandered around the porch trying to decide what to do next. Smashing a window wasn't a viable option, and I had no idea how to break in. Northern Illinois University hadn't offered a class on picking locks.

Ooof. My foot caught on something, and I found my nose pressed up against the porch's floorboards. I pushed myself up to my knees and brushed off my pants. First the tumble at the rink, and now I tripped on the welcome mat.

I looked down wondering if Mack was the kind of guy who left a key hidden in case of an emergency. I flipped over the welcome mat. Aha! Taped to the back was a key. Magnum PI, eat your heart out.

I unlocked the door, stepped inside, and locked the door behind me. Yikes! I suppose the mess in Mack's truck should have prepared me for his house. Still, I guess I'm an optimist. I had hoped for the best. Too bad it was worse.

The living room was strewn with clothes, tools, and what I hoped were empty fast-food bags and pizza boxes. Buried beneath the junk was a purple sofa. The walls were covered by faded red and white gingham wallpaper. Not my idea of country charm. Doreen would have a harder time selling this place than the rink— and nobody had died here.

A good investigator would no doubt search through the cardboard clutter. I, however, just kicked some pizza cartons out of my way and walked the almost cleared path to the dining room. If Mack had a secret, it would have to be in plain sight. I wasn't brave enough to risk dislodging any guests that had taken up residence in the debris.

The mess continued into the dining room, only now it was piled on an old dining room table and six chairs. To my surprise, the kitchen was in better shape. Sure, the floor could use a good sweeping, but there weren't any dishes in the sink, and the counter was free of crap. Baffling, to say the least.

Searching the drawers netted me some silverware and other cooking utensils. No clues. Same with the cupboards. The problem was, I was searching for a needle in a haystack and wasn't even sure I'd know the needle if I saw it.

Finished in the kitchen, I followed the back staircase upstairs to a narrow hallway. The scarred floorboards screeched with every step, making me shudder. I thanked God it was still light outside. Walking around a dead man's house in the dark would have been too creepy.

The first door off the hallway opened into a bathroom. Since I didn't think soap scum and bathtub ring were going to help me, I moved to the next door. Unmade queen-sized bed, scattered clothes, overflowing hamper—must be Mack's bedroom. I rifled though his dresser drawers, trying to ignore the stained under-wear and shirts. Nothing there.

I looked around the room, certain there had to be something here. His bedroom was an obvious hiding place, right? So I had to ask myself—if I were Mack, where in my room would I hide some-thing important?

Looking at the bed, I remembered Pop telling me about people he knew using their mattresses as safe deposit boxes during the Great Depression. They shoved all sorts of savings and important documents among the feathers and springs. What were the chances that Mack had heard the same stories? He already hid a key under a welcome mat. Would he actually hide something important un-der his mattress? It couldn't be that easy, right?

I sent the bedding and pillows flying as I lifted the mattress up and looked underneath. Blinking twice, I grinned. Mack's lack of creativity wasn't very bright, but it was convenient. Taped to the underside of the mattress were three envelopes. I peeled one loose and let the mattress fall back onto the box springs.

Peering in the envelope made me suck in my breath. The envelope was filled with one-hundred-dollar bills. Thirty of them. A quick inventory informed me that the other two envelopes contained the same amounts. Mack had nine thousand dollars under his mattress, and still he was taking deposits from people without intending to do the work. Why?

With a sigh of regret, I tucked the envelopes back under the mattress for safekeeping. A little extra cash would help cover my city apartment's rent while I worked to sell the rink. Still, I couldn't bring myself to take any. Karma had already kicked me in the ass. I didn't need to give it a reason to take another swipe.

Leaving financial temptation behind, I went down the hall. The next room was almost empty except for a few tables, a couple of rolls of packing tape, and a lot of cardboard boxes in a variety of sizes. Not much to find in there. I continued to the last door.

The first thing I noticed was how clean this room was. No wrappers or empty soda cans here. On the far side of the space, next to the window, was a large wooden desk with a laptop computer perched on it. I also saw a combination printer, fax machine, and copier. To my right was a wall of shelving filled with old toys, lunch boxes, comic books, and knickknacks. A little strange but completely dust-free. I appreciated that.

Sitting down at the desk, I put my finger on the START button of the laptop—then stopped. Did computers keep track of every time they were turned on? If they did, and the sheriff ever got out of the daffodils long enough to check this place out, he might wonder why Mack's computer had been used after Mack died.

While the contents of the computer had me curious, looking wasn't worth the risk.

I contented myself with going through the desk drawers. Nothing. That left the contents of the desk shelves. I scanned the labels on Mack's CD cases. He had a few computer games, a couple of office programs, and one CD case labeled BUSINESS. That looked promising. I slid the plastic case off the shelf and opened it. On top of the CD inside were a key and a slip of paper with a name and phone number scribbled on it.

I slipped the CD case and its contents into my purse and gave the room a final once-over. When nothing else jumped out at me, I headed down the hall to the stairway and into the kitchen.

Slipping out the kitchen's back door, I started down the flagstone path to a small gardener's shed. I didn't think it would be a den of clues, but I was here anyway. I poked my head in. Nothing in there but cobwebs and an old riding mower. Big surprise. Well, at least I'd found the CD and key. Who knows, maybe they would lead me to Mack's murderer. The only way to find out required a computer. It was time to head back to the rink.

I walked across the backyard and through the gate just in time to see an Indian Falls squad car pulling up right behind mine. Oh no, I thought. Busted.

Seven

"I thought I told you to let me and the sheriff do our jobs." Deputy Sean sauntered toward me with a scowl. "What do you think you're doing here, Rebecca?"

He leaned on my car. My shoulders tensed as his handcuffs banged against the passenger door. After a year I'd managed to keep the car unscratched, which was practically a miracle, living in Chicago. Getting the first ding from Deputy Pompous would be seriously depressing. Deputy Sean grinned at me and added, "You know, you should be careful. Sniffing around out here might get you more than a little graffiti on your front door."

I stood up straight. That sounded like a threat, and I didn't like threats. Of course, angering the cops after just breaking into a murder victim's house was not exactly my brightest idea. Sean could make trouble for me, and I already had enough of that. I needed to make nice.

"I'm sorry," I cooed, batting my eyelashes. "After finding

Mack's body and getting that message on the rink door, I'm a little edgy. You're a cop, which means nothing frightens you, but I'm scared." *Of staying in Indian Falls for the rest of my life,* I finished the sentence in my head. Taking a step forward, I gave Sean what I hoped was a pleading look. "I know you don't need my help, but I couldn't stop myself from coming out here. Sitting around doing nothing would drive me crazy."

Sean's angry frown eased into a toothpaste commercial smile. "I'll let it go this once. You've had a rough time, but make sure you steer clear of our investigation from now on." He put a hand on his holster. "Don't you worry, Rebecca. We're going to break this case wide open before you know it."

I managed to thank him and get to my car without laughing. Sean had sounded like he'd been reciting lines from a bad action flick. I turned the key in the ignition and noticed Sean watching me. I drove off with a small wave, hoping he didn't dust the house for prints. Mine would be everywhere. Somehow I didn't think Deputy Holmes would let me out of that one with only a Clint Eastwood monologue as punishment.

The Village People echoed through the rink as I walked through the door. Kids skated round and round singing "YMCA" at the top of their lungs. It was the same thing I did at their age. Scary, I thought, some things never change.

Slipping into my office, I pulled Mack's BUSINESS disk out of my purse and slid it into the computer. While the computer was booting up, I examined the key that had been hidden inside the case. It had a square top and a faded number etched in that could be the number seventeen . . . maybe. Besides that, it looked like a plain old key that could fit any number of locks.

The menu for Mack's disk appeared on my computer screen. The disk contained a total of three files. I clicked on the first one, and a spreadsheet appeared.

From what I could tell, it documented Mack's handyman business, organized by month and year. I scrolled down to a year ago. There was my mother's name, a list of the jobs he'd been hired to do, the dates on which he'd contracted them, the dates on which he'd completed them, and then the dates on which he'd been paid. I scrolled back up and found Annette's name. Mack had entered the money received and the date contracted but no completion date. Seven other incomplete jobs—all with money received— gave me more suspects. I scribbled down the names of the customers and clicked on the next file.

It contained a letter, and not a very polite one at that. Mack was demanding fifty thousand dollars in exchange for . . . something. What, I had no idea. The letter was dated three weeks ago, but there was no addressee named at the top. Something told me extortion was a better motive for murder than unfinished work. Maybe Mack had information on someone. Maybe Annette? That my mother's best friend could be involved seemed unrealistic, or maybe I was just engaging in wishful thinking. I clicked on the next file, hoping for a clue to the letter's recipient.

Another spreadsheet, only I couldn't make heads or tails of this one. The first column contained a letter followed by several numbers. The next was date received, followed by date shipped. A dollar amount appeared at the end of each row. Mack didn't provide an explanation of the codes he'd used, so they could mean anything. Nowhere did I find mention of the key I had in my hand.

I was at a dead end with the CD. I grabbed the paper with the scribbled name and number. Theodore Bosikus. Never heard of the guy, but the area code was familiar. It was a Chicago number. I decided to let my fingers do the walking. The mysterious Theodore answered on the first ring.

"Bosikus Investments, Theodore speaking. How can I help you?"

Investments? A guy who hid nine grand under his mattress didn't seem like the type, but what did I know? Doing my best impression of a serious professional, I answered, "Hello. My name is Rebecca Robbins. Mack Murphy recommended your company and gave me your number." Okay, technically Mack didn't give me the number, but I figured Theodore didn't need to know that.

"Murphy? One second." I heard some typing on the other end, and the voice returned. "Oh sure, Mackenzie Murphy. I talked to him a couple of weeks back. He wanted to know my thoughts on markets and stocks. You know, I got to admit I'm surprised he recommended me. At the time we spoke, he didn't have the minimum amount I require to invest."

"He didn't tell me that." At last a moment of truth. "He did say you knew a lot of about stocks and how to get the most out of an investment." That quickly, my brush with truth vanished.

I could hear Theodore preening on the other end of the line. "I do. Although I must admit my strategy is riskier than that of a lot of investors. That made Mack nervous. Me and my clients like going for the big payoffs. The bigger the risk, the bigger the reward— that's my motto. Why don't I get some of your information, then we can talk about your investment options."

My mind whirled. Something was strange about this whole thing. Theodore was way too chatty about Mack's business for my taste. His runaway mouth was good for a beginner detective like me but bad as far as professional ethics went.

I wasn't sure I wanted him to know any of my personal information. I said, "Can I call you back, Theodore? I'm at work, and my other line is ringing." Ring. Ring. "I'll talk to you soon."

Dropping the receiver back in the cradle, I said a small prayer that he didn't have caller ID and leaned back to consider what I'd learned. Besides the fact Mack's real name was Mackenzie, not much. Theodore's company couldn't be the source of Mack's financial need. Mack hadn't invested yet, which I considered a smart move on his part. Big risks might lead to big payoffs, but they also led to big debts. I saw that a lot in my line of work. Mack's mattress retirement plan was a much better option.

"Ms. Robbins?"

I turned to see Doreen's granddaughter hovering in the office doorway, wearing white shorts and a blue T-shirt. Without the goth attire, Brittany almost looked like a normal Indian Falls teenager. If there was such a thing. "Did you need something, Brittany?" I asked.

Brittany took a hesitant step into the office. "I was just wondering how you were after everything that happened. You know . . ." Her voice trailed off.

"I'm fine, Brittany. Thanks for asking."

Brittany took another creeping step forward. "No problem." She nibbled on a lock of hair. "My grandmother said someone like you wouldn't be freaked."

I blinked. "What does 'someone like me' mean?" I was pretty sure I wasn't going to like the answer.

Brittany took a seat in the chair across from my desk and shrugged. "My grandmother said people get murdered in the city all the time. She said you're a city person now. That's why seeing a dead body wouldn't upset you."

Shaking my head, I got up and walked around the desk. Apparently, there were a few misconceptions I had to clear up. "Just because I live in the city doesn't mean I stumble over dead bodies when I walk down the street." If I did, I wouldn't bother to pack. I'd just get the hell out of Dodge.

I leaned forward. "Between you and me, finding Mack in the bathroom really bothered me. I think it would bother anyone."

Brittany's lip trembled. She clutched her hands in her lap. Finally, I understood the problem. I had been doing my best to avoid dealing with my feelings about finding a dead body. Keeping busy solving the crime helped me ignore my emotions during the day. I was a big fan of denial, but Brittany was upset and needed someone to talk to. I was guessing that Doreen wasn't the type to listen. From what I'd seen, the woman's mouth was perpetually switched to the ON position.

Perching on the edge of the desk, I asked, "How have you been doing?"

Brittany sniffled. "Fine."

Sure. Like I believed that. "Not being fine is okay, too," I told her. "In fact, I'd be worried if you weren't upset."

Her eyebrows raised into her hairline. Quietly she said, "My grandmother said I should pretend it never happened."

Forgetting the image of Mack's head stuffed in a toilet was impossible without a lobotomy. Doreen was nuts.

I shook my head. "That's great if it works for her, but I'll never forget."

"Finding him like that really scared me," Brittany admitted, her eyes wide with fear and teenaged fascination. "My friends thought it was cool, but I didn't want to say too much to them. And my grandmother won't talk about it with me."

I smiled. "You can always talk to me. I might not have a lot of answers, but I'm pretty good at listening."

"Thanks, Ms. Robbins." Brittany got to her feet.

"My friends call me Rebecca." Ms. Robbins made me sound old. Brittany smiled back and headed for the door to join her friends. That left me alone to continue staring at Mack's mysterious key.

After a few minutes I got bored with waiting for a psychic message from Mack to point me in the right direction. Sighing, I picked up the phone and called Annette. No answer. I'd have to track her down tomorrow and clear up the matter of her letter to Mack.

Monday morning I blinked as my alarm went off. The rink was closed on Mondays, so I hit SNOOZE on my alarm clock and pulled the covers over my head. My eyes opened again at eleven, and I stared at the ceiling while contemplating remaining in bed the entire day.

Nope. I was awake.

I padded to the bathroom for a quick shower. Damp hair pulled into a ponytail, dressed in jeans and a button-down shirt, I made it to the kitchen as the clock's hands clicked to twelve noon.

Rummaging through the refrigerator, I discovered a major problem. There was no food. With Mack's murder investigation taking up all my free time, I had neglected to go to the supermarket, and Pop's love life must have been too exciting this weekend to do a mundane task like grocery shopping. It was time to remedy the problem.

Slaughter's Market was located in the center of town next to Annette's salon. The store had been around as long as I could remember. Rumor had it that Felix only opened the market to get away from his father's farm and his family. Funny thing was, most of the produce came from his relatives' farmland, which meant no matter how hard Felix worked, he never quite got away from them. A good commentary on families in general, I thought.

I walked through the front door and began my trek up and down the aisles. From across the produce department, I spotted Sean Holmes squeezing tomatoes. I ducked into the cereal aisle before he noticed me. Picking up speed, I steered my cart around a corner. Bang!

"I knew you'd run into me again, but I didn't think it would be this soon."

I looked up into the green eyes of Lionel Franklin and sighed. Why me?

Eight

Today Lionel was dressed in snug jeans and a green dress shirt with the sleeves rolled up. I couldn't help noticing how the shirt brought out the color in his eyes. Too bad he was wearing a superior smile. Although he almost made it work, smug wasn't a look I found attractive.

"Sorry. I didn't see you." For once I was telling the truth. Had I seen him, I would have steered in another direction.

He crossed his arms, and his smile grew wider. "I'm not surprised. You were in a real hurry. Trying to get out before Sean sees you?"

"No." Maybe.

"Worried Sean might want to talk to you about your visit to Mack's house?"

I plunked my hands on my hips and gave Lionel a stern frown. "How did you hear about that?"

"Becky," he grinned, "I hear about everything."

My irritation went up another notch as I backed my cart up

and started to roll it around his. Lionel stepped into my path. Now I was wedged in between his cart and the shelf of cereal. "Would you get out of my way?" I asked. When he didn't budge, I clenched my teeth and said, "Please?"

I was surprised when he stepped aside. "It's nice to know you can be polite. That might come in handy when you want extra toothpaste in jail." He smiled before adding, "Trespassing is a crime Sean Holmes takes seriously."

I blinked. Trespassing? Being arrested for trespassing would be bad, but it was better than breaking and entering. Sean must not know I'd been inside Mack's house. That made me smile. "Can I count on you to bake me a cake when I'm in jail?"

"No, but I'd be happy to testify. I could be a character witness."

"Really?"

He gave me another annoying smile and started rolling his cart down the aisle. "Sure," he said over his shoulder. "Far as I can tell, you're completely nuts." With that parting salvo, he disappeared around the corner and left me and Captain Crunch alone.

I avoided both Deputy Sean and Lionel at the checkout counter and was loading groceries into my car when I heard a distinctive "tsk" behind me. I let out a mental groan and turned. Doreen's eyes glared at me from behind her glittering glasses. Funny, but I couldn't help noticing that the yellow blouse she wore made her skin looked a bit jaundiced.

"Hi, Doreen."

She pushed her glasses up and sighed. "I tried to call you at the rink, but you didn't answer."

"The rink is closed on Mondays." I was certain Doreen already knew that.

She waved off my words, saying, "I think we should officially pull the rink off the market until Mack Murphy's murder is solved. No serious businesspeople will give me the time of day until then."

I should have expected this. Only I hadn't. Somewhere inside I'd continued hoping that the rink would sell in spite of everything.

"Pull the listing," I said with a wince. "Hopefully the case will be solved in a couple of days and we can put the rink back on the market."

Doreen gave a sharp nod. "The minute the murderer is arrested, I'll start making calls."

Thoroughly depressed, I thanked her and turned back to my trunk full of groceries, feeling faint. My vacation time from work only lasted another week. If I didn't figure out who killed Mack soon, I was going to be stuck in Indian Falls for good.

Ten minutes later, I lugged five heavy plastic bags into Pop's kitchen and began loading up the cupboards. As soon as I finished, my grandfather shuffled into the room. Typical male, I thought.

"Missed you at church yesterday morning, Rebecca." He opened the refrigerator door and pulled out the lunch meat I'd just purchased.

"I decided God would understand if I slept in."

"God might, but the neighbors aren't so forgiving." He pulled the newly stocked bread out of the pantry. "Marabelle Thomske got the whole women's group asking me where you were. I told them you were sick. So if anyone asks, you tell them that, or I'll never hear the end of it when I go to bingo."

I sat down at the table and watched him assemble two large sandwiches. Why a salesperson thought it was a good idea to sell my grandfather stonewashed jeans and a tight black T-shirt was beyond me. Pop looked like he was trying to recapture the eighties—and failing.

"If you're worried, don't go to bingo," I offered.

Pop turned. "Don't go?" He gaped like a largemouth bass. "I have to go. It's my turn to pull the numbers. All the women are real friendly to a man handling the balls."

I choked back a horrified laugh while Pop finished making his lunch. He pulled two plates out of the cabinet, piled on the sandwiches, and put both plates in the refrigerator. My stomach grumbled in protest as lunch disappeared behind the door.

"Isn't one of those for me?"

Pop shook his head. "Louise is coming over for lunch. I can make another for you if you want to join us."

I tried to come up with a polite way of saying "no way in hell," but nothing came to mind. I started to sweat as Pop stared at me expectantly. Lucky for me, loud knocking on the kitchen door saved me from agreeing.

"Hello. Is anyone home?"

I knew that voice. It was following me. I put my head down on the table, convinced I should never have gotten out of bed this morning.

I heard Pop shuffle over to the door. "Can I help you with something, Dr. Franklin?"

"Actually, I'm here to see your granddaughter."

I turned my head and opened one eye. Lionel was perched just inside the door, staring right at me.

Pop shuffled back into the kitchen, and Lionel followed behind him. I lifted my head and waited for my grandfather to turn his back. The minute he did, I glared at Lionel. "What are you doing here?"

Lionel smiled. "After you ran into me at the market, I got to thinking that if you hadn't eaten yet we could have lunch together."

"I'm not hungry." My stomach growled on cue. I felt my cheeks grow warm, but no way was I going to take my words back and agree to have lunch with him. Lionel was way too cocky. Being turned down would be a good character builder for him. Come to think of it, my saying no would be a public service for the entire female population of northwestern Illinois.

Lionel's smile widened as my grandfather said, "Rebecca is always hungry, only she doesn't want to hurt my feelings. Louise is coming for lunch, and I invited Rebecca here to join us. If you want, I can make more sandwiches. We're going to be eating in the living room. Louise has a daytime show she likes to watch, and I like being around when she does." Pop winked at Lionel. "There's one character on the show that makes her real frisky."

Visions of my grandfather and Louise getting frisky on the couch made my neck break out into a cold sweat. I had to get out of here. Fast.

I raised my eyes to meet Lionel's. His were crinkled with suppressed laugher, while mine, I knew, were filled with panic. He leaned against the wall, shoved his hands in his back pockets, and raised an eyebrow. I got the message loud and clear. Lionel was waiting to see how desperate I was to get out of here. I clenched my teeth. I was really desperate.

"You and Louise already have plans," I told my grandfather. "I don't think Lionel and I should intrude."

"You wouldn't be intruding." Pop opened the refrigerator and began rummaging through the cold-cuts drawer. "No trouble to make two more sandwiches. You bought more than enough meat at the market."

I mouthed the word "help" to Lionel. For a second I thought he was going to let me suffer. Mercifully, he said, "With work and all, I've been inside a lot lately, so I was hoping to eat lunch outdoors. I even brought a picnic blanket. What do you say, Rebecca? Will you have lunch with me?"

If I'd been sitting on an erupting volcano I couldn't have gotten up faster. "After all the trouble you took, how can I say no?"

Lionel shot Pop an apologetic look. "Maybe next time," he said as he took my arm and steered me out of the kitchen.

Five minutes later, we were traveling out of town in silence. Lionel's enormous black pickup truck looked like it was on steroids, and I had to wonder if its owner was compensating for something. Finally, curiosity got the best of me, and I asked, "Did you really bring a blanket?"

He took his eyes off the road for a moment to grin at me. "Yes, along with a bottle of wine. Both necessities for a good picnic."

That sounded about right to me, and I gave him a tentative smile. "I guess I should thank you. I couldn't have handled a double date with my grandfather and his girlfriend."

"I think you would have survived. How bad could watching daytime television with those two be?"

"Picture *Wild Kingdom* with cheesy background music and old people." Lionel's eyes widened. "Got the picture now?"

"Your grandfather has to be eighty years old." His voice held an almost reverential quality at the idea of a guy Pop's age getting it on. I rolled my eyes.

"Actually he's seventy-six, but he's acting like he's found the fountain of youth. This is the second woman he's gone on a date with this week. The first one slept over."

Lionel chuckled. "That must have been fun."

I shuddered. "You have no idea."

Lionel parked his testosterone-fueled truck, and I hopped down. Wildflowers grew near a small lake sparkling a bright blue, the occasional tree guarding its shoreline. The spot was beautiful, perfect for a picnic. Problem was, I'd been paying more attention to the driver than the roads. I had no idea where we were, and the disorientation was unsettling.

I went to the back of the truck, where Lionel was unloading a large picnic basket. Making myself useful, I grabbed the blanket and followed him down to the lake's edge. I unfolded the blanket while Lionel unpacked the food—and it was a lot of food. The basket reminded me of one of those clown cars. Food, wine, plates, and more food kept coming. Good thing I was starving. There was no way the stuff piled on the blanket was ever making it back in that wicker basket.

Lionel uncorked the wine. He poured me a tumbler, and I took a sip of the burgundy liquid. My entire body sighed with pleasure. The vet knew how to pick camels and a good merlot.

I leaned back and studied Lionel over my glass. "So, do you take all your picnic dates here?"

"Only the ones avoiding law enforcement," he said, opening a carton of colorful pasta salad. "Mostly I come here to fish. I didn't bother to bring my poles today. You don't look like the fishing type."

I sat up straight. I was pretty sure I'd just been insulted. "What's that supposed to mean?"

He shrugged, handing me a plate. "City girls don't like baiting

80

hooks or touching squirming fish. I tried fishing with a city girl I dated in college. By the end of the day I was tempted to throw her into the water."

"What stopped you?"

"I didn't think the fish would appreciate it."

I filled my paper plate with fried chicken, pasta salad, grilled veggies, and crusty French bread. Then, leaning on my elbow, I started to feast. The food was perfect, and my stomach thanked me with every bite. After a minute, I looked at Lionel and reminded him, "I'm not technically a city girl. I grew up here, you know."

Lionel smirked at me. "That doesn't mean a thing."

I blinked. "I lived here year-round for eighteen years. That should count for something." For some reason it was important to me that he agree. Yes, I like the city, but this was my hometown. I felt like Lionel was cheating me out of something I'd earned.

The jerk refilled my wineglass. "Not really. Everybody in Indian Falls knows you never liked it here. That's the reason you're in such a hurry to sell the rink, isn't it?"

"I have a job, friends, and an apartment in Chicago. I can't stay here and run the rink. It's not practical. Anyone can see that." At least I hoped so. I wasn't selling the rink because I didn't fit in. The thought that my mother's friends could think so cut deep into my heart. For a moment I felt like I was back in grade school. Dad's leaving made me feel like an outsider then, and I'd spent years telling myself I'd been wrong. Maybe not.

Lionel shrugged and popped a piece of chicken into his mouth. "It's your life. You can do what you want with it."

I drained my wineglass and concentrated on my plate. Since Lionel was quiet, I decided he was doing the same. The silence was nice for about three minutes; then the ideas he'd raised started replaying in my mind. Trying to avoid the uncomfortable feelings roiling inside me, I asked, "So you were always a small-town boy?"

"Nope. I grew up just outside of Chicago." He smiled at my look of surprise. "My parents are still trying to understand how I ended up treating horses and cows. The biggest pet I had growing up was a goldfish." He opened another bottle of wine and filled my glass.

"Did they ever figure it out?"

He nodded. "I did a school project on zoos. I spent the day with one of the Brookfield zookeepers. That was it. I was hooked. After going to the University of Illinois for my veterinary degree I ended up here."

I had to ask, "Why Indian Falls?" The animals I got, but moving to Indian Falls wasn't something a person did on purpose. Sane people moved away from Indian Falls.

He pulled out a container of fresh fruit from the never-emptying picnic basket and popped it open. "Three years ago the old vet, Dr. Johnson, was moving to Florida. I heard he was selling the practice. So I came out to see it and signed the contracts the same day. Now this is home."

Home, I thought. My body tensed, and I recognized the icky feeling rolling around inside my chest. I was jealous. Lionel sounded happy with the home he'd chosen, and from what I could see, Lionel was accepted here. He really was home.

I wasn't. In Indian Falls I was a city slicker, and in Chicago my friends still thought of me as a country girl. It didn't seem fair, but maybe that was just the wine talking. I was feeling more than a little light-headed.

"Becky?"

"Yes?" I looked a lounging Lionel in the eyes. He must have

skipped shaving this morning; the five o'clock stubble gave his face a dark, rugged look. His green eyes held mine, and the smile spreading across his lips was dangerously flirtatious. An urge to grab him and drag his body on top of mine welled up inside of me.

Lionel tilted his body closer, and my heart kicked into high gear. His mouth opened, but instead of kissing me he said, "The sheriff might be slow on the uptake, but I know you went into Mack's house. So move those sexy lips and tell me exactly what you found."

Nine

"*That's what this picnic was about?*" The languorous feelings in my body vanished. I sat up straight and stared at my tumbler of wine in horror. "You were trying to get me drunk. You just wanted to be with me so I would tell you about Mack Murphy's murder."

To his credit, Lionel didn't deny it. He sat up and shrugged. "It was worth a shot. Besides, I don't know why you're complaining. You liked the food, the location, and the wine."

He was right. All three had been great until I realized they weren't due to my sparkling personality and sex appeal. There's nothing more deflating than knowing an attractive guy was only interested in one thing and it wasn't your body.

"I remember you telling me that I could have asked about Mack instead of trying to deceive you." My voice rose, and I jabbed a finger at him. "Why not follow your own advice?"

He emptied the rest of the wine into his tumbler and put the bottle in the basket. "I would have if I thought it had a chance in hell at working." His eyes met mine with a frank stare. "Honestly, if I hadn't done all this, would you have answered my question?"

"I'm not answering your question now," I huffed.

"What if I said please?"

I shot him a scathing look.

"Okay," he said. "How about I give you one of these?" He pulled a DiBelka bakery box out of the basket and opened it. Inside were two large, whipped-cream-topped chocolate éclairs.

Okay, I was tempted. Chocolate éclairs were my favorite. I couldn't help wondering how Lionel knew that particular Achilles' heel. Somehow I didn't think my mother's friendly stories about her daughter included dessert preferences.

Wincing more than a little, I said, "I don't think so."

Lionel grinned. "How about you get one of these and I'll also throw in a ride on Elwood?"

An image of Elwood's happy camel face sprang to mind, and I caved. "Oh, fine. I found Mack's spare key under the welcome mat and let myself in." I grabbed my éclair and took a big bite. Every nerve in my body quivered with pleasure. Yeah, I sold my secret for dessert and the promise of a camel ride. Sue me.

Lionel leaned forward. "What else?"

While I chewed, I considered how much I should tell him. "Mack is a slob. His clothes are everywhere. Only his office and the kitchen were clean." Lionel glared at me. I decided to throw him a bone. "He also had nine thousand dollars in cash under his mattress. I don't think the tooth fairy left it there."

That got his attention. His eyes narrowed. "What did you do with the money?"

"I put it back where I found it."

Lionel gave me a strange look.

"What's wrong with that?"

He leaned back with a frown. "I talked to Sean earlier. The deputy didn't find any money in Mack's house."

As far as I was concerned, the Indian Falls Sheriff's Department couldn't find their own houses without a road map. "Did they look in the right place?"

"I don't know. After Sean ran into you, he realized he'd forgotten Mack's house keys. He had to go back to the sheriff's office for them."

I licked the filling from the éclair while contemplating Mack's money. It was possible that Deputy Sean was slightly more competent than I'd given him credit for. If so, he would have tossed the mattress. I thought Sean was a jerk, but I didn't think he was a crooked cop who would keep the money for himself and lie about finding it. That meant that during the time he'd gone back to town and returned, someone else had gone into Mack's house and stolen the money. The question was who. Then again, Sean might be completely incompetent, and the money might still be sitting in the bedspring bank.

We shoved everything back into the basket, and Lionel drove us back to town. I had him drop me off at Annette's salon since I had no idea what time Louise's daytime programs ended. No way was I going to witness my grandfather and Louise feeling frisky. Besides, Annette and I had unfinished business.

"Don't forget about my camel ride," I said, hopping down from the truck. "You promised."

Lionel gave me a smile that said riding Elwood wasn't the only thing he was promising. With a wave, he drove off.

Monday apparently wasn't a busy day for Shear Highlights. Annette was in the middle of the salon wielding a blow-dryer on the only customer, a vaguely familiar twenty-something woman. Annette smiled and motioned for me to take a seat. I did and flipped through a magazine while I waited for her to finish. I looked up when Annette and her dark-haired client headed for the cash register. The newly styled woman stopped dead in her tracks. I looked around for the cause of her distress. Considering the lack of options, I had to assume it was me.

Great. Either my deodorant had stopped working or this woman thought I was a potential murderer.

I said, "Hi," and gave her a friendly smile. No serial killer here.

The woman didn't smile back as she made a dash to the counter. A minute later, she bolted out the door.

"What's with her?" I asked.

Annette shrugged and took the seat next to me. "I don't know. She was fine until you got here. Have the two of you had a problem or something?"

"I don't think we've even met." I threw the magazine I'd been reading onto the glass coffee table. "Do I know her? She looks kind of familiar."

"Her name's Danielle Martinez." Annette kicked her feet up onto another chair. With a relieved sigh she said, "Danielle moved here a little over a year ago. She works at the Lutheran church doing secretarial stuff. I heard that her family lives in Galena and that Danielle moved here to get away from them."

I scrolled back through my memory trying to decide why she looked familiar. Nothing. Not that it really mattered. For all I knew she reminded me of someone on television.

Annette arched her back and asked, "So what's up? Do you finally want that haircut?"

"No, I'm avoiding going back to Pop's place. He had a date there when I left. Three is most definitely a crowd."

"Hey, your grandfather's dates are keeping me in business. They keep coming in asking me to help them look their best." Annette peered out the front window. "Where's your car? Did you park at the rink?"

I was tempted to say I walked, but Annette would never believe I'd chosen using my feet over driving. Besides, the town's grapevine was probably already in high gear. Annette was going to find out anyway, so I told her, "Lionel dropped me off."

Annette's eyes widened, and her mouth formed a perfect circle. "Now I think I see."

The problem was, she didn't. "It's not what you think," I said. "He took me on a picnic to try to weasel information out of me about Mack's murder. Speaking of which . . ."

I debated how to approach Annette. Finally, I blurted, "When I was at Mack's place, I found a note you wrote him about the money he owed you."

Annette's smile disappeared. "I'd forgotten all about that," she said, not meeting my eyes. "When Mack started avoiding my phone calls, I wrote that note and left it under his windshield for him to find. I hoped he'd give me back the money and settle the matter." She looked up and shrugged. "You know me. I don't like being angry with anyone."

"Is that why you threatened him?"

Annette looked away.

"Annette, what information did Mack have that was so important you had to threaten him? Was he blackmailing you or something?" Maybe asking for fifty thousand dollars?

"No. Of course not." Annette sprang out of her chair and

walked over to the front desk. She opened the scheduling book and began flipping pages. "Why would Mack blackmail me? I just didn't want Mack going around town badmouthing me because I insisted he give back my deposit. You of all people should know how gossip spreads in small towns. I don't like my business being used as dinner conversation, and I let Mack know it." Annette grabbed a pen. "So do you have time to get that haircut before you go back to the city? I can fit you in any day this week. I figure you're going to be going back soon, and I want to make good on that promise."

I blinked, trying to adjust my brain to the change of subject. "There's no rush. I think I'm going to be here a while."

Annette looked up from her book. "You're staying in Indian Falls?"

I nodded. "For now. This morning Doreen recommended I pull the listing until the murder is solved. So I'm stuck here until then."

"Go back to Chicago, Rebecca." Annette's eyes met mine. They contained no hint of her typical laughter or carefree attitude. At this moment Annette looked deadly serious. "You've worked too hard at creating a life of your own to stay here. Your grandfather will look after the rink until this mess is over. Let me give you a haircut, then pack your bags and drive back to the city. Trust me, it's the best thing you could do for yourself." Annette closed the book on the counter with a bang. "I have to do some inventory in the back, but you think about what I said and let me know about that haircut."

Before I could say anything, Annette gave me a tight smile and brushed past me, disappearing into the back room. That left me alone in the front of the salon, confused and strangely depressed.

For the second time today, I had been made to feel like I wasn't welcome in my hometown. My mother's best friend, the woman who had held me together during Mom's death, couldn't get me out of town fast enough. Worse than that, I wasn't sure I believed everything Annette just told me.

Walking through town toward Pop's house, I tried to get my mind off of Annette's strange behavior by contemplating what Lionel had told me earlier. Mack's money was missing—maybe. A tiny voice inside my head suggested I go back to Mack's place and make sure Deputy Sean hadn't made a mistake. Going there was the only way to find out for sure, right?

I debated the issue until my grandfather's blue two-story house came into view. The sight of its lawn stopped me in my tracks. Smack in the middle was a four-foot-tall scarecrow wearing a Santa Claus suit and a sign around his neck that read MERRY CHRIST-MAS. I blinked twice. Somehow I'd stepped into a festive holiday episode of *The Twilight Zone*.

"Pop?" I peeked cautiously inside the living room. It was empty. Automatically, my eyes drifted toward the stairs. No way was I going up there, at least not until I knew my grandfather was alone. I dropped my purse on the floor, flipped on the television, and plopped onto the sofa.

At three thirty in the afternoon there wasn't much on besides bad talk shows and soap operas. I surfed until I found the Food Network and watched a woman stuff root vegetables up a chicken's butt. Cooking was a hobby of mine, and the show made me homesick for my Chicago kitchen.

I fell asleep as the show's host put the chicken in the oven. The sound of my cell phone ringing made my eyes snap back open. Half comatose, my hand dangled over the couch, I felt around in my purse and came up with the phone.

"Hello?" I said, trying to clear away the haze of sleep.

"Rebecca?"

I bolted upright.

"Rebecca, where in the hell are you and why haven't you called?"

It was my boss, Neil Capezio, and wow, did he sound unhappy.

"Hi, Neil. How are you doing?" I did my best to sound professional.

"How do you think I'm doing?" I held the phone away from my head to prevent hearing loss as his voice boomed, "You left a note on my desk telling me you had a family emergency. It said you'd be gone a week. It's been eleven days. As your boss, I deserve to know what you're doing and when you're coming back."

At the word "boss," I let out the breath I'd been holding. A couple of weeks ago, I ran into Neil just after he'd been stood up by his date. He asked me to join him for dinner, and I felt sorry enough for him to say yes. Since then he'd been hounding me for another date and hinting around the office that I was his girlfriend. Eek.

Oozing sweetness, I said, "I shouldn't have left a note like that, but your cell phone was off." A convenient circumstance since at the time I hadn't wanted to talk to him.

"And yours has been off since you disappeared."

"Sorry," I said. "I had to come to Indian Falls to handle some family problems. I was hoping they'd only take a couple of days to fix. Only I've run into a snag and I need to extend my vacation time."

"What you need is to come back to Chicago. Look, I understand family is important to you. It's important to me too. My brother . . . well, things have been complicated here, too." His voice quavered for a second, then took on its normal barking tone. "Regardless, I need you at your desk handling files." His voice lowered and got all whispery. "Eleven days is too long without seeing your smile. I need you here. Things have been really hard for me lately."

Neil's attempt at romance made my skin crawl, but the genuine panic at the end made me ask, "What's wrong? Did something happen at the office?"

"No. I'd like to talk to you about it, but not over the phone. It's complicated."

If there was one thing I understood it was complicated. "I don't know when I'll be back. Things *here* are a little more complicated than I thought they would be. I hope you can understand and maybe"—I crossed my fingers—"allow me to take a leave of absence for a while. I would hate to come back to Chicago and not have a job waiting for me."

Silence.

I bit my bottom lip and waited as Neil breathed heavily on the other end.

Finally, he said, "I'll think about it and give you my answer in a day or two. Until then, good luck with everything. I'll be thinking about you."

My mouth started to form a protest, but before I could say anything, I heard a click and the line went dead. Damn! I was pretty certain I hadn't just lost my signal. Something told me I'd also lost my job. Promising to get back to someone was how Neil politely ushered a rejected client out of his office.

I went to the kitchen to drown my sorrows in diet soda. Not that I especially liked my job, but I needed it. No check meant no rent, and no rent led to no apartment, which would leave me sleeping in a cardboard box.

"Rebecca." A robe-clad Pop cleared his throat and shuffled into the kitchen with a red-faced Louise trailing behind him. Unless Siegfried and Roy made them magically appear in the living room doorway, they had both come from upstairs. Ick. Ick. Ick.

Pop gave me a big smile and cheerfully said, "I didn't hear you come in."

I didn't want to know why he hadn't heard me. Don't ask, don't tell was a good way to live. "I was just having a soda," I said in a strangled voice. "Want to join me?"

Louise's eyes widened, and she shook her head. "I have to set up for the card party. I'll see you there, Arthur?"

My grandfather's head tilted to one side. "I don't know. Don't bother saving me a seat." He sat down across from me.

Louise stood there for a moment in her frilly pink shirt and tan skirt as if waiting for Pop to say something more. When he didn't, she let out a tiny high-pitched giggle and waved as she walked out the door.

Pop blew a strand of hair off his forehead. "Wow, I thought she'd never leave."

I gave him a hard look. "You invited her upstairs. To a woman it implies that she's welcome to stay as long as she wants."

"Huh. I hadn't thought about it quite that way." He pushed out of his chair and padded over to the fridge for a beer. "How was your picnic with Lionel?"

I frowned. "Men are scum."

Pop smiled. "I guess my date was better than yours?"

93

"Mine wasn't a date since Lionel isn't interested in me like that," I said through clenched teeth. "Lionel only asked me to lunch because he wanted to grill me about Mack's murder."

Pop nodded. "I heard you were poking around town asking questions. Find anything interesting?"

I rested my chin on my hands. "Mack's house key. I kind of let myself into his place yesterday. Turns out Mack had a lot of money stashed under his mattress. Only thing is, the money wasn't there later when the cops tossed the place. Either they missed seeing it, or someone went in after me but before the cops."

Pop gave a low whistle. "You think the thief slipped Mack those pills everyone is talking about, don't you? You do realize going into that house alone was stupid. You could have been killed."

I hadn't thought about it quite like that. Okay. Maybe going back to Mack's wasn't such a good idea after all.

Pop sat down at the table across from me, took a swig of beer, and looked me square in the eyes. "You know what I think? I think we need to go back to Mack's house and make sure the money ain't there."

"We?" What we?

Pop bobbed his head. "You don't think I'm going to let you go alone. That would be dangerous. You need some muscle, and I'm volunteering for the job."

I glanced at Pop's toothpick arms. There might still be a muscle in there somewhere. Shaking my head, I said, "I've been caught once at Mack's house. There's no way Sean will buy that I just wanted to see where Mack lived a second time. If he catches me again he'll arrest me, and you'll go to jail, too."

"I don't mind. Chicks dig dangerous men behind bars. Betty Jean would bake me a cake with a file if I asked, and she makes a great carrot cake with real cream cheese frosting. None of that store-bought crap. Might not be so bad."

"Well, I'm not going to risk it. Breaking into Mack's is off." At least until Pop went to bed. Then I might change my mind.

"What we need is an alibi." Pop snapped his fingers so loud I was afraid he'd broken a bone. "I know. We'll go to the card party at the center tonight. That'll give us an alibi. Once everyone's seen us, we'll cut out and head to Mack's place. Old people have bad memories, so no one will be able to say when we left. It will be dark when we get to Mack's house, which means none of the neighbors will ever know we were there."

Pop grinned. He looked so pleased with the plan I didn't have the heart to tell him his teeth were coming loose. Apparently, so was my head, since it was nodding up and down in agreement. Before I could come to my senses, Pop stood up from the table and shuffled back upstairs to get ready for the upcoming evening. I, however, slumped in my chair wondering what had come over me.

I had agreed to break into Mack's house, again. I was going to do it in the dead of night, and this time I was bringing my grandfather.

Ten

My Monday nights in Chicago were normally spent at Nick's Sports Bar, where I played video poker and watched whatever sporting events were on the big screen.

This Monday night I was sitting at a large folding table in the Indian Falls Senior Center holding a fistful of diamonds and hearts and trying to decide what game I was supposed to be playing now. So far I'd played Euchre, Hearts, Crazy Eights, and a rip-roaring round of Go Fish, and I'd lost every one. I was hoping it was due to my lack of interest rather than the strategic prowess of my opponents. Pop had ditched me the minute we got to the center's makeshift game room, and somehow I had been seated with a woman wearing very red, very smeared lipstick and two men with pants hiked up to their necks.

Lipstick woman smiled at me. "It's your turn, dear."

I put down a card, and the smile disappeared.

"You're supposed to play suit."

"Sorry." I picked up my card and put down another one. I was clueless as to why, but the red-lipped lady nodded.

Mercifully, whatever game I was playing ended. I begged off the next one and headed to the bathroom. Away from the table, I did a scan of the room. No Pop, but I spotted Louise standing in the far corner. My feet started in her direction.

Now that I was closer to Louise, I could see her eyes were red and glassy. She wiped them and straightened her shoulders as she saw me approach. "Good evening, Rebecca. It was very sweet of you to come with your grandfather." It was a nice speech, I thought. Too bad the sniffles ruined her delivery.

I wanted to ask what was wrong. Only I didn't feel it was my place. Besides making crackpot scarecrows and boffing my grandfather, Louise was a mystery to me, and I was pretty sure I wanted to keep it that way. Smiling, I asked, "Speaking of my grandfather, have you seen him anywhere?"

Louise's red-rimmed eyes grew wide. "He's . . . he's . . ." Her eyes started to leak. She bit her lip and pointed toward one of the exits as she wailed, "With her."

"Her who?" The words just slipped out. I knew I had made a mistake the second Louise's sniffles turned to sobs. Big fat tears poured down her scrunched-up face. Louise now bore a startling resemblance to a basset hound. I put a hand on her arm. "I'm sure it's not as bad as you think."

Okay, I was bluffing. It was probably much worse. Pop hadn't bothered to tell Louise that he played the field. He and I were going to have a long talk—if I scrounged up the courage.

Louise's eyes filled with hope. "Do you really think so?" Nodding seemed like the best course of action, and Louise gave me a watery smile. "I'm sorry for being so emotional. Your grandfather and I have become very good friends. A lot of the women here are jealous. It's because he looks like Sean Connery."

My grandfather appeared in a far doorway, all five feet nine inches of him swathed in black. Black jeans, black button-down shirt, black boots, and a black baseball cap that covered his wavy white hair. If I had a couple of martinis and squinted really hard, he might pass for Sean Connery's mailman. Louise was in love. Or she was legally blind.

Pop tilted his head toward the doorway and disappeared. I said good-bye to Louise and found him on the other side of the door. He was grinning like a mad game show host. Come to think of it, Pop looked a lot like Bob Barker before Botox.

"Where have you been?" I asked.

Pop's smile grew wider. "I've been getting cozy with Eleanor Schaffer. She can be really accommodating if you're nice to her."

I clamped my hands over my ears and squeezed my eyes shut. "I do not need to hear this."

"Rebecca Robbins, stop behaving like a child this minute. I want you to listen to me."

It was his tone more than his words that stunned me enough to remove my hands. This wasn't the sex-crazed old man I'd been living with the past two weeks. This was Pop, who'd taught me how to ride a bike and grounded me when my mother couldn't bring herself to do it. This was a man who meant business.

My grandfather gave a satisfied nod. He glanced up and down the hall, then whispered, "Eleanor's been Doc Truman's secretary for years. She has a key to his office. I figured I could get Eleanor to unlock Doc's office. Then while I keep her busy in the back, you can flip through Doc's files. They'll tell you what drug killed Mack."

"That's ridiculous." Pop shushed me, but I ignored him, saying, "Look, even if you could convince Eleanor to go to the office at this time of night, I don't want to steal medical files. It's just not right." Rebecca Robbins, morality police. Breaking into a dead guy's house later tonight, well, that was another story.

Pop frowned. "I don't know what you're complaining about. I'm the one making the sacrifices to help you solve this case. Eleanor isn't my type, you know."

I wasn't impressed. As far as I could tell, my grandfather only had one type—still breathing.

"Arthur, sweetheart? Where did my honey go?" I turned to see the source of the high-pitched voice coming down the hallway. My grandfather's newest conquest was about four inches taller and three feet wider than he was. Somehow Eleanor had sausaged her ample body into a 1980s-style white spandex jumpsuit complete with a shiny gold belt. She was also wearing at least a pound of makeup and false eyelashes the size of tarantulas.

Okay. She wasn't Pop's type, but the Abominable Snowman might give her a whirl.

Eleanor's eyes widened at the sight of my grandfather. Her gold-spangled heels started clip-clopping down the hallway in hot pursuit. She stopped next to him and put a large, possessive arm on his shoulder while crooning, "There you are, pumpkin. You were gone so long that I started to get worried."

"Rebecca here needed to talk." My grandfather winked at me before smiling back at her. "Eleanor, have you met my granddaughter?"

Eleanor tittered. "Not since she was little. I was sorry to hear about your mother, honey. She was a real nice lady."

I don't know why, but genuine sympathy always makes me feel weepy. My throat went dry and tight. I tried my best to smile as I said, "I know." Saying the words made me sniffle, and Eleanor removed her arm from Pop and draped it around me. Before I knew what was happening, I was squeezed against her very ample bosom and turning blue from lack of oxygen.

Pop saved me from the humiliation of passing out by saying, "Are you ready to leave, Eleanor?"

Eleanor let go. "Anytime you are, honeybunch."

I took a step backward. Gasping for air, I shook my head at Pop. I was not going to go to Doc Truman's office.

Pop ignored me. "Eleanor, why don't you say good-bye to some of your friends. I'll get the car, and you can meet me up front. A few ladies might be upset if they see us together." He winked at her. Eleanor winked back and ambled into the main room, blowing him a kiss as she went.

I put my hands on my hips. "Now what?"

"Now we go to the car, and you hide in the backseat. Once we get to the office, you wait five minutes. Then you can come in and find the file. Piece of cake."

Right. "I'm not doing it."

"Okay." Pop gave me an exaggerated shrug. "Eleanor and I will go. You can stay and play Crazy Eights with the Golden Girls. I'll swing back later to pick you up."

Pop put his hands in his pockets and sauntered toward the back exit. I peeked into the lounge. The smeared lipstick lady snored over her hand, and the guy next to her scratched his crotch before picking up his cards. Okay, maybe hiding in the backseat wasn't such a bad idea after all.

I caught up to Pop by his Lincoln Town Car. The car had been my grandmother's. After she died, it sat unused in the garage for years. Then one day Pop sold his truck and started driving it. My mother had tried to get him to trade it in two years ago, claiming it was a death trap. Death trap or not, the car had a roomy backseat.

I got into a cramped but almost comfortable fetal position on the backseat floor. Then my grandfather threw a blanket over my head. Now I wasn't just cramped, I was hot. Yippee.

"Hold on tight, Rebecca. I'll swing around to pick up Eleanor. We'll be at the office in a jiffy."

He hit the accelerator, and my head bashed into the front seat as the car jumped to life with a squeal of tires. A minute later, the car came to a stop. I heard the passenger door open.

"I love your car, Arthur." My side of the car lowered notice-ably as Eleanor climbed in. "I just need to adjust the seat. These long legs need a lot of room."

Oh no. This was not happening. Only it was. The seat in front of me began traveling toward my nose. I held my breath, feeling like I was in an adventure movie I'd watched on cable. The bad guy ended up flat as a pancake, and I prayed the same wouldn't happen to me.

I was about to scream when the seat stopped moving. I let out a sigh of relief. I wasn't comfortable, but I wasn't dead. Life could be worse.

Eleanor chirped, "I'm ready whenever you are, Arthur." Her voice got all husky when she added, "In more ways than you know."

I gagged as the car lurched into gear and hummed down the road, drowning out anything else Eleanor might have added.

Thank God Doc Truman's office was only five blocks away. The car doors opened, and I heard Eleanor's heels click against the sidewalk. A few moments later, a door opened and slammed shut. That was my cue to flip the quilt and get the hell out of Pop's cramped backseat.

Now seated in the very roomy front seat, I debated whether I wanted to go through with my grandfather's plan. Getting the name of the drug that killed Mack would put me a heck of a lot closer to solving the crime. Still, going into Doc's office and taking information was stealing, which was bad. On the other hand, the purpose behind it was good. I was torn.

My fingers brushed the passenger door's handle just as a pair of headlights turned into the tiny parking lot. My heart leapt into my larynx, and on pure instinct, I ducked. I didn't want to go down in Indian Falls history as my grandfather's sexual lookout.

A car door slammed, and footsteps traveled the asphalt. More curious than cautious now, I peeked over the dashboard just in time to see Doc Truman disappear inside the building. Two minutes later (I clocked it), my grandfather came scurrying out with his shirt untucked. A black boot was dangling from his left hand.

"Busted," Pop said as he hopped in the car and cranked it to life. "At least Eleanor and I didn't get very far. I'd hate to have sex with her without you getting that file." I rolled my eyes, and off we zoomed.

We traveled in silence for a few minutes as the reality of what had nearly happened hit me. I had been about to go into that office. Had he pulled up two minutes later, Doc would have caught me red-handed in his drawers. I shivered and vowed that I would only obtain the drug information through a very legal Plan B. I only wished I knew what that might be.

We pulled up to Mack Murphy's house, and Pop killed the engine. He got out, but I didn't move. It was dark. Very, very dark. Not that I was scared of the dark. Good things often happened when the lights were off. Well, not often enough, but occasionally. It's just that I'd forgotten how dark it got outside the city limits. No streetlights. No house lights. Tonight there was no moonlight, either.

"Rebecca, what are you waiting for?" Pop's shadowy outline limped toward my side of the car. Pop still hadn't put on his boot.

I opened the door but shook my head. "We can't do this tonight."

"Why not?" Pop bent over and grunted while tugging on his boot. "We're here. The house is empty." He stood upright. "I say we go in."

I crossed my arms. "It's dark."

"Of course it is."

"We can't turn on the lights or the neighbors will notice."

Pop pulled a flashlight out of his pocket and showed it to me. Turning it on, he started walking up to the house.

I dashed after him. "You can't get in without me, Pop. You don't have the key."

"Damn kids break windows around here all the time." He climbed onto the front porch and studied the door. "Do you think I should use a rock or my boot?"

I moved my grandfather to the side. "Okay. I'll do it." I fished the key out of my pocket and slid it in the lock. Before Pop could protest, I grabbed the flashlight and said, "Stay here. I'll only be a minute."

I slipped into the house and closed the door behind me. My little beam of light pointed toward the debris-filled floor, and I hurried through the house and up the stairs to Mack's bedroom.

Entering the bedroom, I let out a low whistle. Deputy Sean had done a thorough job of tossing the place. The house had been untidy before, but now it looked like a tornado had hit—hard—and the money was gone. Either Deputy Sean had decided to line his own pockets or someone else had come in and swiped the cash. My bet was on the unknown thief. I didn't think Sean was devious enough to keep that kind of secret—at least not for more than fifteen minutes. In high school, the football team always knew immediately after Sean scored with a cheerleader. So who was the thief, and how did I go about finding him?

The floorboard creaked behind me. My chest tightened, and I slowly turned. I panned my flashlight through the door, looking for something to pummel my assailant with. The light hit the doorway, and in bopped my grandfather.

"Did you see all the crap Mack has around here? I could have fallen and broken my hip walking through this place."

I let out a relieved sigh. "I thought I told you to wait outside."

"I'm not a dog, Rebecca. I don't have to stay when someone tells me to." The dim light made his grin look ghostly. "Besides, I wanted to see what Mack's place looked like. Funny, but I thought it would have looked better since Mack stole all those deposits. This place is a dump."

For some reason I felt the need to defend poor Mack. "His office is nice. I think that's where he spent most of his time."

"Huh." Pop glanced down the hall. "After the thing with Eleanor, I'm not really interested in offices." He turned back toward me. "Did you find out what we came here for?"

I nodded. "Lionel was right. The money's gone."

"Too bad. We could have had fun with it on a riverboat casino. Well, I guess we should go." He started down the hall. I caught up to him and led the way down the stairs with my flashlight. Behind me Pop complained, "This trip was a real disappointment. I was waiting to see a bunch of money or a dead body or something. Why do you get all the excitement? All I got coming here was a messy house. I got gypped."

"Next time I break into a house I'll take you along," I promised. I opened the front door and walked right into a brick wall disguised as a chest. Panic flooded through me, and I let out a bloodcurdling scream.

"What's going on out there, Rebecca?" I heard my grandfather's footsteps on the porch, but I didn't turn around. My eyes were riveted on the dark, hulking figure in front of me. The guy was at least a head taller than my five foot six and was dressed like he'd just stepped out of a *Godfather* movie—dark shirt, tie, and suit and all muscle. Holy shit, I thought, taking a step back. Blood pumped furiously through my veins as the man glowered at me.

My grandfather moved to stand next to me. He poked his finger at the guy's chest and demanded, "Who the hell are you, and what the hell are you doing here?"

"Pop." I nudged my grandfather and smiled at the scary guy. "Sorry. We're just surprised to run into someone out here this late at night."

The man stared at me like a wolf sizing up its next meal.

Gulping, I grabbed Pop's arm. "We were just leaving." I began to step around the guy.

Steroid-man moved to the side, blocking our path. "Are you friends of Mack Murphy?" His accent was straight-up New Jersey. Perfect.

I was about to answer no when Pop puffed up his nonexistent chest and chimed in, "What's it to you?"

The big guy took a step backward. "I didn't mean nothin' bad by it. You had a key to the house. I figure you were friends of his. Am I right?"

Pop opened his mouth, and I stepped on his foot.

"We both knew him," I agreed. "How about you? Were you and Mack friends?"

"We were business associates." The guy put his hand in his pocket. I held my breath waiting for him to pull out a gun. His hand came out with a business card, and I took it with a sigh of relief. The card read ANTHONY CATALANO ENTERPRISES. The company was located in Rock Island, Illinois.

"What kind of enterprising stuff do you do?" I asked.

Anthony gave a tense smile. "I like to dabble in a lot of different businesses. Kind of like Mack. He and I were talking about his business interests before he turned up dead."

"Oh," I said. Anthony made it sound like people falling over dead was a common occurrence. I was pretty sure I didn't want to know what kind of work Catalano Enterprises did. I smiled, though I was finding it hard to breathe. "Well, we should get going. It was nice to meet you, Mr. Catalano."

I scooted past the human mountain. Pulling Pop behind me, I headed for the car.

"Hey," Anthony bellowed.

I stopped in my tracks. "Yeah?" My voice cracked.

"You didn't tell me your name."

Hmmm, how could I have forgotten that?

Before I could make something up, Pop yelled, "Arthur Phillips. Don't you forget it."

I shoved Pop into the car, gave Anthony a nervous wave, and hopped in the passenger side. As Pop gunned the engine, I said a tiny prayer that Anthony had more muscle than brain and would promptly forget Pop's name. The idea that he might come looking for us scared me silly.

Not taking his eyes off the road, Pop announced, "I could have taken him. That guy didn't scare me for a second."

The bravado in Pop's voice was ruined by his expression. Pop's face looked like he'd sat on a stun gun.

Sighing, I gently said, "I know, Pop." I closed my eyes for the ride home.

The clock read twelve twenty-two when we pulled into the driveway. The headlights of Pop's car illuminated Cornstalk Santa, causing me to ask, "Why did you put that scarecrow up now, Pop? Christmas is seven months away."

Pop yawned as he guided the long car into the garage. "Louise said her scarecrows are good decorations no matter what time of year. Plus, I'm hoping it'll keep away those damn crows. They keep pecking at the grass seed. This thing should scare them. It scares the hell out of me."

Entering the house, I decided the scarecrow would keep away more than birds. Everyone in Indian Falls had to know Louise made those things, and Pop putting one in his front yard as good as branded him hers. I climbed into bed and shut off the light. Louise was a whole lot smarter than I'd given her credit for.

Bleary-eyed and grumpy, I stumbled into the kitchen the next morning. Pop was already seated at the table drinking his coffee. He looked like nothing unusual had happened the night before.

I chugged a cup of scalding coffee. Then, ignoring the tongue burn, I poured myself another. My mind was in a fog. Even though I'd been dead tired last night, sleep had eluded me for hours.

Visions of the hulking Anthony Catalano had haunted me all night long.

When I opened the rink's front door around ten o'clock, my eyes were finally opened, thanks to the half-pot of caffeine running through my veins. Only problem was, my mind was still asleep, which is why I was seated at my mother's desk wondering what in the world to do next. All my leads were dead ends. I had come to a dead end. I was going to be in Indian Falls for the rest of my life.

I spent the rest of my day renting skates and playing referee during open-skate hours. During my breaks, I tried my damnedest to convince George that being the rink manager would be a great career opportunity. Sadly, at thirty-eight years of age, George was still certain the Ice Capades would call.

The events of the next day were pretty much the same. I even upped my offer to George, saying I'd hire an assistant rink manager to give him some help. No dice, so I called the sheriff's office and chatted up Roxy. By the time I hung up, Roxy had shared that Felix Slaughter was getting a divorce, that Mack's funeral was scheduled for Friday morning, and that Sheriff Jackson and his crack team were no closer to solving Mack's murder than I was.

By Thursday my nerves were strung so tight they were ready to snap. I decided to stop at the DiBelka bakery to get some fresh bagels to ease the tension. Mrs. DiBelka was waiting on a customer as I walked through the door. She gave me a big smile and finished ringing up the order.

Many things in Indian Falls had changed since I left for Chicago. Mrs. DiBelka and her old-fashioned bakery still looked the same. With bleach-blond hair, a spandex leopard-print shirt that exposed her ample cleavage, and four-inch heels, Mrs. D looked like an X-rated Betty Crocker. When I was in high school, the boys would take turns daring each other to get close enough to look down her blouse. Of course, to do so they'd have to buy something. I've always thought that was part of the bakery's grand marketing plan.

The customer disappeared through the door, and Mrs. Di-Belka came around the counter. Her arms wrapped me in a warm hug, and I settled into her embrace with a sigh. Mrs. D. smelled like baking bread.

"How've you been, Rebecca?" Mrs. D. took a step back and looked me over with a critical eye. "You're not eating enough. You're looking so skinny."

I smiled. "They don't have bakeries as good as yours in Chicago."

"Oh, go on." She waved my compliment aside, but I could tell she was pleased. "So what can I get for you?"

I glanced at the case with the éclairs. They had a seductive aura that was working on my psyche. Resisting, I said, "Two apple cinnamon bagels."

Mrs. D. bagged the bagels. She handed them to me, saying, "Doreen Nelson was in earlier. She told everyone you were going to be staying in town longer than she first thought. Is that true? If so, I'll call Angie in Galena. She'd love to come for a visit. The two of you could catch up."

Mrs. D's daughter Angie had been my best friend from kindergarten all the way through high school. She was the only one who'd been able to make me feel better after my father left and the only person besides my family I'd really missed after leaving Indian Falls.

"I'd love to see Angie again. Tell her I might be here a couple of weeks if she wants to swing by." My voice sounded perky. Too bad my heart dropped in my chest as my throat constricted.

Saying the words out loud hurt. They made my extended stay in Indian Falls feel like a reality. The back of my eyes began to burn, but crying in public wasn't an option. Instead I said, "Mrs. D, I need two of those éclairs."

I also bought four doughnuts and two therapeutic chocolate chip scones. Then I drove my Civic to the rink. I waited for George to finish the private lesson he was teaching before showing him the box of doughnuts. Perhaps bribing George with doughnuts was a cheap trick, but bakery goods had worked for Lionel. Right now I'd try anything.

George scarfed down four doughnuts, then turned down my job offer, again. Apparently, all those medical studies about sugar affecting the brain were way off. Either that or George was a medical miracle.

Licking chocolate off his fingers, George glided onto the rink to work off the calories. I turned and went into the office to call my Chicago roommate, Jasmine. Our rent was due in a week, and needless to say, I wasn't going to be there to pay it.

Jasmine picked up at her work extension on the first ring. Her laughter rang through the receiver when I said hello.

"Girl, where are you?" Hearing Jasmine's low-pitched voice made me smile. "I thought you would have been back days ago."

I explained about Mack's murder and the wrench it threw in my plans. Jasmine gasped, then shrieked, "Oh my God. Are you okay? I mean, a dead body would freak even me out."

"I'm fine." Sort of. "I'd be better if the sheriff left his garden long enough to figure out who killed Mack."

Jasmine gave a loud snort and started to laugh. I wasn't offended. It was funny. Years ago, the Northern Illinois University housing department had assigned me and Jasmine the same room in college. Rural me had been a little freaked by Jasmine's very dark skin and boisterous laugh. Now I counted on that laugh to keep me sane.

"Hey," she said. "Neil has been asking about you around the office, and he called our place four times yesterday asking if I knew when you were coming back. I've thought about changing our phone number or telling him you've moved to Mars, only the poor guy has had a bad couple of days. I don't have the heart to crush him like that."

Jasmine and I also worked together. The fact she was concerned about Neil made me sit up straight in my chair.

"What happened? The last time we talked he said his life was kind of complicated, but he wouldn't explain." Neil was a little annoying, but essentially a pretty good person. I couldn't help worrying about the guy, especially if Jasmine was. Jasmine wasn't the worrying type.

"He didn't tell you? His brother and sister-in-law were in a car crash last week. They're in intensive care, and it doesn't sound like either of them is expected to survive."

Yikes! On our one and only dinner together, Neil mentioned that his brother and his family lived in Seattle and were the only relatives he had left. My whole body ached with sympathy. I understood what it was like to lose family. It sucked—and I still had Pop. I could only imagine what Neil was feeling right now.

Jasmine promised to keep me posted and to arrange flowers for the family in both our names if necessary. The call drove home the fact that life went on in Chicago without me. That made me sad, but it also reminded me about the reason I called in the first place. "Hey, are you okay with paying the rent next week?"

I heard a pop on the other end, and my mind quickly conjured the image of Jasmine blowing a bubble. She was the Hubba Bubba queen.

"Yeah," she said. "You left enough to cover it."

Actually, I was fifty dollars short, but Jasmine was too nice to admit it. She was also too good a friend to remind me that next month's rent was only thirty days away and neither of us knew when I'd be back.

I swallowed hard and admitted, "The only thing is, I don't know when this whole thing is going to be over. Do you think you can cover the rent next month if I can't? I promise I'll pay you back."

There was silence on the other line before a subdued Jasmine said, "I didn't want to bring this up, but I have a cousin coming to town, and she's been begging me for a place to stay for a couple of months. I told her no, but she would be willing to temporarily take over your part of the rent. She's desperate."

My vision blurred as blood flooded my head. I put my head down on the desk and tried to take a deep, calming breath. No good. My air intake came fast and shallow.

"Becca? You still there?"

"Yeah," I squeaked.

"Don't freak out or anything. I don't really want her to move in. Just when you mentioned being concerned about the rent I thought it might be a good idea." Jasmine's voice turned soft and sympathetic. "You have enough to worry about without being concerned about stuff back here, my friend. Tell you what, I'll put your stuff in storage so my cousin doesn't do any damage, and the minute you're ready to come back my cousin will be booted. And it better be soon; otherwise there might be a murder here. Trust me, the girl isn't my idea of a desirable roommate."

I rubbed the back of my neck and fought back tears. I hated admitting it, but the idea made sense. A person would have to be insane to want to pay rent in Chicago while living here.

I squeezed my eyes shut. "Okay." My voice squeaked as I choked out the word. "Just make sure she knows I'm coming back soon."

Another Hubba Bubba pop sounded as Jasmine said, "No problem. I'll annoy the hell out of her so she'll be begging to move out by the time you come back." I could hear the concern in her voice as she added, "Hey, you take care of yourself. Let me know if you need any help, all right?"

I hung up the phone with my heart in my stomach. Annette had been right on Monday when she said I should get out of town and trust the rink would be fine without me. Instead of listening, I'd felt sorry for myself. Well, now I was homeless and thoroughly depressed. I grabbed the final éclair in the bakery box and took a bite. By the time I'd eaten the last bits of chocolate I felt improved enough to think logically. Throwing a pity party for myself wasn't going to get me anywhere, but snooping around town trying to solve Mack's murder would. What I really needed was the name of the drug that killed Mack, and maybe Eleanor would be willing to give me the name of the drug in exchange for a real date with my grandfather. Anything was possible.

Grabbing my purse, I headed for the door and stalked through the parking lot with purpose. Then I saw my car, and my feet came to an abrupt halt. My right rear tire was flat. Not just a little flat—completely deflated. I took a step closer, and my eyes zeroed in on a rusty-looking thingy sticking out of the black rubber. My car had been fine when I entered the rink. Someone had stabbed that oversized nail into my tire on purpose.

Eleven

I started to sniffle, but then I heard footsteps behind me. Panic stopped the tears. Acting on instinct, I swung my purse and felt it connect with something.

"Ooof."

I turned in time to see Lionel go down to one knee. That started me crying for real. Not only was my car injured, now I wouldn't get my camel ride.

"What in the hell is wrong with you?" Lionel yelled. He pushed himself off the ground and brushed off his pants while giving me several looks of disgust.

I didn't know what to say, so I just pointed to the car, which apparently was the right thing to do. Lionel immediately stopped looking angry. He walked to the car and knelt down by the tire. A minute later, he walked back with the nail-like thing that had been protruding from the tire and handed it to me along with a folded slip of paper. "I found this under the windshield wiper."

Sniffling, I unfolded the note.

Leave town now or bad things will happen.

My tears were replaced by a strange calm. After being coerced into subleasing my apartment, threats were anticlimactic.

I handed Lionel the note and glanced back at the flattened tire. Finding my voice, I asked, "So do you think I should call the sheriff's department or a mechanic?" Visions of a confused Sean poking my tire sprang to mind. "Never mind the cops," I said. "I don't have a full spare in my trunk, which means I can't fix this myself. Do you have Zach's number handy?"

Lionel looked at me with a confused expression. "I think I preferred the tears. The calm, rational behavior is scary."

My eyes narrowed. "Are you one of those guys who thinks women get irrational during a crisis?"

"No." He shook his head. "But I've come to expect it from you. Rebecca, you are not like other women."

I decided to take that as a compliment. Lionel gave me Zach's number, and I pulled out my cell and dialed the poker-playing mechanic. We sat on the rink's front stoop until Zach and his tow truck arrived. A lump formed in my throat as I watched him load my car onto the back. Zach handed me his card, assuring me the tire would be fixed later today, then climbed back in his truck and drove away with my bright yellow car forlornly trailing behind him.

I took a deep breath and asked, "Now what?"

Lionel's arm snaked around my shoulders. "Now you come with me. I promised Elwood you'd come to the farm for a ride."

Lionel pulled up outside his office. Before he turned off the ignition, I was out of the truck and halfway to the barn. The prospect of seeing Lionel's camel made me feel smiley for the first time in days.

I walked into the dim barn, and Elwood greeted me at the door. Today he was sporting a bright orange construction hard hat. My eyebrows rose, and I turned to look at Lionel.

A smile tugged at the corner of his lips as he disappeared into Elwood's stall. A few seconds later, he reemerged with a motorcycle helmet from the seventies in his hand. The helmet was painted gold and came complete with a chin strap.

Lionel handed the helmet to me. "Your life is a little complicated lately, so I figured you and Elwood should both have some protection."

"Thanks," I said with a frown. The hat was ugly, and I resented Lionel's implication that I couldn't take care of myself. The worst part was that Lionel had a point. During the last week my life had taken on a strange action-movie quality. Maybe extra protection was a good idea after all.

I shoved the helmet onto my head, squashing my hair in the process. Elwood nudged my shoulder, and I gave him a pat on the neck. "So," I asked, "how do I do this?"

Lionel grinned. "Let's go outside in the pasture, and I'll show you."

I followed Lionel and Elwood out into the sunlight. Elwood trotted happily into the pasture, not seeming to mind the rope around his neck. Then, for the first time, I really looked at the camel I was about to ride.

Elwood had short light brown hair and stood about six and a half feet tall from the ground to the top of his hump. His one hump. Somehow I remembered camels at the zoo having two humps. Riding a camel with two humps made sense. You just needed to sit in between them and hold on tight. How did a person go about riding a one-humped camel?

Lionel crooked his little finger in my direction, but I didn't move. "Maybe this isn't such a good idea," I said as my feet shuffled backward.

Lionel grabbed my hand, preventing my escape. "Elwood has been looking forward to this all day. He likes having the people he's friends with ride him. Do you want to fink out and disappoint Elwood?"

I looked into Elwood's sweet camel face. Slowly, I shook my head. I wasn't sure if camels could be disappointed, but it seemed wrong to take the chance. "Okay," I said. "Tell me what to do."

Lionel gave my arm a tug, and I took a step toward him. His hand reached up, and my heart gave an excited skip as he adjusted my chin strap. He chucked me playfully under the chin and turned toward the camel. "I need to get Elwood suited up. Then the two of you can go for a ride."

I watched with fascination as Lionel gave the rope a gentle tug. At the signal, Elwood gracefully lowered himself to the ground. Lionel picked up a large saddle sitting on the grass and settled the thing on top of Elwood's hump. Immediately Elwood stood up, allowing Lionel to fasten the belts. The two of them had clearly been through this routine before.

Ten minutes later, hard-hat Elwood was ready to make tracks. The problem was, I wasn't. The saddle looked really high. Not that I was scared of heights. I just preferred to keep my feet on the ground.

Lionel shot me an amused look. I could tell he expected me to back out. No way. If Lionel could ride a camel, so could I.

I walked over to Elwood and petted his nose. The camel rolled his eyes with pleasure, and I laughed.

"Are you ready?" Lionel asked.

I nodded. "I'm ready."

Another tug on the rope had Elwood back on the ground, and I jumped on board. My butt hit the saddle and kept going. I slid over the saddle and landed on the other side of Elwood with a thud. Elwood turned his head and blinked his thick eyelashes as if asking what I was doing with my ass on the ground.

"Ow." I stood up, rubbing my bruised butt. My eyes met Lionel's. If he laughed, I'd deck him. To his credit he didn't. "Okay," I said, shaking off my humiliation. "What did I do wrong?"

Lionel pointed to the saddle. "You have to hold on to the handle for balance. Try it again."

I took a deep breath. Then, grabbing the handle with both hands, I closed my eyes and hauled myself into the seat. I opened one eye and grinned. I did it. I was sitting on a camel. This was so cool. Elwood looked at me and rolled his eyes. See, I thought, even the camel was proud of me.

"Okay, Rebecca, it's time for you and Elwood to take a ride." Before I could ask what he was going to do, Lionel tugged on the rope, and Elwood clambered to his feet. I jiggled side to side, sending the contents of my stomach rolling. My choice to eat all those pastries for breakfast was looking like a very bad idea.

My hands turned white as they clung to the handle for dear life. I wrapped my legs tight against Elwood's flank as my body tilted precariously from one side to the other. Somehow, miraculously, I stayed seated on Elwood, who was now standing upright.

Lionel looked impressed. "I didn't even hang on the first time I tried that. Good job."

I smiled down at him, and my heart lurched into my throat. The ground was suddenly a long way down. "Thanks," I said, swallowing down my apprehension. I had come this far, and I wasn't going to chicken out now. Straightening my shoulders, I asked, "Does this ride move forward or is it strictly up and down?"

Lionel tugged on the lead rope, and Elwood started forward. At first all I could think about was breaking my tailbone on the ground below. After a few minutes I stopped worrying and began to enjoy myself. The sun was shining, the sky was blue, and I was riding a camel. Did life get any better than this?

Lionel's voice interrupted my Hallmark card moment. "Do you want to go faster?"

I grinned, and Lionel signaled for Elwood to pick up the pace. Now we were trotting. The ride was fun for about five minutes; then my butt started to protest. Riding Elwood was a lot like my life, unexpected and very bumpy.

"Hey," I shouted down to Lionel. "How do I stop him?"

Elwood's head swiveled toward me. His feet came to an abrupt halt, sending my body flying forward over the pommel. In slow motion I watched the ground as it zoomed closer. I closed my eyes, bracing myself for painful contact. Instead, a pair of strong arms caught me and pulled me close.

I found myself looking right into Lionel's deep green eyes. He gave me a sheepish smile. "I should have warned you. Elwood responds to commands from people he likes."

"I'm glad he likes me."

"Yeah. Too bad he's not the only one." Lionel's eyes darkened. My mouth went dry as he dipped his head toward mine. I licked my lips in anticipation of the touch of his lips against my . . . forehead?

I blinked as Lionel set me back on my own two feet. What happened? Did I have éclair breath?

Lionel walked over to Elwood and started unbuckling Elwood's saddle. Over his shoulder he said, "If you're feeling better, maybe we should talk about your car."

My car? "What about my car?"

He gave me one of those "boy, are you dense" looks. "It had a big nail in one of its tires. Remember?"

Shrugging off the returning panic, I said, "Zach is fixing my tire. What else do you need to talk about?"

"Someone flattened your tire on purpose."

I nodded. "I know. Probably the same person who scribbled on the rink doors."

"It could be the same person who murdered Mack." Lionel's voice rang with concern. He squinted at me in the bright sunlight as he tried to judge my reaction.

"I thought of that," I admitted.

"And?"

Elwood nosed my arm looking for attention. I ignored Lionel's pointed stare and scratched Elwood's head. I could see Lionel out of the corner of my eye waiting for me to say more.

Throwing up my hands, I huffed, "And I don't know. The person who wrote on the door used lipstick. That's a little childish for a cold-blooded killer, don't you think?" I also thought that the color was all wrong for a maniac. Charles Manson wouldn't wear Passionate Plum.

Lionel didn't appreciate my logic. "The thing in your tire wasn't childish. Someone wants to scare you out of town."

"I'd love to accommodate them," I quipped. "Only I can't."

Elwood nuzzled me, and I looked around the pasture for some kind of treat. No treats, only Lionel standing leaning against the fence with his hands wedged in his back pockets and his foot tapping the ground. His eyes narrowed.

"Okay," I conceded. "I'll stop by the sheriff's office and file a report about my car. Happy?"

He nodded in agreement, but annoyance lingered in his eyes. Now I was irritated. Two minutes ago I'd been happy after taking a perfectly fun camel ride. Now Lionel was spoiling the moment by not kissing me and dredging up psychotic killers.

I let Lionel drive me to the sheriff's office. As I grabbed the door handle, I felt his hand on my shoulder.

"If you need help you'll call me, right?"

"Sure I will." Maybe.

He leaned close. "I don't want anything to happen to you." My breath caught as his lips brushed mine. A second later, they were gone. "Here," he said as he reached under his seat and pulled out the nail used to deflate my tire. "Give this to the sheriff."

Breathless, I hopped out of the truck. My legs gave a tiny quiver, but I stayed upright as I clutched the rusty spike to my chest and watched Lionel drive off.

Wow, I thought. Either I was desperate or Doctor Lionel Franklin packed a hell of a wallop. If his lips could make me all tingly from a single touch, I couldn't help wondering what they could do with more time.

Roxy was at her desk wielding a compact and a mascara wand. She looked up at me and smiled. "Hey, Rebecca. I was wondering when you'd come by."

"Why?" I asked. Maybe the grapevine had gotten hold of information about my flat tire. "Did you hear something?"

Roxy squinted into her little mirror. "Deputy Holmes said he found you snooping around Mack's place. Personally, I think he should have busted you." Roxy glared at me from around the mirror. "He didn't because Sean's got a thing for redheads."

What luck, I thought.

I dropped the rusty nail thingy on the counter, sending the sound of metal hitting Formica ringing throughout the room. Roxy jumped and almost poked her eye out with the mascara wand.

"What's that?" she demanded. I couldn't help feeling a stab of satisfaction that I finally had her attention.

I shrugged. "Beats me. I found it sticking out of my tire. I guess redheads aren't everyone's type."

Quickly, I related the story of my flattened tire.

Hearing about the note made the pencil-enhanced eyebrows on Roxy's face rise. "Wow, Rebecca. You really pissed someone off."

Roxy handed over the report she'd scribbled out. I read it and signed my name. Then I casually rested my elbows on the counter and asked, "Have they figured out what was used to drug Mack?"

"Yes and no." Roxy grabbed her compact and attacked her nose with the powder puff.

I blinked. "What's that mean?"

Roxy peered at me. The white powder and the dark mascara she'd applied made her look like a mime. "Yes, Doc Truman figured it out, and no, I ain't going to tell you, Rebecca. You need to let the authorities here do their jobs. Now get out of here, and tell your grandfather I say hello." She gave me a fake smile that I returned with one of my own.

I walked out into the sunshine. As far as I could tell, Sheriff Jackson was a gardener and Sean Holmes was annoying, which meant if I waited for them to do their jobs I'd have a lovely garden and a bad disposition to show for it. Neither was appealing.

Clenching my fists as I considered my next move, I felt

something dig into my palm. I looked down and realized I'd forgotten to leave the nail with Roxy.

I glanced back at the sheriff's front door. Nope, I didn't want to go back in there. I dropped the nail into my purse and vowed to come back when Roxy wasn't busy practicing her Halloween makeup.

I checked my watch and pulled out my cell phone. Zach had taken my car four hours ago, which meant he should have gotten the tire changed by now. My fingers dialed the number on the card Zach gave me, and my foot tapped the sidewalk as I waited for him to pick up the phone.

"Yeah."

Eloquent. I identified myself and asked, "How's my car?"

"You can pick it up anytime."

I looked back at his card with a sigh. The address on the card put Zach's shop near the highway. That was over a mile and a half outside of town. While the walk wasn't all that far, I didn't think strolling around town alone was a good idea. A deranged person was plunging rusty objects into things, and I didn't want to be the next target.

With no means of transportation, I did what any woman would do. I played the helpless female card. In my best phone sex voice, I filled Zach in on my dilemma. A couple of feminine sighs cinched the deal, and Zach volunteered to meet me downtown at the diner with my car. Chivalry wasn't dead after all, and this time it came in the form of a mechanic in overalls. I shoved my cell phone back in my purse and, not seeing any homicidal maniacs walking down the street, headed toward the restaurant.

The Hunger Paynes Diner was located about a block from the sheriff's office on the corner of Main and Center Street. Sammy

123

and Mabel Pezzopayne had been running the place forever. There were grease stains on the menus at least as old as me. Still, what the place lacked in originality it more than made up for with its juicy hamburgers, enormous sandwiches, and grease-soaked fries.

I took a seat at the counter, and Sam emerged from the kitchen long enough to say hi and bring me a Diet Coke. I sipped it while I contemplated the faded menu. I decided on a turkey club and a side salad, no fries. If Mack's murderer decided to kill me next, I didn't want to be fat.

A lanky teenaged girl holding a notepad scooted behind the counter. She gave me a toothy smile, then asked me for my order. I gave it to her, and she yelled it back to Sammy. Then, cocking her head to one side, the girl gave me a puzzled frown. Her eyes widened.

"You're Rebecca Robbins, right?"

"Do I know you?" I read her name tag: Diane. I didn't remember meeting any Dianes.

Diane shook her brunette head with a grin. "No, but I've heard all about you. Brittany thinks you're really cool, and everyone is talking about how you found the dead body and how you're asking questions around town like a cop. I bet you're a homicide detective or something in the city, aren't you?"

The girl's mouth moved so fast it was a blur. On top of that, she said the word "city" as if it were "Mars." Funny, but Diane kind of reminded me of me when I was in high school—blue eyes, excitement to spare, and a very active imagination. While I hated to squelch her enthusiasm, I had to say, "Nope. I'm a mortgage broker."

"Oh." Diane's face fell. She looked like I'd stepped on her

puppy. After a few sad-looking seconds, though, her brilliant smile was back. "But you are trying to solve the murder, right?"

I gave a noncommittal shrug.

She acted as if my response had been an enthusiastic yes. "I knew it," she declared. "I heard from my mom you're being threatened because of it and everything. She thinks you're crazy for making yourself a target, but I think it's very cool."

Diane and I had different definitions of the word "cool." "Who's your mom?" I was hoping my grandfather hadn't hit on the mystery woman.

"Roxy Moore. My name's Diane."

The bell on the front door jangled, sending Diane flying around the counter to assist the new customers and leaving me to shake my head. I'd almost forgotten how small this town was. Everyone is related somehow to someone you know.

I sipped my soda and watched Diane whiz around the diner taking orders and chatting up the customers. The girl was fresh faced. No makeup. No hair spray. It wasn't hard to believe that I'd missed the connection between Diane and Roxy, but now that I knew it my mind started to whirl with the possibilities. What else might Roxy have told her daughter?

Diane brought me my food with a smile. Before she could zip off, I began to chatter. "It's hard to believe Roxy has a daughter old enough to work in a diner. How old are you? Are you still in school?"

"I turn seventeen next month. Today was early dismissal, so Sam let me pick up an extra shift. I'm saving my money for when I graduate in two years. Brittany and I are going to get an apartment together in the city just like you."

My appetite disappeared. Diane had made me remember my

lack of living quarters in the city. The camel ride had helped wipe away my problems for a while, but now my depression was back full force.

"Make sure you look me up when you get there. I can show you around anytime," I said, trying to sound upbeat. Then, lowering my voice, I leaned in toward my new ally. "So you know I'm looking into Mack's death. Have you heard anything interesting here in the diner?"

Technically, I was interested in what Roxy said at home, but I thought this was a better way to go. Diane's face clouded. I added, "It's okay if you don't want to talk about it."

"Oh, I don't mind. It's my mother. She told me not to answer any of your questions. Mom said you're causing trouble for her sheriff's department."

"Oh." I pushed the rabbit food around on my plate, disconcerted that Roxy was a step ahead of me.

Diane hurried to explain. "My mom is obsessed with her job. She thinks she runs the place. On top of that she's got a major crush on that stupid Sean Holmes." Diane's nose crinkled with disgust, raising my estimation of the girl by several notches. "I think she's wrong about you causing problems. She told me the sheriff and Sean are having a hard time with the case. I don't see how you could do any worse."

"Thanks," I said, not sure if Diane had actually paid me a compliment. Still, I was certain the teenager had information she wanted to share. I asked again, "What do you know about Mack Murphy?"

Diane bit her lip and did a quick scan of the diner. I craned my neck to look with her. There were seven other people in the place, and only one elderly couple was within whispering earshot.

Considering the way they were yelling at each other, I was betting their hearing aid batteries needed changing. No way either of them could overhear anything we were saying.

Diane must have come to the same conclusion, because she whispered, "Mack met some really big guy in here a couple of weeks ago. I waited on the two of them. They didn't like each other very much."

"Really?" My eyes widened at the possibility of a new lead. "Did you hear anything they were saying?"

Diane's face colored a vibrant shade of pink, and she hung her head. "I was curious, so I pretended to wash the table behind them. The big guy told Mack he had to pay up or give back something."

I leaned forward. "Did either of them say what the something was?" Maybe it was nine thousand dollars' worth of something.

Diane shook her head. "No, but Mack mentioned something about not going through normal channels. He said the guy couldn't prove he had the thing or what it was worth."

Okay, now I was confused. What normal channels was Mack talking about? Diane's eyes darted toward a table to the left. I knew I was about to lose my informant to coffee pouring, so I quickly asked, "Could you describe the guy Mack was with?"

Four thought lines puckered Diane's forehead. "He looked like he was my mom's age, oh, and he was really tall. I remember when he got up I thought he looked like a football player." Diane grinned. "I'm a cheerleader at Indian Falls High."

"That's great," I said. "Is there anything else you can tell me about the guy? I think finding him might be important."

"Really?" Diane's eyes brightened, and she thought for a moment. "He ordered a cheeseburger."

"Diane, table three needs you." Sam's disembodied voice came from the kitchen. He sounded a lot like the Great and Powerful Oz. Diane must have thought so, too, because she gave me a quick, apologetic smile and scurried to the tables behind me.

Damn, I thought. Diane's vague description brought the scary Anthony Catalano to mind, but it could be someone else for all I knew.

I munched on my sandwich while mentally scrolling through the facts of the case. Nothing seemed to go together. The pills, Mack's kicking the cat, the money, Annette's threatening letter, the mysterious object, all the other angry customers—any one could be a motive for murder. I only hoped the killer left my tires inflated and my car drivable until I figured it out.

Twelve

The tinkle of an entry bell made me turn, and I watched a grease-coated Zach step into the diner. I wiggled my fingers in his direction, and he stalked toward me. My keys hit the counter with a clang.

"Your car's in the parking lot. The old tire was too far gone for patching, so I got you a new one."

Grateful, I smiled up at him. "I can't tell you how much I appreciate it. What do I owe you?"

Zach grunted, making me hope he was a better mechanic than a conversationalist. I braced myself for the inevitable checkbook gouging. My car's last visit to a mechanic induced cardiac arrest— and that wasn't same-day service.

An expressionless Zach reached into his back pocket and pulled out a folded piece of pink paper. I swallowed hard, took the paper, and unfolded it. I read the amount and blinked. Maybe stress had affected my vision, because as far as I could tell the bill read thirty-four dollars and ninety-seven cents. I peered up at Zach. Maybe the guy had failed math. "That's it?"

Zach's cheeks turned pink, and his lips curled into a sheepish smile. "This isn't the city, you know."

Why did everyone feel compelled to remind me of that?

I looked back at the bill and realized something was missing. Zach had only charged me for the new tire. I shook my head and said, "I know, but this doesn't cover your time or labor. How can you make money running your business like that?"

Zach's smile disappeared, and he jammed his grease-stained hands in his pockets and took a step toward me. I leaned back against the counter, but even then I had to crane my neck to look up at him.

"Tell you what," Zach offered. "If you don't solve Mack's murder, I'll redo the bill. Then you can pay me for the tire and my time. If you find the guy who killed him, I'll forget the whole thing."

My mouth dropped open. I didn't know what to say, and Zach wasn't waiting for me to regain use of my tongue. He turned on his heel and headed out the door. Grabbing my keys, I threw some money on the counter and raced out the door after him.

"Hey," I yelled. Zach stopped walking, and I caught up to him, panting. Getting in better shape was going to have to become a priority. "Why would you give me a free tire?" I asked. Zach hadn't said much about Mack at the poker game, and I had assumed it was because he didn't know the guy very well. Something told me I was way off.

Zach ran a hand through his hair. When he was done he bore a startling resemblance to a character out of the movie *Grease*. "Mack was my friend," he said, looking away. For a second I thought the macho mechanic was going to cry, but when he looked back his eyes were tear-free and filled with anger. "I don't have all that many friends. Knowing the person who killed him is walking around free pisses me off. I'm no good at poking my nose in people's business, and no one else in this town seems to care. You were always pretty smart in high school. So the way I see it, you're Mack's best shot at justice."

Gee. I blinked twice. I hadn't thought about it quite like that. I sucked in air in an attempt not to hyperventilate as the enormity of my investigation hit me hard in the chest.

Nodding at Zach, I choked out, "I'll do my best."

He gave a whisper of a smile and nodded back. "Let me know if you need any help."

I watched him get in his tow truck and drive off as the weight of my mission pressed down on me. Zach was right. Mack deserved better than Barney Fife and company botching his murder investigation, which left little old clueless me in charge. Poor Mack.

I hopped in my yellow Civic and zipped the five blocks down to the rink. Office work is boring, but I'm good at it. I fired up the computer, checked the answering machine for messages, and returned six customer calls. Every one had called about the same thing. They informed me that the Indian Falls High School graduation ceremony was in sixteen days and the Toe Stop was a great graduation party locale in spite of the murder. I penciled the parties one by one into the rink's schedule, feeling a bit bemused. Most normal kids wanted iPods or trips to Europe for their commencement present. Indian Falls kids wanted to skate in circles. Go figure.

I called back the customers to confirm the date and assure them the place was murderer-free, then logged on to the Internet to check my e-mail. There were nine messages from Neil. I opened each of them, terrified one would contain the official death notice of my job. None of them did. Not a single e-mail mentioned his family problems, either. They were just friendly reminders that he missed me. The last mentioned he was looking forward to seeing and talking to me soon. I typed a quick hello back and let him know I was thinking of him and his family.

That message sent, I switched to a search engine and typed in the name Anthony Catalano. A list of the first twenty entries appeared, and I checked out my options. There were a guitarist, a couple of doctors, one district attorney, a couple of high school football stars, two felons, and a president of a landfill outside Moline, Illinois.

I clicked on the landfill guy. A couple of mouse clicks got me to the home page of Catalano Enterprises. A quick click on Anthony's biography told me the guy went to University of Illinois and had a master's in business. Impressive. The Web site also said he had a wife and kids, but there was no picture. I couldn't tell if this was my guy, since the address of the landfill business didn't match the one on the card he handed me and no other address was listed. I'd have to take a road trip to find out if this was my primary, and currently only, suspect.

A quick search for the guy's home info revealed that he lived in a town only thirty miles away from Indian Falls. I scribbled down the address and grabbed my purse.

I waved to George on my way out to the parking lot, then, steering the car southwest, dialed my grandfather's phone number. It took five rings before Pop's voice came on the line.

"Hey, Pop, I need to ask a favor."

"Do you need me to help you break into another house?" I rolled my eyes at the excitement in Pop's voice. "I could borrow John Markham's gun. Should have thought of that last time, right? I would have taken down that Italian mob guy."

More likely my grandfather would have shot his own foot. "No breaking, no entering, and no guns," I insisted. "I need you to help out at the rink during open skate. There's an errand I've got to run. I'm not sure what time I'll be back."

"Damn. I thought it was going to be something exciting. I already made boring plans with Louise tonight."

Trying to cheer Pop up, I added, "Maybe Mack's killer will return to the scene of the crime. You might get a chance to nab him single-handed."

"You think?"

I could hear Pop's eyes light up and sighed. "Anything's possible."

The minute he agreed I said good-bye, closed the phone, and turned it off. I didn't want to give Pop a chance to change his mind.

Forty-five minutes later, I pulled into the Catalano driveway. I rang the doorbell and took a step back. Running room was always a good idea when waiting for the Mafia's answer to the Incredible Hulk to come to the door. My heart raced as I waited, only nothing happened. I rapped my knuckles on the door, but still no answer. On tiptoes, I looked through the diamond-shaped window. Not a creature was stirring.

Now what?

My eyes cased the house as I tried to decide if the place looked like my Anthony Catalano lived here. It was a big white colonial with blue shutters and an impeccably groomed yard. Stunning rosebushes were flourishing all around the perimeter of the property. The place was perfection—or it would have been if not for two ugly stone garden gnomes guarding the stairs to the front stoop.

"Can I help you?" A gravelly female voice snapped me out of

my thoughts, and I spun around to face the street. A white-haired lady walking a dalmatian smiled.

I grinned back and waved. "Hello. I dropped by to see the Catalanos, but I must have come at a bad time."

The dog eyed me and tugged at the leash. I was thankful the woman kept a firm grip as she checked her watch. "You'll probably find Regina at her store."

Store? That sounded promising. The woman gave me directions to Regina's place and set off with her dalmatian to fertilize a tree. Following her instructions, I pulled up in front of a building with a large sign that read CATALANO'S CURIOS, CURIOSITIES, AND MORE.

The minute I walked through the front door, I understood the garden gnomes guarding the Catalano house. Regina's store was full of them. Medium-sized gnomes gaped at me from shelves. Little ones smiled from tabletops. Four-foot-tall ones glared at me from their seats on the floor.

Displayed between the gnomes were beautiful antique tables and a stunning silver mirror and brush set. There were also ancient metal Brady Bunch lunch boxes, Hot Wheels toy cars, Precious Moments figurines, Beanie Babies, and a collection of Barbie dolls that as an eight-year-old I would have drooled over.

"Hello, can I help you?" a tiny, birdlike woman with olive skin, dark eyes, and harsh features asked as she came out of a back room. My first thought was that she needed Annette's expert help. The woman's ink-black hair was so teased it looked pissed off. She was wearing a bright purple satin blouse that matched her vibrant eye shadow. I noticed the large diamond on her left hand winking at me. Surrounded by this junk, I figured it had to be cubic zirconia. This was a woman screaming to be arrested by the makeover police.

"Are you the owner?"

Her four-inch silver heels clicked across the room, and she held out a manicured hand. "I'm Regina Catalano. Can I help you with something?"

This woman couldn't possibly be married to my Anthony Catalano. The guy might bump people off and dump them in the Mississippi, but he had style. No way could he be married to this freaky-looking woman.

"This is a great store," I lied through a smile.

"Thank you." Regina's lips widened with delight. "I used to collect things in my home. Then my husband suggested getting a shop and selling them. So I did. Now I get to share my treasures with everyone."

My eye caught sight of a rusty robot missing one arm. This woman was off her rocker, but she'd given me the opening I was looking for.

"Your husband sounds like a great guy. Does he help you run the place? It seems like a lot of work for one person."

She nodded her ratted head. "He's president of his own company, but he comes in once in a while to help me with the books and do some inventory. It's hard to keep track of everything since each piece has its own value."

"I can imagine." I didn't really want to, but it sounded like the right thing to say.

The woman cocked her head to the side. "Did you come here to look for something specific or are you just looking around?"

"Definitely browsing."

So that's what I did, although I didn't wander far into the store for fear I'd get lost amid the clutter. Regina's eyes followed me around the room as if I were going to shoplift one of her precious treasures. Far as I could tell, the trip had been a bust. Time to buy something and get out of here. I picked up an inexpensively priced garden gnome and headed for the counter.

A few moments later, I was twenty dollars poorer and the proud owner of a grumpy-looking garden gnome. It was then I noticed the locked case behind the counter. Inside were three beautiful antique china dolls wearing intricate lace dresses.

I pointed to the cases. "Those are lovely dolls."

Regina squealed, "They're my pride and joy. Each doll is from the turn of the century. Are you a collector?" Regina's pleasure was as evident as the cash register sounds going off in her head.

They stopped when I said, "Not really. I don't think I can afford it."

She gave me a knowing look. "I understand. My husband bought me my first doll for our tenth anniversary, and I almost fainted when I learned what he paid for it."

I peered into the case. A tiny price tag next to one doll's foot read—eight thousand dollars? Yikes. Maybe I should have hung on to my Barbie collection. "And you have three of these?"

"Four." She corrected. "The other is being cleaned by a professional restorer." She drifted back behind the counter, which I took as my cue to leave. I grabbed my garden gnome and said good-bye. My hand reached for the front door's handle, and I stopped. There was a picture hanging next to the entrance. In it, Regina's smiling family stood in front of the building. The sign above the store read GRAND OPENING, and the man with his arm around Regina's shoulders was none other than my Anthony Catalano. I'd found him. Only now that I had, I wasn't sure what I was going to do with him.

The sky was turning black as my shotgun-riding garden

gnome and I turned into the rink parking lot. The minute I parked, my passenger door swung open, and Pop appeared.

He put the garden gnome on the floor and hopped in, yelling, "We gotta get over to Doc Truman's office, fast."

On reflex I asked, "Why?" The icky feeling in my stomach told me that I already knew the answer.

Pop strapped on his seat belt. "Eleanor called. She's waiting for me in the back room, and this time Doc Truman won't be surprising us. He's having a romantic dinner with his wife in Galena. That leaves us free to find out what drug killed Mack. Put the pedal to the metal, Rebecca."

My tires squealed leaving the parking lot, and we arrived in front of Doc Truman's office in four minutes flat. I turned off the car and cringed as my grandfather popped a breath mint into his mouth.

"We gotta get this right. I don't plan on doing this again." Pop opened the car door and turned back to me. "Now, give me a few minutes to get her distracted. Then you can snoop around. I'll make sure there's enough noise so she won't hear you."

Yuck. I squeezed my eyes shut. This plan was even worse the second time around. "Why don't we just ask her for the name of the drug?" Honesty was a much better idea than listening to my grandfather make barnyard noises in the back room.

Pop frowned. "Why? That ain't the way real detectives do things. Real detectives are always sneaky. That's how they get the information they need."

"I'm a mortgage broker, Pop, not a detective." Actually I wasn't sure what I was, considering I might have lost my job. Still, Sherlock Holmes I wasn't.

Keeping that in mind, I got out of my car and hit the sidewalk, with my grandfather grumbling behind me. We walked through the front door, and my heart stopped. Eleanor was lounging against the counter with a rose between her teeth. Tonight her ample body was wedged into black leather pants and a matching satin corset. With a whip and a couple of handcuffs Eleanor would be a front-runner in the Miss Dominatrix of Illinois pageant.

The minute she spotted me, Eleanor gave a tiny squeak and dashed behind the counter as if that were going to make me forget her striking ensemble. Or the fact she still had a rose dangling from her lips.

I nudged Pop. He took a step forward and said, "Hi, Eleanor. Rebecca gave me a ride over."

The flower fell out of Eleanor's mouth. Now her face and the top of her large bosom were both the color of an eggplant. I felt a twinge of guilt for interrupting her plans. Pop might not have been looking forward to tonight, but clearly Eleanor was.

Flashing an apologetic smile, I said, "I didn't mean to interrupt your evening, but I was hoping to ask you a couple of questions. I promise to make it quick."

Eleanor swallowed and sat down hard in the chair behind the desk. "What do you want to ask?" Her voice sounded thin and strained with worry, as though she thought I was going to grill her on her sex life. Not in this lifetime. I figured Pop could take care of that all by himself.

I explained, "I've been trying to help the sheriff solve Mack Murphy's murder. I have a few leads, but I really need to know what drug Doc found in Mack's system, and I thought maybe you could tell me. Then I can track down the person who gave it to Mack and the case will be solved. This town shouldn't have to live in fear."

Eleanor's eyes went wide, and her hands clenched together.

For a second I thought she was going to deck me. Instead Eleanor threw back her head, and her robust laughter filled the room. Wiping tears from her eyes, she said, "Is that all?" Still chuckling, she reached into a stack of files and plucked one out. She started to hand it to me, then pulled it back. "You know, I'm not supposed to give this information to you. It could get me in big trouble."

"Come on, Eleanor." Pop sauntered over to the counter. His smile grew wide and a trifle naughty. "The sooner we get rid of Rebecca, the sooner we can get started on . . . you know." He winked, and Eleanor giggled and fluttered her eyelashes.

Kill me now, I thought, before they start talking in detail. I wasn't old enough to hear that kind of thing. No one was.

Eleanor's eyes narrowed, and her lips curled into a big smile. "How about I tell your grandfather the name of the drug after our date tonight?" She winked, closed her eyes, and leaned over the counter, offering her lips for a kiss.

I backed away while shooting a panicked look at my grandfather. Pimping Pop was not on my agenda.

Pop waved a wrinkled hand toward the door with an exaggerated sigh. He was choosing to stay, which meant I was out of here before I saw anything that would scar me for life.

Once out the door, I hit the pavement running. I arrived back at the rink emotionally damaged but one step closer to solving Mack's murder. Tomorrow I'd know the name of the drug. Then all I had to do was find the guy who gave it to Mack.

Thirteen

My eyes fluttered open to sunlight streaming through the window. Today was Mack's funeral. I showered and put on a royal blue skirt with a tan leather blazer. Then I tiptoed out of the house before Pop had the chance to roll out of bed. Yes, I wanted the name of the drug, but I figured it was best to let Pop have some coffee before we did a face-to-face. Pop needed recovery time.

Outside, I admired Pop's front lawn. Last night I'd placed the garden gnome next to the Santa scarecrow. Now, in the daylight, the yard had taken on a warped fairy-tale quality.

I zipped my Civic over to the rink. After sucking down three cups of coffee, I headed for the bank to make the weekly deposit. Since I was downtown I did a few other business-related things. Strange, but I was better at handling rink business than I was at juggling the mortgages I dealt with in Chicago. My mother must have rubbed off on me when I wasn't looking. Good thing. I was determined to keep the place running and profitable until a new owner came along and my life could go back to normal.

I looked at my watch. Nine thirty. Mack's service started in half an hour. I drove my car over to the Lutheran church, where the service was going to be held. An investigator should have a good seat, right?

I planted myself in a back pew so I would have a good view of all the attendees as they filtered in. Not that I thought anything would happen at the funeral. Still, it couldn't hurt to be observant. Ten minutes later, mourners started to arrive. Doreen waved as she walked in with some other women. They were followed by Annette (who I was certain saw me, but didn't smile), Tom the high school football coach, Felix and Barbara Slaughter, Dr. and Mrs. Truman, and Mayor Poste and his wife. The whole town was getting a front-row view of Mack's send-off.

"Rebecca, what are you doing sitting all the way back here? You can't see any of the good stuff from the back."

I turned to see Pop frowning at me. Pop was annoyed, probably more by his date last night than by my chosen seat.

"This is a good place for me to observe everyone. You don't have to sit with me if you don't want to." It seemed like the polite thing to say even though I was dying to ask him if Eleanor had told him the name of the drug.

A man walking by nodded his head in acknowledgment. I did a double take before waving back. Zach was almost unrecognizable in a well-cut charcoal suit and a deep purple tie. There wasn't a speck of grease in sight. He took a seat in the very front row, the one reserved for family.

Pop tapped my shoulder. "Yeah, but what about Mack's body? You can't see that."

I tore my eyes away from Zach's drooping shoulders. "I don't

141

want to see Mack's body," I said. After last Friday in the bathroom I'd seen more of Mack than I'd wanted to.

Pop's eyes widened. "I get it. You're doing surveillance." He danced from foot to foot. "Scootch down. I'll help."

I stayed right where I was. "Why don't you cover the front of the church? You'll be able to hear if someone says anything incriminating."

My grandfather turned toward the front. His eyes narrowed. "I can do that. Oh, wait." He pulled a piece of paper out of his pocket and handed it to me. "Here. Eleanor said that's what you wanted. I read it, but I've never heard of the drug. Must not have to do with kidneys. I've used every drug there is to keep my pipes flushed."

Pop turned, put his chin down, and stalked down the aisle with his head darting from side to side. Pop was on the watch for danger in the pews of St. Mark's. He took a seat near Doc Truman. A few moments later, I saw his head slump. My lookout was asleep.

Heart palpitating, I unfolded the note and read the one word written on it.

Clomipramine.

I'd never heard of the drug either. Maybe the Internet would shed some light.

"Do you have room for me?"

Lionel peered down at me. I scooted over. He settled in and looked down at the paper in my hand. "What's that?"

"The name of the drug someone slipped Mack."

"Really?"

Something in Lionel's tone made my Spidey sense tingle. "Yeah, why? Have you heard of this drug?"

Lionel crossed his arms. "Maybe. I don't know. Let me give it some thought."

I wasn't buying the innocent routine. "I think you know something and you aren't telling me. That isn't fair."

"Becky," Lionel said with a half-smile, "life isn't fair."

The organ started to play, cutting me off. Lionel leaned back in the pew, his forehead scrunched in concentration. He knew something. I was certain of it.

The service began taking my mind off the named but unknown drug. The pastor said some nice things about Mack. My throat tightened up. Doc Truman rose and read a Bible passage that made my eyes start to leak. By the time everyone was asked to sing "Amazing Grace," I was in pretty bad shape.

I took deep breaths, but trying to calm myself just made me sob harder. I was having funeral flashbacks. The last one I attended was a year ago for Mom. Doc Truman did the reading then, too.

Lionel's arm crept around my shoulders. I leaned against him, and he hugged me tight to his chest. To my surprise the tears stopped. I breathed in the warm scent of spicy aftershave and barn animals. It was reassuring and surprisingly sexy.

Pulling away, I wiped my eyes with the back of my hand. I gave Lionel a hint of a smile. "Thanks," I whispered.

He looked embarrassed by my gratitude. He shifted in his seat and nodded toward the front of the church.

Amused, I turned my attention back to the service. Zach was taking his place behind the podium to give the eulogy. To my surprise, the poor guy broke down twice talking about how great Mack was. Zach talked about how Mack was seven years older and had helped coach his Little League team. Mack taught Zach how to hit a curveball, and that summer of baseball had ultimately led to a lifelong friendship.

I sniffled. Zach was going to miss Mack, a lot.

Ten minutes later, the service ended. I followed the procession of automobiles into the Falling Brook Cemetery parking lot. Then I found a spot at least twenty yards away from the burial to watch the proceedings. Seeing the open grave would turn the waterworks on again. I wanted my vision clear for detective work. Besides, all redheads look blotchy when crying.

The ceremony was short, about five minutes. Tom, Zach, and Doc Truman putting flowers on the coffin was the signal it had ended. Then, in a loud voice, the pastor invited everyone to a complimentary luncheon at the Hunger Paynes Diner. That got most everyone moving toward the parking lot. I guess funerals make some people hungry. Not me. I waited for most of the cars to peal away. Then I walked up to the gravesite. Lionel was there waiting for me.

"How do you know Mack took clomipramine?" he asked as I stared at the grave. "Doc said he wouldn't release that information. How did you get it?"

I shrugged. "Pop seduced Doc's secretary."

Lionel shook his head, but I don't think he was surprised. "Your idea?"

"Nope." I studied the gravesite. My eyes latched onto something interesting. "Pop came up with it all on his own."

"You could have said no."

"I tried." I stepped behind the grave and stooped next to a large object covered by a black plastic tarp. "It isn't easy to say no to Pop."

"Eleanor must feel the same."

I shot him a disgusted look. Then I pulled aside the tarp. On the ground in front of me was a beautiful green marble headstone with Mack's name and dates etched into it. Weird. Gravestones typically took weeks to arrive. Mack must have really planned ahead.

I peered up at Lionel. "Did Mack have burial insurance?"

"Burial insurance? Mack didn't have homeowners' insurance." Lionel squatted next to me. He ran a hand along the edge of the headstone. "Mack was the kind of guy that lived one day at a time. He would have thought burial insurance was a waste of time."

That's what I'd thought. So what was with the fancy headstone? After arranging Mom's funeral last year, I had become an expert on all things funeral including the cost of headstones. I was certain this one cost a fortune. Where did the money come from? No one during the service claimed to be Mack's relation. So who liked Mack enough to pay thousands of dollars to mark his burial site?

I stood up. Raising my eyebrow at Lionel, I asked, "Did you buy this?"

"I hate to say this, but buying Mack's headstone never occurred to me." Lionel got up with a frown.

"And if it had?"

"I wouldn't have done it." Lionel shrugged. "Mack would have thought that was a waste of good money."

I understood where Lionel was coming from. My grandfather said that same thing last year when I'd insisted on a white marble headstone for my mother. She was buried on the other side of town in the Catholic cemetery. I'd wanted people who visited the cemetery to know she was important. Maybe Mack's mysterious benefactor felt the same way, or maybe someone was feeling guilty for killing him.

With nothing more to see, Lionel and I walked away from Mack's final resting place.

"Hey," I said as we reached the parking lot. "What do you

know about the drug that killed Mack? You acted strange after seeing the name."

Lionel leaned forward. He gave me a soft kiss on the cheek. Then he climbed into his monster truck with me yelling the question at him again. Instead of answering, he started up the engine and drove away. Damn. He'd gotten away, but one thing was certain. Lionel really did know something, and I needed to know what that something was.

By the time I arrived, the diner was jammed with people. Diane must have been in school, because Mabel Pezzopayne and a woman I didn't recognize were busy taking orders and pouring coffee.

I commandeered a seat at the far end of the counter and scanned the room. None of Mack's poker buddies were here. Annette was also absent. Not that the place could have fit many more mourners. It looked like everyone else in town had made time to eat for free. Again I wondered who cared about Mack enough to foot the bill.

Before I could pursue that thought, Mabel hustled over to my stool with her pen and pad.

I was about to order when a female voice across the room screeched, "How dare you accuse my granddaughter?"

Every head in the place turned. At a table in the back was my Realtor, Doreen. She was standing with her hands on her hips glaring down at the three older women sitting at her table. "I want you all to apologize this very minute. Or else."

"Or else" hung in the air.

"Sit down, Doreen." One of the three women waved at Doreen's chair.

Doreen wasn't listening. No, she danced from foot to foot looking like a boxer ready to knock someone out. "I want you to apologize, now. My Brittany wouldn't deface church property. She's a good girl."

A loud snort from a woman at Doreen's table said this opinion wasn't universally shared. The snorting lady was dressed suspiciously like a leprechaun. Not a person with judgment I would trust.

"Look at the way your granddaughter dresses," the green woman shouted up at Doreen. "She's a troublemaker, that one. I wouldn't be surprised one bit if we find out she was stealing from the church. That's what kids like her do."

Quick as a flash Doreen grabbed the plate of chocolate mousse pie on the table and hurled it at the old lady. Sadly, Doreen wouldn't win any accuracy contests. The pie sailed by her target—splat—into the back of Mayor Poste's head.

Mayor Poste turned around. His fingers felt around the back of his head as he frowned. Doreen turned beet red and stammered, "I'm . . . so . . . sor . . ."

Before Doreen could get the last word out, a tomato slice smacked her right between the eyes. My eyes followed the tomato's trajectory to its source in time to see Mayor Poste's wife reloading. Now she was brandishing a pickle.

"Marion, put that down." The mayor grabbed his wife's arm. The pickle went flying out of her hand. It landed with a splat on a ratted head of white hair three tables down. The woman shook the pickle off her head right onto the little boy sitting behind her.

"Eeeeoo." The kid screamed and launched the pickle at his older sister seated across from him. She retaliated by spooning up her mashed potatoes. They went flying off to the left, smack into the face of Doreen's brightly hued friend. In between globs of mashed potatoes, her eyes narrowed at Doreen. The little boy laughed, his sister reloaded, and the green lady picked up her plate of biscuits and gravy and took aim.

I decided this was my cue to head for the exit. As the door swung shut behind me I heard the crashing sound of a breaking plate. That was followed by several primal screams.

Yep, definitely time to leave.

I zipped over to Pop's house and changed into a comfy pair of jeans and a bright turquoise T-shirt. As I was going out the kitchen door, Pop walked in. I clapped a hand over my mouth, stifling a horrified laugh.

Pop looked like a refrigerator had thrown up on him. A streak of ketchup ran down his left cheek. Smears of meat loaf and mashed potatoes were ground into his black suit pants. What I guessed was melted ice cream decorated his shoulders. Still, it was the cherry wedged deep in his white wavy hair in tandem with the disgruntled look on Pop's face that made my shoulders lurch with laughter. Starving kids in Africa could feed off of Pop for a month.

"Did you win or lose?" I asked, my lips twitching.

He shrugged. "Hard to say."

George was teaching a group lesson when I arrived at the rink. By four o'clock the place was teeming with kids. They were free from the confines of school and ready to race around like idiots. Thankfully we had a couple of high schoolers employed. They helped collect admissions and handed out skate rentals. That left me free to spin CDs in the booth.

I slid a *Best of Motown* CD into the changer and kicked my feet up as "My Girl" blasted over the loudspeakers. I was enjoying the music when I heard a knock on the booth window. Brittany and Diane stood on the other side of the glass waving.

I motioned for them to come into the booth. They grinned like fools and made a dash for the door. Diane and Brittany needed to get out more. A visit to the roller rink sound booth shouldn't be the highlight of any teenager's day.

The two girls piled into the cramped space. I scooted my chair back to accommodate the extra bodies.

Diane looked around the tiny booth with wide eyes. "Wow, I've never been in here before. This is cool." Imagine what she'd say about seeing a building over three stories tall. Maybe she should try out Des Moines before making the move to Chicago.

I smiled at the two of them. "Would you guys like to pick out the next CD?"

They gave me another "I can't believe my luck" look, then dove into the rink's music library. Both wore triumphant expressions as they came up with a CD by a band I'd never heard of. Mom must have been hipper than I was to have bought it.

I let Brittany put the CD in the changer. Turning to Diane, I said, "I missed you at the diner today. There was a big crowd after Mack's funeral."

Diane shot Brittany a look, then said, "I know. I was supposed to work this afternoon, but Sammy and Mabel closed the diner for tonight. The place was a mess. When I showed up there was food and broken plates everywhere. Were you there when all that happened?"

"I left after the first french fries went flying," I said. "I'm still making payments on my leather blazer. Mashed potatoes stain."

Brittany's lip started to tremble, and her chin lifted as she said, "The whole thing was my fault." I thought the pride in Brittany's voice was a nice touch.

I shook my head. "Unless you cut school and were hiding under a table with a fistful of spaghetti, you can't claim responsibility. Trust me. You can't control your grandparent." I understood

149

this better than anyone. Grandparents had sex and threw food no matter how much you wanted them to behave.

Diane put her arm around Brittany. "Rebecca's right. You didn't tell your grandmother to trash the diner. She did it all on her own."

Brittany shook Diane's arm off her shoulder. "My mother told me it was my fault. My grandma's friends told her that I ruined a statue at the church. Only I didn't. I swear I don't know what they're talking about."

Brittany wouldn't be my first choice for town vandal. Pop would. "Why do they think you did it?" I asked. "Do they have any proof you did something?"

"Of course not." Brittany straightened her shoulders. Her trembling lip ruined the defiant pose.

"Then what?"

Diane blurted out, "It's the hair. Ever since she dyed her hair everyone thinks Brittany's out to cause trouble. I said she should dye it back to blond. She won't do it."

"I shouldn't have to." Brittany glared at her friend. "Just because I have black hair doesn't mean I stole a piece of the church statue. I shouldn't have to change my hair to prove it." I nodded in agreement. Encouraged, Brittany said, "Rebecca, you're a detective. If you took my case you could find the real person who ruined the statue and clear my name."

"Wait a minute," I protested. "I'm a mortgage broker, not a detective. I'm only looking into Mack's murder because I feel guilty that he died in my rink." I'd used that excuse so many times I was almost starting to believe it.

Neither of the girls seemed to care. "You're good at asking questions," Diane said firmly.

Brittany nodded. "Besides, you're on my side. I know you can prove I didn't do it."

I studied the two wide-eyed teenagers. They looked so hopeful. Their eyes sparkled with faith—in me. My resolve caved. At least this case didn't involve a dead body.

"Okay," I agreed, blowing a curl off my forehead. "Tell me what they say you did. I'll ask around and see what I can find out."

Brittany launched herself at me. I found myself the recipient of a grateful hug. "You're the best," she said with a happy smile.

I was a pushover.

Brittany gave me a rundown of her problem, with alternative music playing in the background. "I went to church with my family this Sunday at St. Mark's. After mass a bunch of us hung around the back of the sanctuary waiting for our families to leave. The next day a part of the Jesus statue was missing. The pastor 'remembered' I was standing near it the day before." Brittany made quotation marks in the air to emphasize her point. "I guess that's why everyone thinks I had something to do with it, but I didn't."

I promised Brittany I'd do my best to clear her name, and the two girls raced off to the concession stand. They needed sodas. Good for me, since I needed to ponder Brittany's problem without contracting a case of claustrophobia. With the girls gone, the booth felt downright roomy.

I tried to picture the Jesus statue from this morning, but all I remembered was the casket and the flowers. No statue. I was going to have to visit the scene of the crime. That was the only way I could understand exactly what happened.

I left George in charge of changing the music and slipped out the side door of the rink. The early May evening was warm and inviting. The smell of lilacs filled the spring air. I decided to enjoy it by walking.

The St. Mark's sanctuary was deserted when I walked through the double doors. I spotted what might be Brittany's statue on the right-hand side in the back of the church. The thing stood about six feet tall and was a modern styling of Jesus hanging on the cross. The artist had used a combination of copper and silver. Both were extremely tarnished, and while I'd studied the Crucifixion in catechism class, never once did our teacher mention Jesus looked like Herman Munster with a bad perm. No offense to Jesus, but this statue was ugly. It also had a gaping hole in the center of Jesus's feet. The statue was missing a nail.

I glanced at both hands. Both had their nails. Curious, I stood on my tiptoes. I reached for the stake in Jesus's right hand and gave it a tug. The piece of metal slid out of the statue, accompanied by a soft scraping sound. It looked like . . . Wait a minute.

I rummaged through my purse, and my fingers touched metal. I pulled out the thing I'd found sticking out of my tire. It was an exact match of the nail in Jesus's hand.

I swallowed hard. Someone had tried to crucify my car.

"Hello, can I help you?"

I turned to see the skittish woman from Annette's salon. Her eyes grew wide as she looked down at the nails in my hand. *Great,* I thought. She already acted like I was an axe murderer. Now she'd add church vandal to the list.

"Hi." I gave her a bubbly smile. "I heard about the problem the church was having with this statue. Do you mind me taking a quick look?"

The woman took a step back and offered me a stilted shake of her head. "No. Why do you think I would mind?"

The tremor in her voice belied her words. This woman was scared to death—of me. Trying to put her mind at ease, I said, "I don't think we've officially met. I'm Rebecca Robbins." I held out my hand. She glanced at it, but her own hand didn't move.

"I know," she said in a clipped voice. I raised an eyebrow, and the woman quickly added, "I'm Danielle Martinez."

Of course, I thought. Annette had told me that. "Do I know you?" I asked, giving her a closer assessment. Curly brown hair, dark eyes, large chest. I couldn't place where I'd met her before.

Danielle held a hand up to her face. Her breath coming faster, she backed away from me. "I don't think so. I moved here less than a year ago."

I shrugged, thinking I must be wrong, then noticed a tiny butterfly tattoo on Danielle's hand. I knew that tattoo from somewhere. Memories of my boss's birthday party last summer sprang to mind. Or maybe it was Christmas. The office parties were all alike, annoying.

"Have you ever lived in Chicago?" I asked.

All color drained out of Danielle's face. She took several steps backward, almost tripping over a pew in the process. "I really have to go," she stammered. "The pastor is in the back if you need anything else."

I watched the back of her disappear down the aisle. The woman was strange, I thought. Then I looked down at my right hand, which was clutching two of the statue's nails.

Oops. I shoved my tire's nail back into my purse and slid the other one into Jesus's hand with a grimace. I know he was made of metal, but it still looked like it hurt.

I almost skipped back to the rink. I now knew I could prove Brittany's innocence. My car's tire was punctured yesterday around twelve. There was even an official report to prove it. My report combined with a copy of the high school's attendance record would clear Brittany's name. Not bad detective work for a mortgage broker.

Back at the rink I searched the dimly lit interior for my favorite goth teen. She and Diane were flirting with a couple of guys in the concessions area. I stepped out of the way of a young girl racing out of the bathroom on her skates and crossed to them.

"Brittany, can I talk to you for a minute?"

Brittany's dyed hair swished as she looked up at me. "Sure, Rebecca." She gave a cutesy finger wave to the guys before following me back to my mom's office.

I closed the door behind us. Turning, I asked, "Were you in school yesterday?"

Brittany cocked her head to one side. "Yeah, why?"

"Then you're cleared." I smiled with triumph. I explained to her about my tire and how the timing of it all added up to one conclusion—someone else did the deed.

Brittany's eyes lit up. She gave me a quick hug. "I gotta tell my grandma. She'll make sure everyone knows I didn't do it." Brittany took three steps toward the door before stopping. "Rebecca, who took the nail out of the statue and spiked your tire?"

"No idea," I admitted, "but odds are it's someone who attends your church." Staking out the church during Sunday services occurred to me. Only, it not being my church, I'd stick out like a sore thumb. Looking at Brittany gave me an idea. "Would you mind keeping your ears open at church this Sunday? You could let me know if you hear anything unusual."

Brittany bobbed her head up and down. Then, with a happy little skip, she flew out of the office to tell everyone she was exonerated. If only the Mack Murphy case were as easy to solve. Hopefully the Lutheran spy network would turn up a lead this Sunday.

"Holy cow. Would you look at that?"

I bolted upright in my bed. The sound of my grandfather's voice rang through my bedroom. I blinked. It was pitch black in my room. The alarm clock glowing next to my bedside table read three in the morning. I groaned. Flopping back on the bed, I pulled a pillow over my head. I did not want to listen to my grandfather dancing the mattress mambo.

"Rebecca, get out here."

I shoved the pillow to the side and sat up. My grandfather's voice sounded weird. It was more startled than excited. Leaping from the bed, I flung open the door and raced to his bedroom.

No Pop.

I turned and did a fast sprint down the hall to the stairs. My grandfather was standing in the living room looking out the big picture window. The room seemed to glow with a strange light. I walked over to stand next to my grandfather.

"Pop, what's going—" My voice deserted me as I gaped out the living room window. My heart raced with a combination of shock and fear.

There was a cross burning in our front yard.

Fourteen

The orange and gold flames lit up the dark night. The fire created a strangely beautiful glow despite the creepy nature of the source.

I swallowed hard and looked at Pop, who was watching the fire with rapt fascination. I turned back toward the window. Wait a minute. That wasn't a fiery cross at all. The fiery object was Louise's scarecrow Santa.

My eyes welled up, and my lip started to tremble.

The rink had been vandalized. My car tire had been crucified. Now Santa Scarecrow was being burned at the stake for crimes against humanity. The threats were escalating.

Freaked, I ran to the kitchen and dialed the sheriff's department. No answer. I tried the fire department. It took six rings, but finally a sleepy voice answered.

"There's a fire in my grandfather's front yard," I shouted. "Someone needs to put it out." The word "fire" got the guy's attention. He sounded wide-awake while promising to have a truck here in no time.

"No time" took exactly eighteen minutes. Pop and I almost went for the hose ourselves, but the fire was dying a natural death, and we weren't sure if the pyromaniac was still in the vicinity. When the fire truck pulled up to the curb, two guys in dark fire-resistant pants, fire hats, and big yellow jackets jumped out of the cab to do battle with a scarecrow.

After several minutes, they figured out how to turn on the hose. By that time the flames had almost gone out. A little water and the last of the fire was history. Personally I was amazed the scarecrow had burned as long as it did. The lawn decoration wasn't that big. Louise must have used extremely durable materials.

Pop and I moved outside to stand on the lawn. Neighbors from up and down the block were walking down the street toward our house. We all stared at the charred, wet remains of Louise's arts and crafts project. My garden gnome had melted into a black pile of goo. His hat was the only thing left of him. Too bad, I thought with a sniff. I kind of liked him.

Pop shook his head. "We should have got us a bag of marsh-mallows. We could have roasted them before the fire department got here. I still would have lost sleep, but at least I would have gotten a late-night snack."

Someone had played Ku Klux Klan at our house and my grandfather was thinking about campfire treats. I, however, didn't think my stomach would hold down food. My shoulders knotted as the impact of this event hit me. Pop's house could have caught on fire. Pop could have been killed. Pop might be a little sex-crazed, and he occasionally drove me nuts, but he was my family. I didn't have much of that left. I needed him. More than that, I loved him. If anything happened to Pop I . . .

"I'm going to talk to the Sloans." Pop pointed to a gaggle of people congregated by the fire truck. "Wally's going to want to know what happened. He needs the facts so he can tell everyone at the Elks Club tomorrow night. They like to think they're in the know."

My legs shook as I watched my grandfather stroll down the driveway. Slowly I sank to the ground. I wanted to control the panic coursing through me, but I couldn't. I didn't know what to do. Getting in my car and driving as far away from Indian Falls as possible seemed like a really good idea, but I couldn't. At least not yet. My mother needed me to take care of the rink until someone else could be found. I had to stay no matter how much the dripping, charred remains of the scarecrow terrified me.

"Becky?"

I looked up at a disheveled Lionel peering down at me. Before I could say a word, he leaned down and took me in his arms. He held me tight. His hands stroked my hair until my trembling subsided. Even then he continued to hold me. I felt safe, and safe wasn't a commodity I had a lot of right now.

After a few minutes of being a wimpy girl I pulled away. There was no way Lionel saw the flames from his farm ten miles away. "What are you doing here?" I asked.

Lionel shoved his hands in his jeans pockets. His mouth flashed a lopsided grin.

"I'm a volunteer fireman. The kid who got your call didn't know what to do, so he called everyone on the list."

I looked toward the street. The two lone firemen were struggling to get the hose loaded back onto the truck. "Where is everyone else?"

"If they're smart, they're still in bed."

I raised an eyebrow. "So what does that make you?"

"A guy who should have his head examined." He ran a warm hand down my bare arm, causing little goose pimples to appear on my skin. "For some strange reason, I care what happens to you."

Wow, I thought, that had to be the most romantic thing anyone had ever said to me. That either meant I was having a great moment or my life was completely pathetic.

"I'm going to have to find another place to stay," I told him. "I don't want to put Pop in danger."

"Don't you think you should let him make that choice?"

"I know what he would say." I looked out toward the road. Pop's hands were gesturing furiously at a group of curious neighbors. He looked like a choral conductor leading a slumber-party glee club. A vise clamped around my heart and tightened as I watched him smile. "No. I can't chance it. He's all I've got. I'm not going to sit here and wait for Pop to get hurt. Tomorrow morning I'll look for a new place to live." I gave Lionel my best stoic smile. Despite my bravado, the water pressure rose behind my eyes.

Lionel dropped my hand. He jammed his in his back pockets and stared at me for a good long time. Looking away, he muttered, "You can move in with me."

Huh? I tried to inhale. My lungs had forgotten how to work. Did he say "Move in with me"?

His head tilted downward. "I have a guest bedroom. You need a safe place to stay. It makes sense."

Only if I wanted to be the town Jezebel. Funny, the offer, along with the ensuing gossip, could have sounded tempting had Lionel offered to share his bedroom. Only I wasn't looking for a relationship. Something told me Lionel was the church-ceremony-and-wedding-cake type. Sex I could handle on the rare occasion I had it. Commitment was something very different, especially if the guy liked living in Indian Falls. I lived in Chicago, and despite my recent setbacks, that wasn't going to change no matter how great the guy or the sex. So why tempt myself?

"Thanks for the offer, but I don't think it's a good idea. Besides"—I swallowed hard—"I already have a place to stay."

"You do?"

I closed my eyes and nodded. "I'm going to stay at the rink."

I stood with my suitcase in the open doorway of Mom's rink apartment. Nothing had changed since I'd come in here with Doreen. The Cleaning Fairy hadn't come along with a can of furniture polish to save me the job. I'd have to dust the place myself.

If I ever got past the entryway.

I couldn't move. My feet refused to take those extra steps. Not without Mom. The back of my knees began to sweat, and my heart raced. How was I going to live here if I couldn't even make it as far as the bathroom? My life was going to get awfully messy if I couldn't figure it out.

"Hello?" Pop's voice made it up the stairs. A few moments later, he walked past me into the apartment. Pop turned with a frown. "What are you doing here, Rebecca?" He gave a pointed look at the suitcase at my feet.

Darn it. It appeared I'd underestimated my grandfather's psychic abilities.

Shuffling my feet, I answered, "You said you were going to the sheriff's office to file a report about last night."

"Roxy isn't there." Pop gave me a stern look. "And neither were you when I got home. Lucky for me that Harold from across the street saw your car heading downtown. Now I want to know what the heck you're doing here."

"Moving in." I gave him what I hoped was a chipper smile. "You're used to your privacy, and I didn't want to overstay my welcome."

"That's a lie, and you know it." Pop wagged his finger. "Tell the truth. You didn't want me to get killed by a scarecrow-burning murderer." My jaw dropped. Pop grinned. "You were a terrible liar as a child. You need to work on that, because all the good detectives lie like champs."

"I'm a mortgage broker," I replied.

Pop shrugged off my comment and wandered around the living room. "Right now you're working on Mack's murder, and you're cutting me out of the action."

"That's not what I'm doing," I protested.

He shook his head. "I may be old, but I'm not stupid. Now, I appreciate you caring about my health and all, but I don't like you moving out without talking to me first. I'm your grandfather, and I deserve at least that much respect."

"I didn't want to worry you."

"I'm not worried, I'm pissed off." Pop stalked around the sofa glaring at me. "You run around town asking questions. You stir up trouble and have fun. Meanwhile I'm stuck with Louise and her Santa scarecrow crap." He sat down on the sofa, sending up a puff of dust. "I'm tired of being left out of the good stuff."

Good stuff? "What good stuff?"

Pop huffed. "You look for clues and shake things up. You're looking for the truth about Mack. I can help you do that, but not if you're living here."

I rolled my eyes. "This isn't Zimbabwe. Your house is four blocks away."

"That's my point." Pop slapped his hand against a seat cushion. Another wave of dust flew through the air. It was going to take more than a little furniture polish to get this place livable.

Pop didn't seem to notice the dust. He bounced on the couch, waving one hand in the air. "All the exciting stuff will be happening here. I'll be stuck at home doing nothing."

Apparently, winning gold in the Bedroom Olympics had lost its luster. Pop's cheeks were flushed with emotion. His eyes were bright with hurt and resentment. Both chipped at my resolve.

"You're very important to my investigation, Pop. You got the name of the drug out of Eleanor, and you're my best source of Indian Falls gossip. I need you."

"Then move back home." He gave an imperious wave of his hand.

"This is my home, Pop." The words echoed in the room. Pop gave me a sharp look. I took a deep breath and corrected, "This was my home, and moving in here makes sense. I need to clean it up and get it ready to sell, and living here will help me do that."

I turned away from Pop and reached down for my suitcase. Before he could say another word, I forced my feet down the hall to the second door on the right. I took a deep breath and walked into my old bedroom.

When I was a kid the room was filled with posters of Chicago. Chicago Cubs, Michael Jordan, the skyline—anything that was the city and not Indian Falls. Now the tribute was gone. The walls were painted a light green, while the high ceiling was a bright white. It matched the molding around the two windows that looked out on the parking lot and a small park. Mom had redone the room a little over a year ago, along with the kitchen and the rest of the rink. I'd never had a chance to stay in it before she died. I'd never even seen it.

Standing here, I could feel my mother's touch. I bit my lip as a wave of sadness hit deep in my chest. Mom knew I was never going to live here again, but she'd made this room beautiful anyway.

I walked to the window and looked down at a framed photo sitting on the sill. I picked it up and smiled. The picture had been taken two years ago. Mom and I were smiling at the camera. Behind us was the skyline of Chicago. Mom had loved me enough to let me find my own life even if it meant her beloved rink would have to be run by someone else someday. I missed her so much, yet somehow standing here in the room she'd decorated made me feel less alone.

I dropped my suitcase and headed down the hall to the utility closet. It was time to make Mom's place clean.

I conned Pop into beating the dust out of cushions and vacuuming. For a home-cooked meal Pop would do anything. I washed the floors and got the kitchen in serviceable condition. Once the place was aired out and dust-free, I drove us both to the sheriff's. Roxy wasn't there, but Deputy Holmes was lounging against the counter. Looking at him made me chuckle. The guy was eating a doughnut.

Pop sauntered up to the counter. "Hey, Sean. We missed you at the barbecue last night."

Deputy Sean straightened his shoulders and did his best impression of a cop. "I heard about your problem. Too bad I slept through the call." He winked at Pop, making me cringe. I was positive I didn't need to know about Sean's sex life.

I stopped the two men from comparing sexual notes by inter-jecting, "My grandfather and I would like to file a report."

Deputy Sex God shrugged and went in search of the appropri-ate paperwork. A few minutes later, Pop signed his name to the bottom of an incident report. Handing the clipboard back to Sean, Pop said, "Hey, any news on the Mack Murphy case?"

Sean's doughnut froze halfway to his mouth. A lazy grin spread across his face. "We're closing in on the perpetrator."

Pop threw back his head and let out a cackle. "You don't have a clue, do you? Maybe you should think about asking my grand-daughter here for some help. She's a crackerjack investigator, you know."

Sean's eyes narrowed, and the doughnut dropped to the coun-ter with a soft thud. Uh-oh. That was definitely our cue to leave.

I grabbed Pop by the arm. He shot me a dirty look as I dragged him out the front door.

"What do you think you were doing in there, Pop?" I de-manded.

"Getting information."

He looked so innocent I almost believed him.

Before I could respond Pop asked, "Where are we going next?"

I pointed to the car. "To the grocery store, then back to the rink."

"What about the case?" Pop frowned. "We should be out run-ning down clues. What about finding the bad guy?"

I'd already upset Pop once today. I didn't have the heart to upset him again, and I did have one person I needed to question. It couldn't hurt to take Pop along. Lionel could lie to me, but maybe he'd have a hard time lying to my grandfather. The vet was the respect-your-elders type, and Pop was definitely elder.

I opened the passenger door for my grandfather and said, "Get in. We're going to Lionel's."

Lionel wasn't in his office when we arrived, but his monster truck was parked in the driveway. That told me the man was around here someplace, so we ambled down to the barn.

Elwood greeted us from his stall. Today he was wearing a big Uncle Sam top hat with two little holes cut out for his ears. Elwood was celebrating Memorial Day two days early.

I left Pop with the camel and walked down the center barn aisle to the back room. Pay dirt. There was Lionel sprawled out on the leather couch, asleep. Lionel's hair was disheveled. His jawline was covered by dark stubble, and his mouth was parted just enough to kick my imagination into full gear. God, this guy was sexy.

I leaned over him. Feeling flirtatious, I planted a light wake-up kiss on his forehead. Lionel's eyes fluttered open, and before I knew what was happening, I found myself yanked off my feet. I landed on top of his chest with a thump.

"What are you—" I managed to say before Lionel shut me up with his mouth . . . and what a mouth it was. His lips pressed hard against mine, and his tongue slipped in between my lips, making the lower parts of my body zing with pleasure. Lionel's kiss had definitely been worth the wait. All the reasons for not getting involved with an Indian Falls man flew out of my head as my blood pressure started to rise.

Strong hands ran down my back. They dipped enticingly under my shirt, and I snuggled closer without losing contact with Lionel's mouth. God, he felt good. My disposition was feeling better and better with every touch.

"Rebecca, what the heck are you doing over there?"

Surprised, I rolled off Lionel and smacked my ass on the hard cement floor. I blinked at Pop and Elwood both grinning from the doorway. At least I think Elwood was grinning. It might have been an effect of the silly hat.

"Lionel was asleep," I explained, out of breath. "I was waking him up."

Pop shot a meaningful look in the direction of Lionel's crotch. "Looks like you did the job."

My face burned hot. I tried to sputter a response, but Lionel got there first. "Arthur, Rebecca didn't tell me you were here."

"Don't seem like she was saying much of anything." Pop showed all his false teeth. Now it was Lionel's turn to look uncomfortable. Served him right, I thought. A chivalrous guy wouldn't pin this mess on the girl.

I shoved myself off the floor and brushed off my jeans. Time to get to business. I stood next to Pop, straightened my shoulders, and in a matter-of-fact voice informed Lionel, "Pop and I are here to ask you about clomipramine. You didn't answer me yesterday, but I'm pretty sure you know something about it."

Lionel's sexy mouth stayed closed. So much for respecting elders, I thought as I gave him a sharp look. Lionel's eyes darted away from mine, and I decided it was time to play hardball. "Tell me or I go to the cops and tell them you know something. I think Sean will listen to me, since I've heard he has a thing for redheads."

Pop sucked in air, but Lionel didn't flinch. I was ready to hyperventilate. I was certain Lionel could tell I was bluffing. No way the cops would take anything I had to say seriously. Still, if Lionel knew something incriminating about one of his friends, he might not want to chance it.

Lionel glanced at me. "Okay. I might know something."

I pulled out a chair and sat down at the table. "Spill, and make sure you don't leave anything out."

Pop and Lionel joined me at the round table. Lionel said, "Clomipramine is a psychiatric drug. It helps people with anxiety and behavioral disorders. In my field clomipramine is prescribed for dog anxiety. The FDA hasn't given the feline version its stamp of approval, but in the past couple of months I've prescribed it for a local cat."

"Any cat I know?" I asked, surprised at the turn the conversation had taken.

Lionel nodded. "Nothing else worked for Precious. That's why I tried the clomipramine. The drug worked like a charm."

My heart sank as the pieces clicked together. "Agnes killed Mack," I said. Pop looked stunned. Lionel looked sick. I was both. Mack drop-kicked Agnes's cat, and to get even Agnes fed clomipramine to Mack. I didn't like the scenario, but it made a warped kind of sense.

"I can't believe Agnes could kill someone," I said. Taking away a library card for defacing a book I could see, but murder by cat pills was beyond me. Besides, Agnes cared too much about her cats. Wasting their meds on someone she disliked seemed out of character. I asked, "Why would she use Precious's pills? Did they have a warning label or something that could have given her the idea?"

"Yeah, does the stuff induce heart attacks or something?" Pop's eyes were wide with interest.

Lionel shook his head as he leaned back in his chair. "Not usually. The bottle says clomipramine might cause lethargy, and it says to bring the pet into a vet if it stops eating or has other symptoms.

There's nothing printed on the label that would inspire anyone to use it for murder."

Okay, now I was confused. "If it only causes drowsiness, how did Mack end up in the toilet?" I doubt he mistook the porcelain potty for a pillow.

Lionel raked a hand through his hair. "Doc said Mack had a thyroid problem. People taking thyroid medication don't take clomipramine. Combined the two drugs can cause blackouts, cardiac arrhythmias, or worse. That's what happened to Mack."

"So if Agnes gave Mack the pills, she didn't mean to kill him." I stood up. I paced the floor as my mind whirled.

Lionel shook his head. "Not unless she knew about Mack's thyroid condition, which I doubt. Mack never told me about that, so I don't think he would have shared it with her. The two of them weren't on the greatest of terms."

"Besides Precious," I asked hopefully, "do any other animals around here take this drug?"

"Not that I know of," Lionel answered, "and people around here aren't the types to go to shrinks. At least none of them talk about going. So our options are limited."

Damn, I thought. Having Agnes arrested was really going to ruin my day.

The sun was setting as I pulled into Agnes's driveway. Pop climbed out of the passenger's side and sauntered behind me up the sidewalk to the front door. I'd tried to drop Pop off at the rink, but he had played the guilt card. Hearing him say I didn't need him anymore really hurt even though I knew it was a ploy. My grandfather played dirty.

A couple of cats were on the porch, but no Agnes or Precious. I pressed the doorbell as Pop reclined against a porch railing. A few moments later, Agnes appeared at the screen door with a delighted smile.

"Rebecca, dear, it's so nice of you to drop by." She opened the door and shuffled onto the porch in a pair of pink bunny slippers.

Pop snorted at her footwear, and I elbowed him. "Is Precious around?" I asked.

Agnes frowned. "I'm keeping her inside for a couple of days. Precious doesn't like it, but I have to. She's been hissing a lot."

"Any reason why?"

Agnes glanced at Pop, then back at me. Hanging her head, she said, "Precious hasn't had her medication in a few days. I ran out. But don't worry. I'll go see Dr. Franklin and everything will be back to normal."

Pop snorted. "Don't count on it."

Agnes's eyes widened, and she shot me a fearful look. "Rebecca, what does Arthur mean by that?"

I glared at Pop. "Mack Murphy died because someone slipped him some medication. The same medication Precious takes for her . . . problems."

Agnes clutched her chest. Her mouth formed the word "no."

I shook my head. "I'm afraid so, and the minute Sheriff Jackson finds out Precious takes those pills you're going to be the number one suspect."

"You're going to the slammer, Agnes." My grandfather wagged his gnarled finger. "Your cat's pills killed Mack Murphy, and we know all about it. The jig is up."

"But I didn't do anything. I swear." Agnes pressed against the side of her house. Her voice got small and scared. "I would never give Precious's pills to anyone. You have to believe me, Rebecca. This is a mistake."

Agnes's face was pale and her eyes were wide. A fluffy orange cat rubbed against her leg. Agnes didn't look down. She didn't smile at her baby's attention. No, Agnes just stared at me with those wide eyes.

Watching the old librarian made my heart quiver. I was putting the fear of God into a woman who looked like Betty Crocker. How awful was that? To top it off, I believed her. Agnes was scared, but it was a confused fear. This wasn't the "Oh my God, they caught me and I have to get out of this" kind of terror. Agnes looked innocent.

I put a reassuring hand on Agnes's arm. "I'm not accusing you of anything, Agnes." I shot a look at Pop. He opened his mouth, took one look at me, and closed it. Good. Without Pop's assistance, I might get some answers out of Agnes.

"Why don't you have a seat," I offered.

Agnes nodded gratefully. She shuffled over to a chair and sat down. "Thank you, Rebecca. You're a good girl."

That made my heart squeeze tighter. She was thanking me after I accused her of murder. The woman was either a saint or a brilliant psychopath, and since I didn't trust Indian Falls' finest, it was my job to figure out which.

I sat down in the chair next to Agnes. "Agnes, the last time I was here, you said you'd forgotten to give Precious her medication. Did you give it to her after I left?"

Agnes started to nod up and down, but then her head changed directions and bobbed side to side. "I couldn't find it." Her hands clutched her faded pink skirt. "I always leave the bottle on the windowsill in the kitchen. Then one day the pills weren't there. It was just like what happened to my last set of teeth."

Pop's expression went from threatening to sympathetic. "Nothing worse than losing a good pair of teeth. I did that a couple of years back. I had to suck soup for four days before Doc Singe got me a new pair."

"Took me over a week," Agnes said. "They had to be made special by another doctor in Minneapolis."

I hated to break up the bonding moment, but I had to ask, "When was the last time Precious had her pills?"

Agnes scratched her head. "Over a week ago. I'm afraid I don't know the exact day, but *Wheel of Fortune* was on. I always give it to her during *Wheel of Fortune*. My nephew hates watching it with me, but Precious likes the lights."

Wheel of Fortune was on six days a week. No help there. I tried a different tack. "What did you do when the pills went missing?"

"I searched all over the house for them. I even checked my garbage for the pills before putting it out on the curb."

"Garbage pickup is on Friday," Pop said with authority.

"That's right." Agnes nodded. "The last day Precious got her pills was a day or two before that. I'm sure of it."

Agnes and Pop looked pleased with their powers of deduction. I was less impressed. Knowing when garbage got picked up wasn't going to help prove Agnes didn't kill Mack.

"Agnes, did you call Dr. Franklin about the missing pills?" Lionel hadn't mentioned getting a call, but it wouldn't have been the first time Lionel had hidden the truth.

"No," Agnes admitted as her head drooped. "I wanted to. Precious really needs her pills, but I didn't know what to tell Dr. Franklin."

"How about the truth?" I asked. That seemed like the obvious choice. Of course, that might not work if the sweet little old lady had used the pills to bump off the pesky handyman. Then the truth might not look so good.

"I can't say I lost them," Agnes protested. "People will think old age is making me lose my mind. They won't let me live alone anymore, and all my babies would be taken away from me."

Now I was really confused. Who needed medication more, Precious or Agnes? "People lose things all the time, Agnes," I said.

"Yeah," Pop chirped. "I lose my keys all the time. Nobody's saying that I'm losing my mind."

"That's because you have a nice family, Arthur." Agnes dabbed at her eyes with her shirtsleeve. "My nephew is looking for a reason to put me in an old folks' home so he can get his hands on my house and my savings. If I admit to losing the pills, he'll say that's proof I'm senile. The courts aren't nice to senior citizens. They'll rule against me. Then what will happen to all my babies?"

Several fat tears rolled down Agnes's face. Pop immediately handed Agnes his handkerchief. While she wiped her face, he patted her shoulder and asked about her health. They compared aches and pains as my mind kicked into gear. The explanation about the pills was strange enough to be true. Face it. I wanted it to be true. Problem was, Pop had trouble keeping secrets. I needed to find out who took those pills before Pop spent a whole day at the senior center. Agnes would be a goner for sure if anyone else found out about Precious's pills.

Too bad I didn't have a clue how to track down the pill thief. Maybe Agnes's greedy nephew would.

"Hey," I said, stopping Pop mid-colonic-sentence. "Who's your nephew, Agnes? Do I know him?"

Agnes leaned down to pet a fluffy cat. "I don't know. He moved here a couple of years ago after you left for the city. His name's Tom. Tom Owens."

Tom Owens? I screwed up my face. Visions of a wasted guy with drool hanging out of his mouth popped into my head. Tom Owens was one of Mack Murphy's poker buddies. The only one I hadn't talked to since cleaning out his wallet. At the time, a drunken football coach hadn't seemed like a good source of information. I'd just changed my mind.

I awoke the next day disoriented by the sounds of Britney Spears. Then I remembered where I was—Mom's apartment with its fabulous gourmet kitchen. Pop and I had eaten well last night, and I'd sent him home too stuffed to grumble about my new living arrangements. All part of my nefarious plan.

I struggled out of bed trying to recall why I'd chosen to get up at eight o'clock. It was Sunday. Sunday morning I usually slept in unless struck by guilt. Then I attended church.

I slapped my forehead. Last night, I'd set the alarm so I could go to mass this morning. Brittany and her grandmother would be spying at the Lutheran church, and I figured I should cover the building across the street.

I grabbed the only dress in my suitcase. Glancing at the mirror, I sent up a prayer that the Ladies' Guild would have something better to talk about than my attire. Not that I looked bad. In fact, I looked too good. The dress was scarlet red with a just-above-the-knee hem and spaghetti straps. I'd bought it because it made my waist look smaller and my breasts bigger. Today it was doing both. I grabbed a white cardigan and sighed. The fashion gods would frown on covering up such a great dress, but successful snooping required blending in. Something I was bad at even on my most understated day.

The church was near capacity by the time I arrived. Pop was up in front sitting next to Mrs. DiBelka and her husband. No Lionel. He must not be Catholic, I thought, feeling mildly disappointed. I took a seat in the back and waited for someone to act incriminating.

Sadly, nothing suspicious happened. Not much had changed since I'd last attended Sunday mass in Indian Falls. The organist was loud, the soloist slightly off key, and the priest, while kind and good-natured, was long-winded. During the moments of silence, I plotted my next course of action.

I spotted Lionel walking a gray stallion in a fenced-in area next to the barn. Hips swaying, I stripped off the modesty cardigan and walked over to lean on the fence. I could tell the moment Lionel spotted me. For a second he went still. Then his eyes traveled up my entire body. He smiled, and my skin started to tingle.

Okay, I admit that coming here had nothing to do with the investigation. The priest had talked about Sunday being a day of rest, so I was following instructions and taking a break from Mack's murder. A little flirting seemed like a great way to recharge my batteries.

I smiled as Lionel crossed the grass. He was wearing faded jeans, a worn flannel shirt, and a pair of leather boots. Add wind-tossed hair, and I had the sexiest man in the Midwest approaching.

"I like the dress," he said.

"The women at church think I'm scandalous."

Lionel's eyes smoldered. "Am I supposed to help you live up to expectations?"

I bit my lip. Maybe playing with fire wasn't such a good idea after all.

His finger hooked one of the dress's spaghetti straps, and he gave it a tug. I had to take a step closer or lose my dress. "What's wrong?" he asked. "Scared?"

Scared? Me? "Never," I fibbed.

I saw a brief smile twitching at the corner of his lips a second before they touched mine and I stopped thinking altogether. Dr. Lionel Franklin's lips were potent. I dropped the sweater. My arms snaked around his neck, and I pressed myself close. The length of my body rubbed up against his. The friction made parts of me zing with excitement.

Lionel's hands ran down my hips. That's when I seriously contemplated dragging him into the barn.

Then he was gone. Lionel's hands left my hips. His mouth disappeared from mine. My eyes popped opened just in time to see a fist connecting with Lionel's jaw. Seeing Lionel go down made me fly into action.

Without thinking, I leapt onto the back of Lionel's attacker. We both fell to the extremely hard ground with a thud. I rolled to my knees and grabbed the bad guy by the shirt. Yanking him up, I looked into his face and sucked in my breath. Looking back at me was the pasty, pockmarked face of my boss.

Fifteen

"*Neil,*" *I yelled.* "What the hell are you doing here?"

Neil struggled up to a sitting position. He picked a piece of grass off his green-and-yellow plaid button-down shirt. "What am *I* doing here?" he demanded with a huff. "I should ask you that. I needed to talk to you, and since you weren't coming back to Chicago, I came here. Good thing I spotted your car and followed you, otherwise you would have been mauled by this cowboy."

Yeah. Good thing. I might be naked and happy right now.

I got up and stood beside Lionel. He was rubbing his jaw and glaring at my out-of-shape, pencil-pushing boss, who apparently had a decent right hook.

"Are you okay?" I touched the red spot on Lionel's face, and Neil growled behind me.

Lionel gave a clipped nod. "I'm fine. Thanks for defending me against Captain America here."

His jaw tightened as Neil awkwardly climbed to his feet. Lionel took a step toward him. "Now, if you don't mind me asking, who the hell are you? More important, why are you on my property?"

Neil pushed out his chest and shoved his hands into his beige Dockers pants pockets. "My name is Neil Capezio. Rebecca here is my employee and a very close personal friend."

Lionel looked at me with one raised eyebrow. "Is that right?"

"Yes, he's my boss." Neil wrote out my checks and helped with some of my more complicated mortgages. Once in a while we talked. I didn't think that counted as a close personal friendship, but I didn't want to say that and hurt Neil. Clearly, family problems were affecting his judgment.

Neil grabbed my arm and pulled me away from Lionel. "Look, I forgive you for being with this guy. Being in the middle of a crisis can make you do impulsive things. Now, is there somewhere we can go and talk? I really need to talk to you."

I shot Lionel a "please be patient" look and asked, "Is it your brother?"

Neil's eyes widened.

"Jasmine told me about the accident," I explained. "Are your brother and sister-in-law okay?"

Neil smiled. "They're both out of the woods. The doctors say it's a miracle."

I let out a sigh. "That's great, Neil. I'm really happy for you."

"I knew you would be. You know, since the accident I've been taking a hard look at my life. Time passes so quickly. It's easy to take people for granted. You only realize how important they are when they're gone."

My mother's warm smile popped into my head. "I know how you feel. It's important to appreciate the people you love and stand by them while you can."

"See, I knew you would understand." Neil's smile grew wider. "That's why when you didn't come home I knew I had to come find you. Life doesn't wait. So will you marry me?"

I blinked. "What?"

"I want you to marry me. This whole thing with my brother made me realize there was more to life than money. I want more. I want you."

I heard Lionel chuckle, but I didn't have time to deal with him now. Not while Neil was sinking down onto one knee with a goofy smile plastered on his face. He had to be on drugs. Either that or he needed a shrink to give him some.

"Look, Neil," I said, pulling the guy back up to his feet. "I'm really flattered, honest, but I don't want to get married." At least not now, and definitely not to him.

Neil's eyes narrowed, and his face turned three different shades of red. "This is because of him, isn't it?" His jaw tightened as he glared at Lionel.

Lionel took two steps toward Neil and cocked his head to one side as if daring Neil to take a swing. Neil's fists clenched and un-clenched at his sides as the two men locked eyes. Yikes!

I stepped in between them and gave Neil what I hoped was a sweet, understanding smile. "Look, Neil, I think you're a really great guy. I like working for you. But getting involved with some-one you work with is a bad idea. You should look for someone who doesn't work at the office."

Neil's face scrunched up. For a second I thought he was going to throw a tantrum. Then he surprised me by nodding.

I sighed my relief. Neil was going to return to earth from whatever dimension he had been visiting.

"You're right," he admitted. "Married couples shouldn't work together." Neil looked at Lionel, then back at me. "Rebecca, I hate to do this, but you're fired."

"What?" I gasped. Okay, I was pretty sure he was going to fire me a week ago, but the indignity of hearing the words hit hard. My stomach dropped into my shoes.

My ex-boss's mouth spread into a goofy grin. "I agree with you, Rebecca, and I still intend to marry you."

Was this guy for real?

Before I could recover from another trip to Neil's alternate universe, my ex-boss started toward his Volvo. With a glance at Lionel he said, "Sorry I had to hit you, but I care about Rebecca. I don't know what I'd do without her."

Lionel crossed his arms while I wondered what I'd done to deserve this. We both watched Neil climb into his car and drive away.

"Well, that was interesting." Lionel gave me an indecipherable look.

I shook my head. "Interesting is a book or a movie. That was a disaster. I don't know why he would ever think I'd marry him."

"Could be because you're sexy as hell and not smart enough to realize when a guy is getting the wrong signals."

I sputtered my indignation. Lionel added, "Next time your boss attacks me, I'd appreciate you staying out of it. I don't like women fighting battles for me."

He turned on his heel and stalked back to the barn, leaving me alone to consider giving up men entirely. I didn't need stubborn and irritating in my life, which meant it was good Neil showed up when he did. Sexual exploits with Lionel would have only confused me. Right? Now I could focus all my energy on solving Mack's murder and getting myself out of town and back to Chicago where I belonged.

. . .

Memorial Day dawned, and I was up and out of Mom's apartment early. Indian Falls believed in celebrating Memorial Day in style. Ever since I was a kid, everybody turned out for the Memorial Day parade, which included floats made by the Elks, the Masons, the various women's guilds, and almost every extracurricular group at Indian Falls High. The best float won a traveling trophy. When I was a kid the thing looked worn and dented. Now it probably resembled shrapnel.

Following the parade was an all-day picnic held in the park, complete with music and a softball game. The senior citizens' group always played bocce ball. Major excitement.

I would have stayed on my sofa watching Bob Barker instead of the parade, but Pop never would have forgiven me. Besides, I reasoned Tom Owens would be one of the first to show up for the softball game. When he did, I'd be there in a pair of flattering red shorts and a low-cut white tank to cheer him on. If I didn't get a reputation after yesterday's dress, today's outfit would do the trick.

The streets were filled with people when I stepped outside. I staked out a shady spot underneath a tree and from there watched the floats stream by. As the high school marching band stumbled past, I studied the crowd. No Lionel. No Pop. Annette, resplendent in a flag T-shirt and blue platform high heels, was standing two trees away. After the way she acted the other day in the salon I wasn't sure she'd welcome my presence, but I trotted down to join her anyway.

Annette looked surprised to see me, then smiled at my outfit. "Someone's trying to get a certain vet's attention."

"Nope," I said, relieved my friend was back to acting normal.

The Girl Scouts waved as they marched by. "But I am looking to catch the football coach's eye."

Annette's jaw went slack. "Tom Owens?" I nodded, and she perched a hand on her hip. "What happened to Lionel?"

I shrugged. "He got a little irrational yesterday."

"Honey," Annette put one French-nail-tipped hand on my arm. "Guys get irrational when a woman's would-be fiancé turns up."

"Okay," I said. "How do you know about that?"

"Your boss stopped by the diner. Doreen was there."

Oh God, I thought. Doreen put Paul Revere's communication skills to shame. That meant everyone within a hundred-mile radius knew about Lionel getting decked.

Annette's laughter made me turn my attention back to the parade. The senior center's float was rolling by. I did a double take. In the middle of the float was my grandfather, wearing an enormous black wig and strumming a guitar. Several blue-haired women lounged on the float, batting their eyes at Pop. Elvis's version of the "Battle Hymn of the Republic" blasted from the sound system. Thank goodness the real King drowned out most of Pop's enthusiastic rendition. Pop sang like a hedgehog.

Annette commented, "Well, that's not something you'd ever get to see in Chicago—and neither is that."

Trotting happily down the parade route was Elwood, resplendent in his Uncle Sam top hat. Lionel walked next to the camel, holding his lead rope. Not that Elwood needed to be led. The camel walked confidently down the road, swinging his head from side to side. Kids cheered and waved, and the camel rolled his eyes in response. Elwood was in his element.

When the parade mercifully came to an end, Annette and I strolled over to the park. Even though it was only eleven o'clock, the grounds were jammed with people. The smell of grilling meat made my stomach grumble.

"So," Annette asked. "What's got you interested in Tom Owens?"

"He's Agnes's nephew and was a friend of Mack's. I thought it might be a good idea to chat with him."

"He was Mack's best friend, but you should watch yourself," Annette warned. "Tom is a lot like the football players he teaches— loud, immature, and aggressive. He hates when he doesn't get his way."

Sounded like most of the men I'd known. Thinking about that reminded me to ask, "Hey, Annette, do you know of anyone who sees a psychiatrist? I know people around here don't typically talk about it if they do, but I thought you might know." Precious's pills might not be the only clomipramine in town.

Annette gave me a funny look. "Rebecca, are you looking for yourself? Do you need someone to talk to?"

"Well, it's not—"

"Talking to a psychiatrist isn't anything to be ashamed of. After everything you've been through, I think it's a good idea that you see a professional."

I shook my head at her assumption. "I don't really need to talk to anyone. Honest."

Annette wasn't listening. She dug through her purse and smiled as she came out with a bent business card. "Here, call Dr. Skinner. I see him every week."

The admission made my feet stumble, but Annette didn't seem to notice as she gushed, "He's a great listener, and he really helped me through some tough times. You don't know this, but I suffer from panic attacks. Not as much now as I used to, but

Dr. Skinner's helped me by prescribing a couple of different medications to prevent them. The most recent one works great. I haven't had an attack in over three months. The man's a genius."

Part of me wanted to ask what drugs she was taking, but I wasn't sure what I would do if the answer was clomipramine. Probably throw up. I took the card and shoved it into my pocket. That seemed to be all the answer Annette required. She beamed at me before looking around the park for a place to sit. Annette spotted something glittering in the sunlight and pulled me toward my grandfather. How I missed seeing him was a testament to how dazed her admission had left me. Only the Vegas strip and Pop's tacky suit could generate that kind of wattage.

Pop waved to us from a picnic bench. He had ditched the wig and now looked less like the King and more like Liberace.

"So what did you think of the float?" he yelled as we approached.

I perched on the weathered picnic bench, trying to ignore the icky feeling growing in my stomach since Annette's admission. "You got our attention," I answered Pop.

Pop grinned. "The center went all out this year to win best float." He looked up Annette. "Think we got a chance?"

She tilted her head to the side. "You were definitely the most original float out there."

"That's what we were going for." Pop turned back to me. "You disappeared awful fast after church yesterday. Louise and I wanted to invite you to lunch."

Boy, was I ever sorry I missed that. "I had some things to take care of."

"Like your former boss?"

"Did Doreen tell you?" I demanded.

"Nope." Pop stripped off his Elvis scarf and used it to pat the sweat off his forehead. The temperature was on the rise. "Ran into the boy myself. There he is now."

A lead weight settled into my chest as my eyes followed Pop's bony finger past the hot dog stand and cotton candy booth. Sure enough, there was Neil in purple plaid shorts and a yellow polo shirt. To make matters worse, he was heading right for us.

"Hi, Rebecca." He strolled up to the picnic bench. To Pop he said, "Hello, Arthur. Your name is Arthur, right? I sometimes have a hard time remembering people's names, but I always remember faces. Your face is one I'd never forget." Neil's excited voice tapered off.

Pop blinked. He gave me a look as if to say "I can't believe you actually associate with this guy." Like Pop was one to talk.

I stood up. Looking my ex-boss in the eyes, I said, "Neil, what are you still doing here? I thought you were going back to the city."

"I like parades," he said with a shrug. Two bright red stains marched across his cheeks, killing his attempt to look casual. "The motel had a sign posted advertising the parade and picnic, so I decided to stay. Gives me a chance to get to know the place where you grew up. I should know about the woman I plan on marrying."

"I said no." And got fired for it.

Neil folded his arms across his chest. "Only because you haven't had a chance to think it through. You're going to realize how compatible we are and change your mind. I want to be right here when that happens."

"Makes sense to me," my grandfather interjected.

"Look, Neil," I gave Pop a "stay out of it" look. "I'm not going to marry you. You're not my type."

Neil's nostrils flared. "That cowboy from yesterday is?"

"You betcha." Pop slapped the table. "My granddaughter has good taste. She gets it from me." Pop wiggled his bushlike eyebrows at Annette. She rewarded him with a giggle.

I watched Neil's face fall. There was nothing sadder than a pouting guy in ugly plaid shorts.

"Neil," I said in a consoling tone, "I think you'll be happier back in Chicago."

Neil shook his head. "If there's one thing I learned in business, it's persistence. You're a smart woman. Pretty soon you'll realize that cowboy has nothing to offer and you'll come back to Chicago with me. Until then I think I'll have some cotton candy and enjoy the weather."

"I love cotton candy," Pop said. "Especially now that I don't have to worry about rotting my teeth. I'll go with you."

Neil gave me a wink, and off they went in search of spun sugar. Shaking my head, I waved good-bye to Annette and took off at a power walk to the opposite side of the park. I wanted to get away from Neil's lecture on persistence, any reminder of my jobless state, and my growing concerns about Annette's involvement with this case. All three were more than a little unsettling.

Tom was easy to spot when I reached the baseball diamond. He was wearing an Indian Falls Varsity T-shirt and barking orders to some younger guys. By the dull-eyed look of them, I was guessing they were members of the high school football team.

Tom's eyes widened as he spotted me in my short shorts. I waved and sauntered over to where he was standing.

Doing my best Marilyn Monroe impression, I said, "Hi, Tom." Tom's eyes dropped down to my chest, and I arched my back to give him a better look. His jaw went slack as I cooed, "I haven't seen you since poker night at Lionel's."

He nodded. "I'm afraid I didn't make a good impression. I was a little out of it on that night."

"Mack's death was hard on the whole town. I know the four of you guys were close. You had every reason to be upset." I gave him a sympathetic pat on his arm, then left my hand there. Maybe my touch would distract him into saying something interesting. Tom wasn't a suspect, but he might have important information about Precious's medication—maybe a wayward fact that would clear Agnes of all wrongdoing.

"It's been hard," he admitted as his shoulders slumped. "Mack was my best friend." His hand covered mine.

I smiled sympathetically. "You've also had your Aunt Agnes to deal with. That must be hard, too."

Tom pulled back. His eyes lost that glazed "I'm sad, but I want sex" look. "What did you hear about my aunt?" he demanded.

Time to go in for the kill.

With a vacuous smile I explained, "I heard you were related to Agnes Piraino. I know how hard it is to be responsible for an aging relative. Even if they're in good physical health, you never know when they'll forget to turn off the stove or lose their medication." Or have sex with a dominatrix. "It's a big responsibility."

Tom struck what I guessed was a masculine pose. Hands on hips, he blustered, "My aunt is a sweet lady. I love her, but she shouldn't be living on her own. Aunt Agnes has a number of serious mental problems."

My fingers twitched. They really wanted to slap the guy silly, but that wouldn't help my fishing expedition.

Warming to the subject he said, "Thing is, Aunt Agnes doesn't want my help. I tried to find her a nice place in an assisted-living facility, but she won't leave those goddamn cats." Tom's face grew serious. "If you visit my aunt, watch out for Precious. The cat is on serious medication, and Agnes sometimes forgets to give it to her. I was over there a week or two ago when she forgot. The minute I stepped inside, Precious went nuts. I had to get the pills from the kitchen and give them to Precious myself. I haven't wanted to go back since."

Precious was pretty smart for a druggie. "Did you put the pills back?" I asked. This was what I was really interested in. Tom's eyes narrowed with suspicion, so I forced an empty-headed giggle while adding, "Your aunt has so many problems. I'm sure you put the pills back where you found them. Otherwise who knows what might happen the next time Precious needed her medication."

Tom grinned. "Of course I did. That's just the kind of guy I am."

A burly man approached and informed Tom that the game was starting. Tom gave me an apologetic smile. "I hate to go," he said, "but duty calls. Maybe we could get together sometime and . . . talk?"

"Sure." Not. A guy who wanted to lock away his aunt wasn't my idea of a dream date. Especially since he didn't appear to know anything useful.

Tom gave my shoulders a long squeeze before jogging to join the players in the baseball diamond.

"I didn't know you liked baseball."

Lionel's voice echoed behind me. I didn't turn around. "I guess you don't know a lot of things about me," I answered lightly.

"I've been thinking about that. We really don't know each other very well. The whole thing with your boss came as a pretty big surprise." Lionel walked directly in front of my view of the field. "Maybe we should think about that before we tear each other's clothes off."

I blinked. "I still have my clothes on, so it doesn't look like that's a problem."

Lionel raised an eyebrow before leaning down and tilting my face up toward his. "It will be. You know it. That's why I was thinking the two of us should spend some time together. Get to know each other first."

"Like a date?" I took a step back. A date implied the possibility of long-term interest. Unless Elwood was happy trotting down Michigan Avenue, I wasn't interested. Lionel's green eyes caught mine. My breathing sped up. Okay, maybe I was interested. Still, that didn't mean I was going to do something about it.

Lionel's smile grew wider. He moved closer until only an inch separated us. "Don't tell me going on a date with me scares you."

I lifted my chin. "Of course not." *Fibber,* my mind scolded.

"Good." He hooked an arm around my shoulders and dropped a kiss on the top of my head. "Why don't we spend the day together? We can see how it goes. I'll even spring for hot dogs and funnel cakes."

Someone hit a home run, but I barely noticed. The promise of sticky, deep-fried dough had my attention.

"Okay," I said. "You got yourself a deal."

We strolled around the park eating hot dogs, drinking soda, and savoring a funnel cake slathered in strawberries and powdered sugar. Finally, after Lionel was asked by a couple of Indian Falls residents to look at overheating dogs, I got up the nerve to admit, "Annette just mentioned she goes to a psychiatrist."

Lionel swiped some of my calorie-intensive food and shrugged, asking, "Does that bother you?"

I stopped walking. "No, but she also said she was taking medication for anxiety." I waited for his reaction. He looked at me as though I were in need of a shrink myself, so I added, "When I searched Mack's place I found a note from Annette threatening him, and when I asked her about it she got really weird. The whole thing feels off."

"You think Annette killed Mack?"

"I don't know," I answered, feeling a little panicky. "Annette was my mother's best friend. She helped me get through Mom's death. I don't want to believe that she could kill someone. That's why I'm telling this to you."

"You want me to tell you Annette didn't do it."

I nodded.

"Okay," Lionel agreed, stealing another piece of funnel cake. "Annette didn't do it. She's a good woman, and unless you find out she's taking clomipramine, I wouldn't worry about her being involved. Lots of people threatened Mack, including me. You don't think I killed him, do you?"

I shook my head no.

Lionel ate the last bit of funnel cake and tossed the sticky plate into the nearby trash can. Smiling, he took my hand and asked, "Speaking of Mack, how did your conversation with Agnes go yesterday?"

A lightbulb went on in my head. This was just like the picnic he set up. Lionel knew I had talked to Agnes, and he'd even spotted me talking to her nephew. The skunk asked me on a date to find out what I'd learned from them. Last time he tried to use liquor, and this time he bribed me with sugar. The man was a menace.

My eyes narrowed, and Lionel's smile disappeared. "What's wrong?"

"I want the truth," I demanded. "Did you really want to go on a date today or did you just want to pump me for information about Agnes?"

Lionel's jaw clenched, and his face turned red. The man looked ready to blow. Instead he nodded and said, "Maybe you're right. I was curious about Agnes. I figured after you told me about Annette that you wouldn't mind talking about Agnes. I guess I was wrong about that and about this date. A guy would have to be nuts to want to date you."

Before I could respond, Lionel turned and stalked away.

The date was over. If it was a date. I had to admit that the prospect of Lionel using my attraction to him to manipulate me hurt more than it should considering I didn't want a relationship.

Thoroughly depressed, I hugged my arms tight to my chest and looked around the park. There was Neil, watching me from under a large oak tree and wearing a lovesick smile. Frustrated, I turned and walked back toward the rink with Neil trailing behind me.

Oh goodie.

Neil was still following me the next day. Two minutes after I walked into the bakery, Neil moseyed through the door. I stopped at the diner, and again there was Neil. The self-declared persistent Neil was everywhere, and wow, was he hard to miss. He was wearing a pair of white jeans and a bright purple shirt with the collar open. John Travolta, eat your heart out.

At this moment, he was parked outside the rink, which meant I was locked in my office with a can of soda and the mail to keep me company.

There were bills, a credit card application, and two advertisements for stores ten miles away. The last envelope made me smile when I saw Jasmine's name on the return address. I pulled out the folded piece of paper, and something dropped to the floor.

I spotted a key on the ground and stooped down to pick it up. The key was gold with the number 174 etched into it.

By the time I got to the end of the letter, my head was spinning. The key was for the self-storage unit that Jasmine had rented for me. Now my things were sitting in a dusty, dark garage waiting for me to reclaim them.

It was official. I was homeless.

My stomach rolled. How had my life tanked so quickly? I'd come back to Indian Falls to sell the rink. Now I was jobless, homeless, and completely stumped on Mack's murder case. I didn't know who drugged Mack, if Annette took the same drug, where the missing money went, or what that damned key . . .

Wait. I snatched my storage key off the desk. Heart pumping, I opened my top desk drawer and flipped open Mack's CD case. Sitting inside was Mack's key.

Sure enough, the two keys were almost identical. Unless I was wrong, Mack had a storage unit somewhere, and inside might be a clue to who killed him. Now all I had to do was find it.

Sixteen

Booting up the office computer, I did an Internet search for storage companies in the area. There were four within a twenty-mile radius. I grabbed my purse and rifled around inside. Aha! I came up with the gas receipt I'd found in Mack's truck. The town on the receipt matched one of the storage company's addresses. Bingo.

I grabbed Mack's key and headed for the door. It wasn't until I reached the front door that I remembered my problem.

Neil.

In my excitement I'd forgotten the matrimonial campaign he was waging outside my rink.

Damn.

Tiptoeing to the rink's front door, I peered outside. There was Neil's car, but no Neil. I craned my neck. Neil was standing at the corner having a chat with Danielle Martinez. Maybe she'd convince him I was a homicidal maniac.

I calculated the odds of getting to my car without being noticed. They weren't good. If Neil didn't see me, Danielle would. Either way I was screwed.

I considered my options. I dialed my grandfather, hoping he could pick me up at the back entrance. I'd have to bring him along on the storage locker search, but letting my grandfather play Sherlock Holmes was preferable to facing Neil.

Pop didn't answer.

Now what?

Annette was working, and I wasn't about to call Lionel. That left one option. I sent a text and hoped for the best. Brittany and Diane arrived at the rink's back door five minutes after classes were dismissed. Score one for technology.

"I need to track down a lead," I explained. "Problem is, that man out front is following me, so I need you guys to tell him you saw me across town somewhere. That way he'll leave to chase after me, and I can slip away."

They looked at each other and grinned.

Ten minutes later, I was cruising out of town, and Neil was scurrying after a figment of Diane and Brittany's imagination. Things were looking up.

I took two wrong turns, but at four o'clock I steered into Store-for-Less. The place reminded me of a one-story motel. A sign over one door read RENTAL OFFICE, while the other doors were marked with numbers. For a second I considered questioning the office staff, and just as quickly I discarded the idea. I would have to explain about Mack, and any conscientious staff member would then call the cops. Not the result I was looking for.

I looked at each numbered door, and my eyes latched on number seventeen. I marched over, slipped the key in the lock, and held my breath as I tried to turn it. Nothing. Jiggling the key, I tried turning it again. Maybe it was my imagination, but I thought I felt the key shift. Putting my not-so-toned arm muscles into it, I gave the key another turn and let out a triumphant cry as the door swung open. I held up my arms in victory, then felt inside the door for a light switch. Light flooded the garagelike space. I stepped inside, curious to see what Mack was hiding that might have gotten him killed.

Inside the unit was . . . Barbie dolls.

Barbie dolls sitting on a very large, sealed cardboard box. They weren't just any Barbie dolls, either. They were the ones stores displayed behind glass—Eliza Doolittle Barbie, Scarlett O'Hara Barbie, and several that looked like they might be original Barbies from the fifties. Each one was still in her box, and none looked as though it had ever been touched by human hands. Each was marked with a numbered Post-it, one through twelve.

Fascinated, I walked over to a box that wasn't taped shut and gave the flaps a pull. Inside were Strawberry Shortcake dolls from the eighties. All perfect in their boxes. Like the Barbies, each had a numbered Post-it note on the top. For a macho kind of guy, Mack sure had a lot of dolls, which was probably why he needed the storage locker. Barbie and Strawberry Shortcake were hard to explain to the boys on poker night.

Tearing open another box, I discovered Cabbage Patch Kids, also numbered. In the next were old *Star Wars* action figures. Mack's image was on the upswing as I came to the last box. I opened it expecting to find more pop culture toys. The lid flew open, and a jolt of surprise stopped my heart.

Inside the box was a glass case. Sitting in the case was a beautiful china doll like the three I'd seen in Regina Catalano's store.

I drove back to the rink pretty sure that the china doll now residing in my trunk belonged to Regina. Regina thought the doll was at a professional restorer. How Mack had gotten it was beyond me. Anthony had to be the man Diane saw eating with Mack in the diner. They had been discussing the doll. Anthony wanted it back, and Mack wasn't giving it up without a fight or a lot of money. Fifty thousand dollars, according to Mack's ransom letter.

Fifty thousand dollars was a lot of money for one of those dolls, but maybe not too much to keep your wife from catching you in a lie.

My Civic pulled into the rink parking lot, and I scanned the area. Neil's car was there, but not Neil. The girls must still have him chasing shadows.

Music was pumping when I entered the rink with my cargo from the trunk. I went directly to my office and locked the door behind me. Setting the doll's case on the floor, I took a seat at the desk.

Now what?

I tapped my fingers on the desk. I should call the cops and give them the doll and Mack's storage key. Then they would have to arrest Anthony Catalano. Problem was, they'd also have to arrest me. While I could probably justify entering the storage locker, explaining how I got that key might be a little harder. Breaking and entering wasn't a good résumé builder.

Besides, I didn't know if Anthony had actually committed a crime. He did have a motive, but Anthony didn't strike me as the "drug the guy and wait to see what happens" kind of person. He looked more like the "beat the dude to a bloody pulp" type. I decided to hold off on calling the authorities until I was certain I'd solved the case. With luck, the cops would be delighted with my discovery and baffled enough by Mack's strange fascination with girlie dolls to overlook my missteps.

Wait a minute. I slipped Mack's disk into the computer and selected the file with the letter demanding fifty grand. I printed the letter out, then moved on to the previously indecipherable spread sheet.

The first entry was listed under the letter *C*. The next column was the number fourteen, followed by a date and a price of seven hundred dollars. The spreadsheet was still confusing, but now that I'd seen the stuff in Mack's storage I was willing to bet money that the *C* stood for Cabbage Patch Kids. The number was probably the same one written on the Post-it note.

The next entry started with the letter *B*. Barbie? Since the number was three with a price of five hundred and fifty dollars, I decided I'd cracked the code.

The list was about one hundred lines long, most with two sets of dates, but the last few entries only had one. Mack was doing a brisk trade in dolls, and there was only one place I could figure he was doing it. I logged on to eBay. Sure enough, all the Barbies I'd seen boxed in Mack's storage unit were being auctioned. The seller was mmurphy23, and the bids were high enough to make my eyebrows raise. Wow, I thought. With all the toys in that unit, Mack was making a fortune. Who knew selling old toys could net enough to buy a small country?

Still, was an old toy reason enough to commit murder? Maybe the doll wasn't the only problem. Could be Anthony was Mack's partner in this and Mack was cutting Anthony out of the action.

Mack didn't seem like the type to share a business, but after finding the Barbies I had to admit anything was possible.

There was only one person still living who had the answers.

I picked up the phone, and a tired Jersey voice came on the line. Anthony sounded like he hadn't slept in weeks.

"Hi. I don't know if you remember me, but you ran into me and my grandfather outside Mack Murphy's house."

"I remember." Anthony sounded awake now.

I took a deep breath and said, "I came across some unusual things of Mack's and thought you might be interested in them. One of them in particular. Can you meet me tonight to talk about it?"

He didn't hesitate. He also didn't waste words. "When and where?"

I asked Anthony to meet me at Papa Dominick's Italian restaurant in one hour. Then I hung up the phone and let out a whoosh of air. I had a date tonight—with a possible murderer.

I drove over to the edge of town where Papa Dom had been serving pasta and hot, crusty pizza since I was in high school. I was early, so I commandeered one of the two empty tables near the bar and ordered a Diet Coke and some calamari. I wasn't sure if I could eat. Still, the act of ordering made sitting in the restaurant seem more normal. When meeting a potential homicidal maniac, anything normal was good.

Dom himself brought out the golden calamari and told me in his thick accent how sorry he was about my mother's death. "She was a very nice-a lady," he said. I nodded my thanks as Dom sighed and shuffled back to the kitchen.

I took a big sip of my soda and tried to swallow down the lump in my throat. Dom was right. Mom was a great woman. Somehow she'd made the whole town love her, which was a trick I hadn't mastered.

"Rebecca Robbins?"

I looked up. The voice had a New Jersey accent, and it didn't come with fried food. This one was stuffed into a charcoal gray suit, complete with an angry scowl.

"Yes." The word barely squeaked out of my mouth. I nodded in case Anthony didn't speak mouse and gestured to the chair across from me. He sat down with a grunt.

Yikes. Seeing this guy on Mack's dark porch was scary, but in the light everything, including his neck, looked three times larger. This guy was a walking billboard for steroids.

"Thanks for meeting me on such short notice," I said.

Another grunt. The guy was pithy.

Now that Anthony was seated across from me I doubted the brilliance of my plan, but I couldn't get up without him following me, and I definitely didn't want to be alone with him outside. I was stuck.

The waitress came over, startling me from my building terror. I ordered the eggplant Parmesan. No need to count calories when faced with a hit man, right? Anthony ordered a glass of white wine and the linguine with clam sauce.

We stared at each other across the table, and knots of tension formed in my shoulders. Quiet made me edgy. "So," I said. "You and Mack were business partners?"

Anthony's eyes narrowed as he grunted again. Strange, but this time I wasn't intimidated—probably because he had a deep-fried tentacle he'd pilfered from my appetizer dangling from his lips. Not that I minded. As long as I stayed alive, the man could eat anything he wanted.

He nodded as he swallowed. "Not exactly."

"What's that mean?" I asked.

"Let's just say the two of us shared a mutual interest."

"Like an eBay account?" He looked at me blankly. "Did you guys run a company together based on online auctions?"

"Nope. Mack did that stuff all on his own."

So much for that theory. That just left the doll. "How were you and Mack getting along in your mutual interest?"

Anthony's massive shoulders shrugged. "Not good. Mack and I had different ideas about how business should be conducted."

I wondered if medicating his partners figured into Anthony's financial strategy. "I heard you fought with him at the diner."

Anthony gave me a flat stare. "I don't like people poking into my business," he growled.

"Well, I don't like dead people floating in my toilets." I straightened my shoulders, trying to look confident even though I was sure everyone in the restaurant could hear my knees knocking. "Finding Mack's body in my rink gives me the right to ask a few questions, don't you think?"

He tilted his head and nodded. "You might be right." The tone of his voice turned pleasant. "I apologize. This whole thing with Mack has me disturbed."

I blinked, not knowing what to say to that. Heaping plates of food arrived, allowing me to regroup while Anthony sucked down his meal. The red sauce Dom had prepared smelled fabulous, but I couldn't eat while my stomach was churning.

When Anthony slowed his gastronomic assault, I peered up at him and said, "I think it's time for us to lay all our cards on the table." Anthony nodded, so I continued. "From what I can tell, Mack's got something that belonged to you. He was willing to sell it back for fifty thousand dollars, but you didn't want to pay. How am I doing so far?"

Anthony pushed his plate to the side and placed his elbows on the table. "Do you know what Mack stole from me?"

"Would it be a turn-of-the-century china doll?"

"I'll be damned." Anthony sat straight up. "He told you that?" I shook my head no, and Anthony slapped the table, making the silverware dance. "You're good, girlie. Now." His eyes darted across the room, and his voice lowered to conspiracy level. "You wouldn't happen to know where the doll is, would you?"

I leaned forward, trying to look more in control of the situation than I felt. "Tell you what," I whispered. "You tell me how you killed Mack and I'll tell you where the doll is." Right after I called the cops and had him locked up for murder.

The space between Anthony's brows disappeared, and his mouth tensed into a tight line. When his eyes narrowed, my palms started to sweat. Either Anthony had indigestion or he was plotting ways to off me. My eyes darted toward the door.

Anthony's mouth twitched, and he began to chuckle. The chuckles evolved into a full-blown belly laugh.

"You think I knocked off Mack?" Anthony asked as his thick fingers wiped tears from the corners of his eyes.

I crossed my arms. "You had a motive."

He took a sip of his wine. "Look," he said. "I bought some things from Mack on eBay. He was always real reliable with payment and shipping. Mack had a good business going. He was a top-rated seller. Then one day I decided to try my hand at it. I put one of my wife's china dolls up for auction with a minimum selling price. Mack was interested in the doll, but he didn't bid the minimum amount. No one did, so I pulled it."

Anthony leaned back in his chair with a sigh. "Mack wouldn't take no for an answer. He e-mailed me privately and offered me ten grand for the doll. I accepted, and we agreed to meet. I exchanged the doll for his check, only his check bounced. When I told him I wanted the doll back he refused."

"I don't get it. Why didn't you report him to the authorities?"

A pink shine colored Anthony's cheeks as he cleared his throat. "I don't want my wife to find out. She thinks the doll is at a professional restorer. Mack knew that."

Anthony clutched his hands on the table. "My Regina is trying to sell her dolls out of a store, and I suggested she try the Internet. My wife can be very hardheaded. She told me no one would ever pay top dollar on the Internet, so to prove her wrong I listed one. I've been trying to get it back before she finds out what I did. I don't want to get a divorce over a doll." My heart went out to the big lug. "Kid, I didn't kill Mack. My wife would never let me buy a gun. Besides, I was in Vegas when it happened. I got back from my vacation and tried to contact Mack. That's when I found out he was dead. I might have wanted to put my fist into the guy's face, but I didn't kill him."

Taking a sip of water, I considered Anthony's story. Maybe I was naive, but I bought it. To top it off, Anthony said he didn't have a gun. Mack wasn't shot. Not exactly proof of innocence, but something told me Anthony could also prove he was in Vegas at the time. The evening had removed Anthony from the top of my potential murderer list.

The waitress wrapped my uneaten meal while Anthony paid the bill. I thought that was decent of the guy, seeing as how I had just accused him of murder. We left the restaurant, and he followed me back to the rink. Leaving him waiting in the parking lot, I retrieved his wife's prized doll from the office and walked back to the parking lot. Anthony stared at it for a moment, then clutched the thing to his chest. I swear I saw tears glittering in his eyes.

"Thanks," he said with a watery smile. "I hope you catch the guy who knocked off Mack. Remember, if you ever need anything thrown in a landfill, give me a call."

Asking him to dispose of Neil seemed like a bit much, so I bit my lip and waved as he drove away. Strange, but for a brief second I felt a sense of satisfaction at reuniting a man with his doll. Then the satisfaction was replaced by dejection. Anthony might think I was a good detective, but I knew better. I had no idea who gave Mack the pills, who took the money, or who was torching lawn ornaments in my grandfather's front yard. Basically, I was clueless.

I was walking toward the rink with my foam-encased leftovers when a voice called out, "Who was that? A hot date?"

I blinked and spotted Lionel striding toward me. His expression suggested that he could benefit from some of Precious's pills.

Calmly I explained, "It wasn't a date. The guy was my suspect in Mack's murder."

"Right." His left eyebrow twitched. "You expect me to believe that you went to dinner with a murder suspect?"

I shifted the container of eggplant in my hands and waited. Lionel's jaw dropped. "You did? You actually went out to eat with a murder suspect? Are you nuts? How could you be so stupid?"

"I'm not stupid," I yelled back. I was willing to admit that dining with a potentially homicidal maniac wasn't my brightest idea, but that didn't give Lionel the right to call me names. "You should give me a little more credit."

"You want me to give you credit?" Lionel raked his hand through his hair and tilted his head up toward the dark sky. Under his breath he muttered, "You are definitely *not* girlfriend material."

Girlfriend? Horror movie music began playing in my head as visions of china patterns and homey gingham curtains danced in front of my eyes. Who said anything about girlfriend?

Our eyes locked, and Lionel sighed, "All right, I'm sorry for the girlfriend comment, but the rest still applies. Going alone to an Italian restaurant with the Godfather is not a smart thing to do."

I cocked my head. "How did you know we went out for Italian?"

"It's a small town, Becky. Three different women called tonight to tell me you were having dinner with another guy. They didn't know you were in mortal danger." He shoved his hands deep in his pockets as he started to pace. "You should have called me."

"After you got angry and stormed away when I asked a perfectly reasonable question about your motives? Now who's being stupid?"

Lionel's face looked ready to pop.

"Look," I said. "Dinner might not have been the smartest move, but I now know that Anthony didn't kill Mack."

Curiosity bloomed in Lionel's eyes. He said, "Tell me."

I walked Lionel through my discovery of the storage locker, Mack's eBay business, and the extortion letter he wrote to Anthony. Finally I told him about the china doll. I saw Lionel's hands twitch and could tell he wanted to throttle me for giving the doll to a guy who could have been lying to get back evidence. To Lionel's credit, his face stayed expressionless until I finished. I asked, "What do you think?"

"I don't want to tell you what I think. I'd yell, and I don't want to yell right now. Let's save that for tomorrow. I think you've had enough excitement for one day." Lionel stepped toward me. His hand cupped my chin. "Did you have dessert tonight?"

My heart gave a little skip, and my mouth started to water. I know I was supposed to be upset with him, but a little taste couldn't hurt. Right?

My voice was a little breathless as I said, "I skipped dessert."

Lionel leaned down and nuzzled my neck.

"We should do something about that," he said as his lips traveled up my jawline. My legs went deliciously weak, and all arguments for avoiding a relationship with Lionel disappeared from my mind by the time his lips reached my ear. I heard Lionel whisper, "Do you have any ice cream upstairs?"

If I didn't, I'd make some. Milk, sugar, some ice . . . how hard could it be? I even had a few ideas about what we could do while we were waiting for the ice cream to chill.

I grabbed Lionel's hand. Together we walked toward the back entrance. I had to force myself not to race for the stairs. People were already gossiping about my eggplant Parmesan. An ice cream social with Lionel would really get their panties in a bunch.

The minute I opened the back door, Lionel gave me a gentle shove inside. A second later, he had me pinned against the wall. His lips pressed hard against mine, and the temperature in the stairwell rose ten degrees. When tongue touched tongue, the thermostat broke and my body began to overheat. Forget ice cream, I thought. Lionel was better than dessert.

We broke apart, panting. Lionel's eye traced a path up the stairs. The two of us moved at the same time. Lionel took the stairs two at a time, but when I actually went to the gym I was a StairMaster champ, so I beat him to the top and flashed a wicked grin. He grabbed me and kissed the smile from my face. A pretty good prize for victory, I thought. Not breaking contact with his mouth, I fumbled for my key. I tried to slide it into the lock, but the door floated open the minute the key touched it.

I pulled back from Lionel and stared at the gaping door. My blood ran cold, and an image of a flaming scarecrow flashed through my mind. Pointing a shaky finger at the door, I whispered, "I locked that door, Lionel. I know I did."

He stepped in front of me and gave the door a shove. It swung open. Lionel felt around the wall for the light switch, and the lights sprang to life. I peeked into the apartment and gasped. There on the floor was a man. The man was lying on his side with his back to me. His hands and feet were bound.

I rushed over and carefully rolled him onto his back. My breath caught in my throat.

It was Neil.

Seventeen

Neil's eyes were closed, and a dish towel was stuffed in his mouth. Worse was the large gash in his forehead. My stomach went all squishy as blood oozed from the cut. I yanked the dish towel out of Neil's mouth and pressed the already moistened fabric against the wound. With the blood stopped for now, I assessed the damage.

He was breathing, which was good, but he wasn't talking. Normally, a mute Neil was a pleasant Neil. In this instance, it was bad.

Lionel knelt on the floor next to me and began to work at the ropes binding Neil. A minute later, Neil was lying spread-eagle on the hardwood floor, still unconscious. Lionel leaned back on his heels and passed me Neil's restraints.

I clutched them between my fingers. The ropes looked like shoelaces. I looked down at Neil's feet. Sure enough. His shoelaces were missing.

Lionel shook his head. "Who would do something like this?"

I was about to say I didn't know when a terrible thought swept over me. Cringing, I croaked, "I swear they weren't supposed to kill him."

"What?" The vein in Lionel's neck started to pulsate.

My hands clenched and unclenched. "Neil was following me all morning. I had to go to Mack's storage unit, so I asked Brittany and Diane to distract him." Neil gurgled, and I looked down at his pasty face. Guilt hit me hard. "They were just supposed to talk to him. They were going to say they saw me on the other side of town. I thought that's what they did. I swear to God. They weren't supposed to hurt him."

I bit my trembling lip and stole a look at Lionel. He was looking at me with a combination of disbelief and amusement, neither of which made me feel any better.

Lionel climbed to his feet with a half-smile playing on his lips. "Why don't I call Dr. Truman?" he suggested. "Doc can come over and take a look at Neil. Make sure he's okay. In the meantime, you should take a look around up here to make sure nothing is missing. Then go downstairs."

"Why downstairs?" I asked, scrambling to my feet. "Shouldn't I stay here? It is my apartment, you know." Which was why I wasn't calling the sheriff. Sean would arrest me for assaulting Neil, just for fun. No doubt Lionel was aware of this.

Lionel sat down on the couch with his cell phone. His fingers began pushing buttons. When I didn't budge, he looked back at me with a sigh. "Becky, you should go talk to the girls. I have a feeling they aren't responsible for this."

Now Lionel thought I was amusing. Perfect. "Stay here,"

I commanded. I turned on my heel and marched around the apartment looking for signs of robbery. Nothing was out of place. Everything was just as I left it—aside from Neil on the floor. After conveying the lack of theft to Lionel, I gave Neil a quick pat on the hand and headed for the door. I was halfway down the stairs before I admitted that Lionel was right. The girls were good kids. They might tie up a dorky guy with his own shoelaces, but they wouldn't bash him over the head.

I took the rest of the stairs two at the time. Since it was Tuesday night, the rink was on the empty side. No Brittany and no Diane on the floor. I made my way down the sidelines to the snack area.

Bingo.

My shaky legs carried me to where Brittany was aggressively batting her eyelashes at two pimply-faced teenage boys.

"Brittany," I interrupted. "Can I talk with you a minute?"

The girl jumped up from her seat as her face broke into a wide smile. "Hey, Rebecca. This is Brent and Emilio. They're on the football team." The way she said "football team" you would have thought they belonged to the Chicago Bears.

I smiled at them and turned back to Brittany. "Can we talk in my office? I promise it'll only take a minute."

Brittany rolled over to me, her eyes drifting longingly to the guys. I could tell she was worried they would disappear the minute she did.

So I offered, "Why don't the guys have a few pieces of free pizza while they wait for you. They'll hang around. Right, guys?"

The boys' eyes lit up at the prospect of free pizza, and Brittany shot me a grateful smile. When the guys were safely stuffing their mouths, I led Brittany back to the office and shut the door.

"How did you and Diane keep Neil from following me?" I asked.

Brittany's eyes brightened with triumph and words began tumbling out of her mouth. "You'd be really proud of us. Diane and I walked up to Neil and started talking to him. I asked him what he was doing in the parking lot, and he said he was a friend of yours. That's when Diane pretended to be helpful. She told him that we just ran into you at the coffee shop, and I said you were getting a vanilla latte because details are important in making a story believable. After we said good-bye he took off down the street. We did good, right?"

I swallowed hard. "Yeah, you did great. Thanks."

"Anytime. Oh, I also ran into Pastor Rich this afternoon. He said to tell you to come see him because you might be able to help figure out who stole that piece from the statue. I tried to ask him if he'd give you a reward, but he was busy paying attention to his secretary by then. I think they're dating."

Brittany gave a little shiver. I guess to a sixteen-year-old, dating a pastor had a high ick factor. She turned and slipped out the office door, and I headed back outside and up the stairs to my apartment.

Dr. Truman was kneeling beside Neil when I walked into the room. Lionel stood up from the couch, walked around Neil's body, and put his arm around me. Grateful, I leaned against him.

A loud moan made us turn in time to see Dr. Truman helping Neil into a sitting position. Neil started to cough, and Dr. Truman thumped him on the back.

I took a step forward. "Is he going to be okay?"

Dr. Truman nodded. "Yep. Although he's got a heck of a concussion. I'd like to take him back to my office and put a couple of stitches in to close that cut of his. But don't worry, Rebecca. I promise he'll be fine."

I let out a sigh of relief as Neil struggled to stand up. Dr. Truman moved closer to help, and between the two of them, they awkwardly made it to their feet. I was watching them stumble to the couch when something on the floor caught my eye. On the spot recently occupied by Neil's butt was a folded piece of stationery.

Acting casual, I leaned down and grabbed the paper. Standing up, I shoved the note deep into my pocket, then settled into the chair across from Neil. He was now looking around the room with a combination of confusion and interest.

"Neil," I asked, "do you remember how you got here?"

He nodded. I noticed his eyes were filled with pain and tears, which made my chest ache. Sure, the guy had been stalking me, but he didn't deserve to have the crap scared out of him. He licked his dry lips and said, "About five o'clock, I came up here looking for you. I knocked on the door, and it swung open, so I decided to come inside. You know, to make sure everything was okay. I wasn't trying to sneak in or anything."

Something told me that was exactly what he was doing, but I let it slide. I stood up and went to the kitchen to get Neil some water. Handing a cup to him, I asked, "What happened then?"

"I don't know. I turned the light on and took a look around. The place is homey. I like it." Neil leaned forward on the couch. "I figured the two of us could talk better about the future if we were alone, so I waited. I was watching *Wheel of Fortune* when I heard a noise. At first I thought it was one of the sound effects on the show, but then I realized it was coming from the stairs, so I got up to take a look. I opened the front door and *pow*. All I remember is dark hair and a flash of light. Next thing I knew I was lying on the floor with this doctor standing over me."

"Well, that doctor wants to take you to his office. You need stitches." Doc helped Neil to his feet while giving me and Lionel a stern look. "Soon as I'm done taking care of Neil, I'm calling Sheriff Jackson. I know he hasn't had much luck finding Mack's killer, but he needs to know about this."

I had opened my mouth to protest when Lionel's foot stepped on top of mine. Ouch. "We understand, Doc," Lionel said.

It took all three of us to get the unsteady Neil down the stairs and into Doc's car. Doc assured us Eleanor would help with Neil on the other end. I knew Eleanor was more than capable.

Once Doc's taillights disappeared, Lionel and I headed back up to the apartment, and I collapsed on the sofa. With Neil being cared for, I could contemplate the fear gnawing at my stomach. Neil had been bludgeoned, tied up, and left bleeding in my apartment. Who hit Neil over the head? Better yet, why were they coming to my apartment in the first place? The hair on the back of my neck stood on end as I realized that they wanted me.

Had I been home, I could have been killed. Up until this moment, I'd never believed that was a possibility. The graffiti and my flattened tire had been unsettling. The flaming scarecrow had been disturbing, to say the least. This was more than that.

I took two big gulps of air and closed my eyes, hoping the room would stop spinning.

"So are you planning to show me that note you picked up, or do I have to wait until you fall asleep to read it?"

My eyes snapped open. In the commotion I'd forgotten about

the note. My trembling fingers dug into my pocket and pulled out the slip of paper. Opening it, I read:

Wheat Germ
Bean Sprouts
Skim Milk
Whole Grain Bread
Tofu

Huh? I blinked and read it again. The other notes had been intimidating and a little frightening. This one was only scary if I was supposed to eat the food on the list. Wheat germ? Yuck!

I held the paper out to Lionel and watched as his face went from concerned to completely baffled in ten seconds flat.

"What the hell is this?" he asked.

"I don't know." I took the paper back from Lionel. "But the handwriting is familiar." I grabbed my purse and upended the contents on the couch. There was the note we'd found along with my flattened tire. "See," I said, pointing to the writing on both. Same precise script handwriting with the same small flourishes on the final letter of every word. I had to give my psychopath credit for great penmanship.

"Sure enough. But why did Mack's killer leave you a grocery list?"

I felt my forehead wrinkle with thought. "I don't think it was left intentionally. Think about it. Whoever did this must have heard that I was at dinner with Anthony, figured the place was empty, and panicked when Neil was here. This list must have fallen while tying him up, and I'm pretty sure the person who did it was a woman."

My powers of deduction amazed me, and I waited for Lionel to applaud.

No applause. Instead he asked, "Why do you think this was done by a woman? You've always referred to Mack's killer as a he before."

"No guy in this town would eat the food on this list. Would you?"

Lionel made a face. "Not even on a bet. All that tells us is that the killer makes mistakes and *he* has bad taste in food. With luck he'll make another mistake so we can catch him. We need to put an end to this."

"Maybe we should put an end to it before the killer does something else." Like killing me. That would be bad.

Lionel nodded as he dropped an absentminded kiss on my forehead. "Sounds like a good idea, Becky." He caught sight of the clock and sighed. "I have to get back to check on a sick horse. Are you going to be okay by yourself tonight? I can come back here if you want."

Letting Lionel's warm body chase away my fears was tempting, but the threat of the rumor mill buzzing about Lionel sleeping over was too much for me to handle now. Not that my reputation really meant all that much. Still, this was Mom's place, and her reputation mattered.

Reluctantly, I said, "No, but thanks."

"Call me if you change your mind." Then Lionel gave me a kiss good-bye that almost made me do just that.

I didn't sleep well during the night. Every creak and moan of the old building made me jump. By two o'clock the fear had sunk in so deep I was shivering under three layers of quilts. By seven the fear had turned to anger. I preferred the anger. Anger was powerful. Anger didn't feel so cold.

By eight o'clock I'd used the power of that anger to get showered, dressed, and ready to solve the mystery of who clocked Neil over the head. I had a plan. I was going to shake the trees in this town. Then I'd sit back and see what fell out.

My first stop was Something's Brewing. I needed caffeine, and Indian Falls' lone coffee shop was known for its high-octane brew. I ordered a large quadruple-shot latte, and after one large sip my brain turned on. Sufficiently caffeinated, I walked across Main Street to the bakery, then to my real destination—the sheriff's office. When entering enemy territory, always bring gifts. In this case, Bavarian cream and chocolate sprinkled doughnuts.

Roxy's eyes narrowed as she watched me approach. My lips spread into a cheesy smile as I chirped, "Hi, Roxy. How are you doing?"

She glared at me from behind the counter. "*I'm* doing a lot better than you. Doc Truman called in an assault last night. He says it happened at your place."

I nodded. "Doc said he was going to call, and I thought I should come in and answer any questions you might have about it." Lying to the cops had turned into one of my favorite hobbies. Besides, I couldn't tell her I was here to dig up information on Mack's death. Again.

Roxy cocked her head to one side as she studied me. Finally her perfectly manicured fingers rifled through a few papers and passed over the report filed by Doc. "Read this and tell me if anything is missing."

I scanned the paper. Doc did pretty well. I added a few details, like the time we discovered the body and the fact that Neil's shoe-laces had been used to tie him up. The note I kept to myself. Some-how I didn't think the cops would be impressed by a health-food list. Besides, call me crazy, but I wanted to take a whack at the clue before the sheriff got hold of it.

I passed the clipboard back to Roxy with my thanks, and she snorted. Roxy didn't look to be in a sharing-information mood. I plopped the box of doughnuts on the counter. Roxy's nose twitched, and she took a Bavarian cream. Two bites later, she was smiling. I waited for her to take her second doughnut before say-ing, "There are a few other things I should tell the police, but I'm nervous about talking to the sheriff and Deputy Holmes. You were friends with my mom. I feel I can trust you."

The doughnut stopped halfway to Roxy's mouth, and her eyes lit up. "Of course you can trust me," she said, leaning forward. "Why don't you tell me what's on your mind."

I felt a surge of triumph as Roxy took the bait. Nodding, I rummaged through my purse. My fingers closed around Mack's storage key, and I held it out to Roxy. "This key turned up at the rink. I did a little investigating and discovered it belonged to a storage locker registered under Mack's name. I thought the sheriff might be interested. It could be important."

"Anything is possible. Is that all?" Roxy took the key, her face filling with disappointment. A key wasn't good gossip material, but I wasn't done gossiping yet.

I looked from side to side as if afraid of being overheard. Then I said, "One other thing. I was talking to Agnes Piraino about her pets. She mentioned that her cat's medication turned up missing one day, which sounds suspicious to me."

Roxy frowned. "Agnes is a hundred years old. She probably

threw the medication away by accident or fed it to the fish. I wouldn't worry about it."

She went back to her doughnut, and I let out a very audible sigh. "Yeah, I guess you're right. I was just concerned because the drug the cat was taking is the same one that someone slipped Mack. If you don't think it's important, though, I'll stop worrying about it."

That got her attention. Roxy looked like someone had given her a wedgie. "How do you know it was the same drug?"

I shook my head. "I don't want to get anyone in trouble." Not to mention not wanting the story of Eleanor and Pop to get around. "I do know about the clomipramine in Mack's system, which is why the missing prescription bothered me. I thought maybe the person who took it was the one who bumped off Mack, but I guess I was wrong. Thanks for listening to me, though."

I headed for the exit as the distinct sound of a receiver being yanked off its cradle followed me out the door. The Indian Falls phone tree was about to kick into high gear.

After some power walking, I strolled through the front door of Doc's office. Eleanor waved at me. "Hi, Rebecca. How's your grandfather doing?"

"He's fine."

"I was so excited when they announced the senior center won best float. I tried to congratulate Arthur, but there were too many people around. Let him know I'm looking for him, will you? Tell him we should celebrate his victory in private."

Every nerve in my body cringed. "Okay," I said before quickly switching subjects. "Doc brought in a guy for observation last night. Do you know how he's doing?"

"Neil Capezio?" she asked. "What a nice boy. I can't imagine who would want to hurt someone like that."

Neither could I, but I was going to do my best to find out.

"So, he's going to be okay?" I asked.

"Sure is, honey. He's still a little confused because of the concussion. He keeps saying that you were going to be his fiancée but that he's not sure about that anymore. He wants to go back to Chicago and think about it."

Maybe a bump on the head was what Neil needed to bring him back to his senses. That or Neil didn't want the mother of his children to put them in mortal danger. Either was good by me.

"Thanks for taking care of him, Eleanor," I said with genuine feeling. Deliberately, I added, "Mack's murderer already killed one person in my rink. I couldn't bear it if he succeeded with another."

Eleanor's eyes grew wide. "You think Mack's killer hit that boy over the head?"

I tried my best to look solemn. "I'm sure of it—but don't tell anyone, okay? I don't want to scare half the town. Besides, the cops will catch the suspect soon. I heard they have a lead."

Mission accomplished, I headed for the door. "Oh." I reached into my pocket and pulled out Neil's bondage shoelaces. "Give these to Neil and tell him to have a good trip back to Chicago."

Next on my agenda was Shear Highlights—the hub of gossip. Besides, I had to find out what drugs Annette's shrink had her on in order to get her name off my suspect list. Since my nails were looking a bit ragged, I figured I could weasel information out of my friend and get a manicure all at the same time. Can I multitask or what?

Annette was arm-deep in chocolate brown hair coloring when I walked in the door. I signed in at the front desk and took a seat in the full waiting area.

Magazine in hand, I was contemplating whether the new Victoria's Secret bra would actually do wonders for me when I heard, "Hi, Rebecca. Are you going to finally let me cut your hair?"

"No, but I'll let you paint my nails, and you can use any color you'd like."

"Works for me. Give me one second, then I'll get you started." Annette led me to a manicure table located about four feet away. It was the perfect location for being accidentally overheard but not great for pumping Annette about her psychiatric issues. The drug questions would have to take a backseat until I caught Annette alone.

"So," she said, arranging bowls and files on the tiny table, "is it true you hit your ex-boss over the head?"

I blinked. "Who told you that?"

Annette put my hands in a bowl of soapy water. "Marietta Espinoza. She talked to Eleanor just before she came here to get her hair done. Eleanor said your former boss was in Doc's office nursing a concussion."

One of the problems with gossip was the inaccuracies that popped up, but I was more than happy to spread the "truth" to every busybody within the sound of my voice. "Lionel and I found Neil tied up on the rink apartment's living room floor last night." Out of the corner of my eye I could see several magazines lower as the yentas tuned in. "It looks like Mack's murderer was after me. I guess I was asking too many questions, only he beaned Neil instead."

"Wow." Annette jumped in her seat, sending several nail files

218

careening to the ground. "You figured out who killed Mack, didn't you? Are you going to tell me?"

I shook my head. "I can't, but I've talked to the sheriff. They should wrap up the case any day now. Once that happens, I'll fill you in on everything."

"Good. Then you'll be able to get out of this town and back to Chicago where you belong." Annette gave a relieved sigh as every woman in the place reached for her cell phone.

Fifteen minutes later, I left the salon with Rustic Red nails and a mostly satisfied smile. I might not know what drug Annette was taking, but between Roxy, Eleanor, and the yentas, the whole town would know the cops were about to nab the killer. If that didn't shake the killer out of hiding, I didn't know what would. I just wished Annette weren't so eager to kick me out of Indian Falls. Her desire to send me packing made my minor victory feel hollow.

Next stop on my agenda was Slaughter's Market. There could only be a handful of people in this town who would purchase the items on the killer's grocery list, so all I needed to do was find out who those people might be. Easy, right?

A tall, scrawny white-haired guy with a vague expression was manning the register. His name tag read NIGEL. I smiled at him. "Hi, Nigel. My name's Rebecca Robbins. I'm the owner of the Toe Stop roller rink. Do you mind if I ask you a question?"

He blinked, which I optimistically chose to take as a yes. "I'm starting a gourmet club here in town, and I was hoping you could tell me which customers like tofu?"

"Huh?"

"Tofu." I carefully enunciated the word. "Do you know which customers buy tofu?"

"Hair goo? Hair care is in aisle three."

Something told me Nigel needed to change the batteries in his hearing aid. Abandoning the tofu questions, I raised my voice and inquired, "Is Felix in the store?"

"How should I know if Felix snores? You'll have to ask him yourself. He'll be in after two."

My brain aching, I left the market. Outside, the temperature was climbing. I walked down Main Street, retrieved my car from the rink parking lot, and pulled up to the Dairy Queen drive-up window. All the talk about tofu had made me hungry.

Armed with chili dogs and fries, I aimed the car toward Pop's house. Roxy and company should have spread the word about my detective skills. Now I needed Pop to find out what they were saying.

The charred remains of the scarecrow were now in a pile at the end of the driveway, the first stop on a journey to its final resting place at the county dump. Saying a silent farewell to Louise's arts and crafts project, I pulled up next to Pop's maroon Lincoln Town Car, grabbed the Dairy Queen bags, and carefully listened at the side door for any noises. If Pop was entertaining a guest, I wasn't going in.

Nothing.

I opened the side door and dropped the bags on the kitchen table. Grabbing a soda from the fridge, I went in search of Pop. I could hear the television blaring in the living room, and my nerves tightened with dread. Peeking around the corner, I let out a relieved sigh. Pop was sprawled on the love seat, snoring away in a pair of boxers. A long purple scarf was draped around his neck. His black Elvis wig sat slightly askew on his head. After some of the strange outfits he'd been wearing, this was a good look for him.

"Hey, Pop. Wake up." I nudged his shoulder. "I brought chili dogs."

Pop's eyes snapped open. "Chili dogs? Where are they?" Pop swung his legs to the floor, and before I could blink he was up on his feet. Growing up, there were two constants in my life—my mother and Pop's addiction to chili dogs.

A few minutes later, the two of us were seated in the kitchen dividing up the hot dogs. Three for Pop. One for me. Both of us got fries and onion rings. I chomped down on a french fry, and my body hummed with pleasure.

When the last piece of hot dog was devoured, Pop leaned back in his chair and belched. "So why the chili dogs? What do you want?"

"I need you to tap your resources and find out what the gossips in town are buzzing about. I set a few things in motion this morning, and I need to know if they worked."

"I can do that." Pop pushed away from the table and shuffled over to the phone. "I gotta make it quick, though. I have to start practicing for my new job."

"What job?" I asked. "I thought you said you couldn't take care of the rink anymore because working was bad for your health."

Pop shrugged. "This isn't a nine-to-five job like that. See, winning the float competition got me thinking. I really like the King, and all the women told me I looked just like him yesterday. You can see the resemblance, right?"

Maybe if I stayed out in the sun too long and was hallucinating. "So what's the job?" I asked.

Pop grinned. "I'm going to be an Elvis impersonator, and my first gig is Friday night at the senior center. The bingo crowd is a rowdy group, and everyone who's anyone will be there. You should bring Lionel. I'll make sure you get a scarf." Pop began to gyrate his hips, and he slid the purple scarf off his neck and swung it around in a circle, causing a muscle in my neck to twitch. The jerky movements made the black wig slip over Pop's eyes. He stopped dancing in order to readjust the rug on his head and quipped, "I'm still trying to figure out how to get this hair to stay on during my dance routines. Maybe Annette can give me some advice."

I pointed to the phone, and Pop started dialing while I buried my head in my hands. The image of Pop doing a hula in his shorts was going to haunt me for the rest of my life. If my grandmother was alive, this would have killed her. Grandma Phillips was the steady-as-a-rock, everything-in-its-place type, and growing up I'd thought Pop was, too. Boy, did he have me fooled.

Several phone calls later, Pop shimmied back to the table with a large grin plastered on his face. "I don't know what you did, but the whole town is abuzz. Everyone's saying there's evidence pointing to Mack's murderer. They claim you have it. Do you?"

"Maybe." Pop was great for getting gossip, but he was also a champ at spreading it. Telling him I was bluffing would ruin everything.

Pop's eyes were wide with curiosity, and he added, "Edna said something about Mack storing dead bodies somewhere and that Agnes's cat drugged Mack. I don't know if I should pay any attention to her, since she also claims to hear the voice of Abraham Lincoln giving her racing tips. Edna plays the ponies every Saturday."

"Anything else?" I was hoping someone would crack under the pressure. A confession would make my life a lot more comfortable.

He shrugged. "Marjorie Buckingham said she'd come over

later and help me with my pelvic rotations, but I wasn't sure you'd want to know about that."

The chili dog lurched in my stomach. Pop gave me a concerned look, and I gave him a big, if sickly, smile while asking, "Why isn't Louise helping you with your Elvis career? She'd make great costumes."

"Louise and I called it quits. She wanted me to put another one of those death traps in my yard. I said no way in hell, and that's when Louise said I was ungrateful and broke up with me." Pop turned on the sink and filled his glass with water. "Good thing, too. I wanted to end it for a week, only I didn't know how to do it. I hate seeing women cry."

Pop gave me a hug good-bye and started gargling at the sink. Getting in my car, I could hear my grandfather's out-of-tune voice wafting through an open window as he gave the neighborhood a sneak preview of "Don't Be Cruel"—Pop style. Talk about irony.

I stopped by the rink. A quick peek assured me the upstairs apartment was quiet. Downstairs, George was on the floor practicing jumps in a pair of bright blue spandex shorts and a matching shirt. I briefly wondered if he'd like to be in Pop's new act and decided to keep my mouth shut. Indian Falls wasn't ready for that.

"I have a few more errands to run," I yelled to George as he rolled by. "Are you okay running things by yourself?" I could see every muscle beneath the spandex move as George pushed himself along the floor and skidded to a stop in front of me.

"I'm fine." His voice sounded tense, though, and his forehead scrunched up, which made me doubt his statement.

"What's wrong?" I asked.

"All but two of my lessons canceled for today, and Mrs. Ramirez canceled Miguel's birthday party. Between the murder and the guy you found bleeding upstairs, no one wants to let their kids come here." George sniffled and wiped his nose on the back of his hand. "Your mother would be disappointed."

The guilt trip scored a direct hit to my heart. George was right. Mom would be disappointed.

"Don't worry, George." I put my hand on his spandexed arm and gave it a reassuring squeeze. "A couple of days from now this will all be behind us. Mack's killer will be arrested. Everything will go back to normal."

George's big brown eyes glistened with hope. "Then it's true? Everyone's saying you know who Mack's murderer is, but I figured it was a big joke."

"No joke. The case is good as solved." George was so happy he never noticed me crossing my fingers behind my back.

"That's great. Oh, I left the messages on your desk along with the mail. You know where to find me if you need me." George skated back to the center of the rink, looking a lot happier than when I came in.

Ducking into my office, I flipped through the mail. Nothing exciting. I read through the messages George had scribbled down. People calling to express concern about the rink's safety or cancel their events. I prayed what I said to George turned out to be true; otherwise, the rink would be in serious financial trouble.

I noticed there was a new message on the machine, so I hit PLAY. Agnes Piraino's anxious voice filled the room.

"Rebecca, dear, could you please come see me? I'm having a little problem, and you're so nice that I thought you might be able to help. I promise I won't take much of your time. Oh, one more thing. Don't come to the house. You see, the sheriff has locked me in jail."

Eighteen

Oh God, I groaned silently. My quest to shake loose the killer had landed Agnes in the clink. While I was certain Precious's pills led to Mack's death, I was equally sure Agnes wasn't the guilty party. Too bad I had no idea who really did it.

When I arrived at the sheriff's, several people, including a reporter for the local paper, were loitering outside. Our esteemed newspaper editor, Carter Ostrowski, raced over to me yelling, "Hey, Rebecca, do you know anything about Agnes Piraino being arrested for Mack Murphy's murder?"

"Nope. Sorry, Mr. Ostrowski." I walked as fast as my low-heeled sandals would allow.

The reporter trotted at my heels. "That's funny. Several people say you're the one who found the evidence that put Agnes behind bars."

I stopped in my tracks. "Me?" I croaked.

"Yep. Roxy said Sheriff Jackson called you a heroic citizen. Do you have any comment?"

Yeah, Roxy inhaled too much nail polish, and Sheriff Jackson was a nut. "Maybe later." I raced into the sheriff's office. Roxy was on the phone, no doubt spreading confidential cop business to anyone who asked. When Roxy finished her conversation, she waved me over.

"If it isn't the woman of the hour." Roxy came around the counter, and I found myself squashed in a big, heavily perfumed hug. "I told the sheriff about your tip, and he went right over and arrested Agnes. Who would have guessed the old lady was a killer?"

"Not me." I took several steps back. The scent of decaying lilies was overwhelming. "Speaking of Agnes, she called me after the sheriff brought her in. Would you mind if I talked to her?"

Roxy's lips pursed tightly together. "I'm not sure what the policy is since we've never had a murderer in jail before. Wait here. I'll ask the sheriff." Her heels echoed down the small hallway while I twiddled my thumbs in the lobby. It wasn't long before I heard Roxy's return.

"Sheriff says it's okay. Follow me."

We both clopped down the hall past the sheriff's office. When we reached the last door on the left, Roxy gestured toward it. "She's all yours."

I poked my head into the room. There were four decent-sized cells along one side and a small, kitchenette-sized table and chairs on the other. Agnes was in the last cell, the only one with a window. Her face lit up the minute she spotted me.

"Rebecca, dear, I knew you'd come. I'm so sorry to bother you with this, but I had no idea who else to call."

Seeing the animal-loving librarian in jail twisted every soft, squishy emotion in my body. "Please don't apologize, Mrs.

Piraino. I'm glad you called, and I should be the one apologizing to you. This whole thing is all my fault."

"Your fault?" Agnes blinked. "How could you possibly think this is your fault?"

"Well." I looked down at my shoes. "I was talking to Roxy this morning, and I mentioned how Precious took the same pills that killed Mack." I looked back at Agnes, and the knife of guilt cut deeper. The older woman looked like she'd aged ten years since Pop and I saw her. "It never occurred to me that they'd arrest you, because I'm sure you didn't do it."

Agnes plopped her hands on her hips and gave me a stern frown. I braced myself for a tongue-lashing. "Oh, heavens, dear. Don't blame yourself." Agnes grabbed a steel bar in each hand. "If anyone's to blame for this mess, it's that nephew of mine. He's the reason I was scared to say I lost the pills. As a matter of fact, he's the one that got me arrested today."

Being absolved of guilt must have scrambled my brain, because I didn't understand. "What does Tom have to do with you being in jail?"

Agnes let out a heavy sigh. She walked over to the tiny cot against the wall and sank down. "When you told the cops about Precious's pills, they came to see me. I told them exactly what I told you, that the pills were in my kitchen one minute and the next they were gone. Sheriff Jackson was very sympathetic. He told me it could happen to anyone."

Probably because it happened to him all the time. "Then what happened? Why are you here?" It sounded like the sheriff had been willing to leave Agnes alone.

The old librarian's eyes filled with tears. "The sheriff and Deputy Holmes were about to leave, but then Tom showed up.

Tom started waving his arms around, saying things like 'my aunt can't help herself' and that he tried to make sure I didn't hurt anyone, but he couldn't watch me all the time. Before I knew it, Deputy Holmes was cuffing me and reading me my rights. I just can't believe my own flesh and blood would stoop this low to get my money."

Neither could I. I mean, there were times I'd have cheerfully traded my family for a new car, but that's when I was sixteen. I could blame the stupidity of youth. What was Tom's excuse?

Agnes clutched her hands together and bowed her head. Anger flooded through me as I looked at the tiny and helpless librarian standing behind steel bars. In my best authoritative voice I said, "Let me talk to the sheriff. I'm sure I can make him understand what's going on. You'll be out of here in no time. I promise."

Her head came up, and hope shined bright in her eyes. "You really think so?"

I nodded. "Let me handle it." Only this time I'd be careful about what I said; otherwise, I might get Agnes burned at the stake. So far my meddling hadn't turned out the way I'd anticipated.

"Oh, Rebecca," Agnes cried. "Could you also stop by my house? I don't want to put you to any trouble, but Precious needs her medication. I just got a refill from Dr. Franklin today, and I didn't have time to give it to her before the sheriff showed up. I don't want Precious to bite anyone by accident."

Unless it was Tom, I thought. Tom deserved whatever he got. I agreed to medicate Precious and feed the rest of Agnes's cats. She told me where I could find a spare key, and I said good-bye. Wandering down the hallway, I poked my head into a variety of rooms looking for the sheriff. He was nowhere to be found, but

Deputy Sean was. While throwing darts at a board in his office, Sean told me the "big man" had gone home. Probably back in his garden smelling the daisies.

By the time I hit the pavement, the local paparazzi and the other curious townsfolk had disappeared. Sheriff Jackson's floral palace was about three miles outside the town limits. I pulled up the gravel drive and immediately spotted him. The sheriff was kneeling next to a large flower bed and watering what I guessed were azaleas.

"Sheriff Jackson," I yelled across the yard. "I need to talk to you."

The sheriff continued turning dirt into mud, so I yelled a little louder. "Sheriff Jackson. Do you have time to talk?"

His head came up. Slowly he looked around the large lawn. I cleared my throat loud enough for someone to hear in Kansas, and his head swung in my direction.

"Oh, Rebecca." He stood up and wiped his dirty hands on his overalls. Hooking his fingers through the bib straps, he asked, "What are you doing here? I thought you'd be busy talking to Doreen about selling the rink. It'll sell now that Mack's murder has been solved."

"But it hasn't."

He frowned at me. "Of course it has." He turned back to his pansies and grabbed a watering can. "You gave us a tip about the pills, and we brought in Agnes. Case closed. Sell the rink, Rebecca. Go back to the city."

My shoulders tensed. He was trying to get me to leave town, just like Annette and my stalker. "Look." I marched through the manicured grass toward him. "I said Agnes's cat took clomipramine.

I didn't say Agnes killed Mack, and I know you don't believe she did it, either. You've known her forever. Does she strike you as a homicidal maniac?"

The sheriff squinted up into the sun. "Can't say she does, but criminals are like that. Normal one day, and the next they just snap."

True, but this was Indian Falls. When someone here snapped, everyone noticed.

"Agnes said you weren't going to arrest her today, but then her nephew showed up. What did he say to make you change your mind? Did he have proof Agnes killed Mack?"

"Now, see here," Sheriff Jackson blustered. "Agnes is getting up there in age, and I know better than anyone how the mind can play tricks on you. Tom only pointed out that Agnes is older. She overreacts to certain situations, especially ones involving her cats. Mack was mean to her cats, and Agnes decided to get even. She had the motive. She had the drugs, and she gave them to him. Knowing her, she probably didn't mean to kill the guy, but that's what happened. What more proof do you need?"

Gee, maybe something tangible. The sheriff's case would never convince a jury, not that it would get that far. Not with Tom as the star witness. One look at his motives would make anyone doubt his story. I hoped that included Sheriff Jackson.

"Seems like you're placing a lot of weight on Tom's opinions," I said. "How well do you actually know the guy?"

The sheriff rolled his eyes and shifted his weight from foot to foot. "I know he got our team to the regional finals last year. That says something about a man."

Yeah, that he could coach football. What that had to do with anything else was unclear to me.

Trying a different tack, I asked, "Did you know Tom has been looking to commit his aunt? He wants to put her in an old age home so he can get his hands on her estate."

The sheriff stopped fidgeting and gave me a hard stare. "You know this for a fact?"

I nodded. "I'd say money is a pretty big motive for lying." The two of us locked eyes. Neither of us blinked.

"That's an interesting theory." He chewed the inside of his lip. "Only problem is, we got Agnes sitting in jail right now. We don't have any evidence against anyone else."

Plopping my hands on my hips, I said, "For the sake of argument, let's say Agnes did do it. How do you know she didn't have help? Someone had to tell her about Mack's thyroid condition? The clomipramine only caused him to black out because it was mixed with the thyroid medication. Normally, it would have been harmless." I smiled. "You said yourself that she's getting up in age. Do you really think she could have pulled this off on her own? Maybe you should say you're looking for additional suspects. Put pressure on anyone else that might be out there. Chances are they'll make a mistake." I hoped. At least that's what always happened on TV.

"Not a bad idea." Sheriff Jackson stroked his chin. A moment later, he nodded. "You know, it couldn't hurt to keep the case open. I don't want to stop the investigation if there's a chance we have the wrong person." He squinted at me with a puzzled expression. "You're a pretty good investigator. Funny, I thought your grandpa said you were involved with a bank or something. Did I get that wrong, too?"

Sighing, I replied, "I'm a mortgage broker." Although I no longer felt the same sense of pride admitting that.

Leaving the sheriff playing with his flowers, I headed over to Agnes's house to help ensure the town's safety. I needed to medicate Precious.

I pulled into Agnes's driveway behind a white van with the words MISSISSIPPI RIVER ANIMAL RESCUE stenciled on the side. I raced up the sidewalk and in my haste almost barreled into a middle-aged woman wearing a khaki-colored uniform and ball cap. The woman was lugging two cat carriers, each containing a loudly meowing cat.

I blocked the woman's path to the van. "Who gave you permission to take these animals?" I demanded.

She frowned at me as one cat carrier began to swing from side to side as its resident tried to escape. "The cats' owner called and asked me to come get them. He said they were more than he could handle." She adjusted her grip on the swinging carrier. "Now if you'd like to get out of my way, I can do what he asked."

The woman took a step forward, but I didn't budge. "Agnes Piraino is the owner of the house and the cats."

"Agnes Piraino is dead," the lady shot back. "Her nephew is sitting inside broken-hearted about giving these cats away, but he had no choice. The poor man's allergic."

I sucked in air. Tom Owens was about to have a real medical ailment, because my fist was about to be implanted in his mouth.

"Agnes is not dead," I informed her in a loud voice. "She happens to be away for the day. If you don't believe me, I can call the cops, and they can help us sort this out."

I flipped open my cell phone. The upside to my property being vandalized multiple times was having the Indian Falls Sheriff's Department on speed dial. The animal rescue lady set both carriers on the ground with a thud. One of the caged cats let out an angry growl. I peered inside. The pissy cat was Precious, and for once I didn't blame her for having an attitude. If you put me in a box, I'd be pissy, too.

Roxy answered on the fourth ring, and I gave her a rundown on my newest problem. Passing the phone to the catnapper, I watched as sweat appeared on her forehead. Her eyes grew wide. Finally, she closed the phone and shot an angry look toward the front door.

"How could he?" Her face turned several shades of angry. "That guy cried while talking about his aunt, and I bought it. The whole time he was just playing me."

The woman stalked toward the front door. I reached out and pulled her back. Sure, it might have been fun to watch the animal woman tear Tom limb from limb, but I kind of wanted to do it myself.

"Why don't you leave him to me," I offered with a tense smile. "I'll make sure he doesn't get away with this."

The woman took a long look at the door, then nodded. Taking a deep breath, she put down the two cat containers and handed me her card. "You might not want to let that one out of its cage right away. I'll come back and pick the carrier up later."

Good advice. I left Precious in her cage but let the other cat out. Meanwhile, the animal control lady jogged over to the back of her van. She hauled out several other carriers, and a few minutes later, six cats were bounding toward the house. By their meows I could tell they were ecstatic to be freed from kitty jail. Now all I needed to do was get Agnes out from behind her bars and life would be happy again for everyone involved.

Except Tom, I thought as I grabbed Precious's cage and walked purposefully into the house. I put Precious down in the living room and looked around. Two suitcases sat in the middle of the floor. Either Tom was bringing clothes to his aunt or he was moving in. My guess was the latter.

I strolled through the kitchen, where the pill bottle above the sink caught my eye. Precious's medication. I opened the bottle and took out one of the pills. Following a tip from Agnes, I rummaged through the fridge for some cheese. A few seconds later, a still-caged Precious was busy chewing a cheese-coated pill. I figured I'd give the pill a couple of minutes to take effect before letting the cat out to play. Precious scared me.

Once the cat was mellow, I headed back through the kitchen to the den. The place was stuffed with oversized furniture; a television in the corner blared a Chicago White Sox game. No Tom.

I flipped off the game to protect my eardrums and heard water running upstairs. Tom must be taking a shower. I hoped it was a long one, because I wanted time to snoop. There had to be a big reason Tom was pushing so hard to get his aunt incarcerated. I wanted to know what it was so I could get her sprung for good.

I backtracked into the kitchen. On the Formica table were grocery bags bursting with lots of barbecued potato chips, two jars of processed cheese dip, and three bags of cheese puffs. According to the receipt at the bottom of one of the bags, the junk food had been purchased today. That told me one thing—Tom wasn't my stalker. He would never touch tofu or wheat germ. Too bad. Having Tom arrested for assault would make my day.

Back in the living room, Precious was purring loudly, so I flipped the latch on her cage and watched the cat stroll out. When she didn't attack me, I heaved one suitcase onto the coffee table and unzipped it. Inside were dozens of T-shirts and Tom's under-wear. Cringing, I pawed around the suitcase for anything that might interest the cops.

Nothing.

I zipped that suitcase shut and moved on to the next one. The odor of stale shoes wafted out the minute I moved the zipper. Sure enough, a flip of the lid revealed two ratty pairs of Nikes. Under them were some jeans, a couple of polo shirts, and a lot of socks. I was about ready to give up when I hit upon a stack of papers.

Pay dirt. The papers were Tom's bank statements and bills, and from the looks of things Tom hadn't been a very good money manager. In fact, his bank balance made me look like Bill Gates. Now I understood why he wanted to steal Agnes blind. Tom was over his limit on every credit card.

I pocketed Tom's most recent bank statement to show Sheriff Jackson and put the rest of the papers back in the suitcase. Taking Tom's bank documentation wasn't technically legal, but neither was convincing the cops to lock up a cat-loving old lady. In my book the whole thing was a wash.

I turned back toward the kitchen and let out a scream. Tom was standing in the doorway, clad in a pair of jeans. His hair was still wet, and the weird smile he wore was directed right at me.

"What are you doing here, Rebecca?" he asked. "I didn't hear the doorbell ring."

The bank statement felt like lead in my pocket. I ignored it and frowned at Tom. "The lady from the animal rescue let me in. Turns out someone called her to take the cats away. The person told her that Agnes was dead. You wouldn't know anything about that, would you?"

I waited for Tom to look guilty. Nope. No guilt, just a smug smirk. "It's for the best. Aunt Agnes can't take care of all those cats from jail, and I don't like sharing my new house with furry little critters. I'm allergic to the things."

His running nose and red eyes made me think the guy was telling the truth. It was a better reason for Tom giving Agnes's cats the bum's rush than plain old meanness. Still . . . "It's not your house," I informed him.

"It will be once Aunt Agnes is convicted. She killed my best friend. She deserves to lose her house."

"Agnes didn't kill Mack." I insisted as something furry rubbed against my leg. I looked down, and Precious looked up at me with a purr.

Tom sneezed. He sniffled and started sneezing again. He saw the cat, and his face turned purple. Not a good look with his swollen red eyes. "What the hell is that cat doing here?"

Risking rabies, I picked up the cat and scratched her behind her ears. Precious purred louder, and I smiled up at Tom. "Lucky for me, I arrived just in time to stop animal rescue from kidnapping Precious and her furry friends. Agnes asked me to look in on them. I don't think she expected you to move in. Especially not with your allergies. You did ask her permission, right?" My eyes shifted to the two suitcases on the floor, and for the first time Tom looked concerned.

"I'm family," he said with forced bravado.

I gave him a sage nod. "Of course you are. I'm sure the cops would be interested that you moved in here, especially since you were the one who claimed she was losing her mind. Do you think they might be suspicious of your opinions, knowing how badly you want your aunt out of the way?"

Precious started to squirm, and I set her down while keeping one eye on Tom. Sweat dripped down his face, which I thought was a good sign. "Look," I said, "Agnes has put me in charge around here until she gets out of jail, which means you need to take your bags and leave." Tom's hand clenched at his side. I pulled out my phone and held it up. "If you don't, I'm going to call the cops and let them sort it out. It's up to you."

Tom grunted. His narrowing eyes met mine. A vein on his neck began to pulsate as his neck turned red. Suddenly I wished I hadn't given Precious her medication. An angry cat might come in handy if Tom got physical.

Tom sniffled and let out a loud string of sneezes, causing him to double over. When the sneezes stopped, he rubbed his eyes and said, "Fine. I'll leave. I need to get some more Benadryl anyway." He grabbed his suitcases and scowled at me. "Just make sure these cats are gone when I come back for good."

Tom kicked the screen door open and stalked out, leaving me and Precious alone in the living room. Following Agnes's instructions, I set out several bowls of dry cat food. After giving Precious a few affectionate scratches, I locked the front door, hoping that Agnes would be out of jail by the time Tom had second thoughts about abandoning his new home.

I found the sheriff still working in his yard, apparently not all that motivated to get back to the office.

He squinted at me from his perch in the dirt. "Did you forget something, Rebecca?"

"No." I crossed the lawn and thrust Tom's bank statement into his hands. "This is Tom's. It shows that he's in serious need of money."

Sheriff Jackson struggled to his feet. He wiped at his sweaty forehead with the back of his hand. "Don't tell me you broke into his house. I don't want to arrest you, too."

Knowing I wasn't on the sheriff's hit list made me smile. Shaking my head, I explained how I stopped by Agnes's to feed her cats and found Tom in residence. The minute I finished my story, the sheriff scratched his chin and grinned. "Let me talk to the county's attorney. I'll show him Tom's bank statement and let him know what you found today at the house. We'll need to get a warrant for the actual bank records so the courts will consider it. Still, this combined with the lack of substantial evidence should be enough to get Agnes released sometime tomorrow. We can always rearrest her if we find something more incriminating."

I skipped all the way to my car.

Driving down Main Street, I saw a space in front of Slaughter's Market. I took that as a cosmic sign and pulled in. I let out a sigh of relief when I saw Felix standing at the counter making the cash register buzz. Now maybe I'd get answers about the flavorless food list.

The line at the counter was six people deep. I grabbed a cart. Might as well get some shopping done while I waited. Milk, bread, apples . . . stuff that tasted good. I also paid a visit to the tofu and wheat germ sections of the store. Sadly, the psycho health food nut wasn't shopping just now. The tofu was completely stocked, as was the wheat germ. Nobody in Indian Falls was interested in those items, at least not today. Big surprise, I thought, since I didn't want to eat them, either.

The checkout counter was clear of customers when my cart and I pulled up. In no time Felix had my groceries packed, double bagged, and ready to go.

Passing over my money, I did my best to sound casual as I asked, "I noticed that you carry tofu here. Do many people actually buy that stuff in Indian Falls?"

Felix carefully counted out change. Handing it to me, he admitted, "Not many. We don't get a lot of those vegetarian types here in Indian Falls, but I try to stock vegetarian friendly things just in case. Although, I got to say I can't imagine why people actually like tofu. Have you tried the stuff?" Felix's body quivered with disgust.

"Lots of places in the city serve tofu." Felix looked at me as if I were crazy. I shrugged. "It's not too bad when you cook it right." Although I personally had never had that experience. Still, I was sure it was true. Why else would people eat squishy, flavorless white stuff?

Felix chuckled. "If my wife can make brussels sprouts taste good, I suppose anything's possible."

I stopped myself from asking for her recipe. Cooking tips wouldn't help me find the psychotic shopper. "I'd love to talk to your wife," I said truthfully. "You see, I've always wanted to start a food club."

Felix blinked twice. "A what?"

"A food club," I repeated. "It's a group that gets together every week to cook and sample different kinds of foods."

Felix's eyes brightened. "I've heard of those kinds of clubs. My wife would love it. Heck, even I think it sounds like fun, and it would be good for business."

I thought it sounded like fun, too, and someday I really was going to start one. Just not in Indian Falls. Felix and his wife would have to spearhead their own.

"I was hoping you could help me figure out whom in Indian Falls to invite," I explained. "They have to be interested in trying new things. That's why I was asking about the tofu. I figure anyone who likes tofu would be gastronomically adventurous."

Felix offered, "There are the two guys who live on the old Vanderbeek farm. Must be bankers or something, because they dress so well. Anyway, they love the stuff." He looked up at the ceiling and snapped his fingers. "There's also one woman who moved here about a year ago. She buys all sorts of unusual stuff. I think she must have come from California." He leaned forward and whispered, "You have to eat wheat germ and alfalfa sprouts to live out there."

"Could you give me their names? I'd love to talk with them about joining the club." And melting my garden gnome.

"Sure thing. The guys are Reginald and Bryan. Don't know their last names because they only come in once in a while. You probably already know the girl." I held my breath, hoping Felix didn't say Annette's name. "She works here in town. Name is Danielle Martinez."

I did a mental double take. "Danielle Martinez?"

Felix slapped the counter. "Yes sir. Danielle took over the secretarial work at St. Mark's when Beatrice retired. Rumor is Danielle and the pastor will be getting engaged any day now, which I think is a bad match. The pastor is a meat-and-potatoes kind of guy. He would never eat tofu."

Huh. A pastor's girlfriend didn't have any reason to whack Mack, not to mention vandalizing my property. Two unknown guys living on a farm seemed a long shot, too. There had to be another tofu lover in Indian Falls. "Is there anyone else you can think of who buys tofu regularly?"

A woman with an overflowing cart steered her way into the checkout line. Felix turned his attention to her while saying, "That's all I can think of for now, but I'll give you a call if I think of anyone else for your club."

Felix began bagging frozen vegetables, and I carted my groceries to my trunk—depressed. Walking in there, I thought I was on the verge of busting the case wide open. Now all I had to show for my effort was a pack of bagels, the ingredients for corn chowder, and the names of three people who ate tofu but probably didn't have anything to do with Mack's death. Of course, I could be wrong. Actually I hoped I was. That would prove my suspicions about Annette were unfounded.

I decided to pay the health food nuts a visit. I'd start with the guys, since Danielle and I didn't have the best rapport going. The woman freaked at the sight of me. That was going to make conversation difficult. Besides, the Vanderbeek farm was only two miles away from Lionel's place. It would be impolite to go all the way out there and not stop by.

Nineteen

I headed to the Vanderbeek farm in my cutest outfit—a low-cut purple top that flattered my complexion and a tulip-hemmed gray skirt that showed off my curves. A snazzy black and purple scarf completed the look. Technically the ensemble was for Lionel's benefit, but I figured it wouldn't hurt to look appealing while interrogating the tofu-loving men. If they were straight they'd admire my legs. If they were gay (and the fact they liked tofu made me think they were) they'd love my sense of style. It was a win-win situation.

The farm looked different than my childhood memories. Every Halloween, Mom brought me out here to pick out a pumpkin and cut cornstalks. Didn't look like Bryan and Reginald were growing things for October. In fact, it didn't look like they were growing anything at all. The fields were overgrown with wildflowers and weeds, but on the upside the lawns around the house were perfectly manicured. Strange way to run a farm, I thought, but what did I know?

I walked up to the baby blue farmhouse, admiring the fresh paint, and knocked on the front door. A few minutes later, the biggest man I'd ever seen appeared in the open doorway. He had dark brown skin, long dreadlocks, and a diamond twinkling from his left earlobe.

I took a step back.

The guy stepped out onto the porch to join me. "Hey," his deep voice boomed. "Can I help you?"

My throat squeaked out, "Hi, my name's Rebecca. I own the Toe Stop roller rink in Indian Falls."

The guy's mouth broke out in a wide smile. "I love that place. Bryan and I have gone there a couple of times."

This must be Reginald. Picturing the man wearing skates made me smile as I admitted, "I haven't seen you there."

Reginald looked embarrassed. "It's not easy for me and Bryan to go places around here. People don't know what to make of us." Reginald twisted the gold band on his left hand, and I knew my suspicions were right. Standing in the middle of rural Illinois was a gay married black man. Wow. Talk about a social experiment.

Briefly, I wondered what Bryan looked like. If he was anything like the guy in front of me, people would have to be nuts to get in their way. Reginald looked like he could take on the Chicago Bears—all by himself.

Curious, I asked, "Why did you guys move here?"

Reginald's broad shoulders shrugged. "We wanted to try organic farming. I was a business major, and Bryan has a degree in environmental science with a minor in agriculture. Owning a farm has been our dream. It's just been hard for people to accept us."

My heart went out to the big guy. My dream had been to move

out of Indian Falls. I never thought people dreamed about getting in.

"Sorry." Reginald tilted his head. "I'm sure you had a better reason for coming here than hearing about my problems."

Since the guy gave me a perfect opening, I said, "I was thinking about starting a gourmet club. Felix at the market said you and Bryan might be willing to join."

Reginald clapped his hands together with delight. "That would be great. I love to cook. Bryan tends to burn things, but I'm sure he'll be thrilled to join. When do we meet?"

Good question. Too bad I didn't have an answer. "Why don't you give me your phone number, and I'll call you when I find other members. You're the first people I asked."

I swear to God Reginald looked like he was going to cry. He raced into the house and returned with his phone number scribbled onto a yellow square of paper along with an exuberant smile. "This really means a lot to us."

The guy was so sincere in his gratitude. Knowing that I was lying to him made me feel like dirt.

I pocketed Reginald's number and told him, "I'll call you in a couple of days to give you an update. Oh, one other question. Do you guys go to the Lutheran church?" I figured it didn't hurt to ask, on the long shot that Reginald and Bryan were annoyed with the town and took it out on my Civic.

Reginald shook his head. "No. We don't go into town much, but maybe that will change now."

His hopeful smile followed me all the way to Lionel's place. By the time I pulled up next to Lionel's muscle truck, I'd created a potential club membership list. It wouldn't hurt to have one meeting of the club before I left town, right?

Elwood stuck his visor-clad head out of a stall and greeted me as I walked into the barn. I gave him a quick hug, and the animal took advantage of my closeness by placing a long, wet camel kiss on my cheek. The slobber was a little on the nasty side, but I smiled anyway. Things couldn't be all bad if a camel loved you.

I petted a couple of goats and scratched a pretty brown horse on my way down the aisle of the barn. Turning the corner, I ran smack into Lionel's very muscular, very sexy chest.

Lionel held me for a moment, then leaned back to get a good look at me. "Did something else happen I don't know about?"

I thought about the rink cancellations, Agnes's arrest, and my new friend Reginald. "Nothing we can't talk about later," I said, batting my eyelashes.

Lionel gave me a peck on the lips. When I tried to go back for seconds, Lionel held me at arm's length. "I hate to say this, but we're going to have company soon. I told you yesterday that we were having a game tonight. Doc, Zach, and Tom should be here in an hour or so. That leaves us with just enough time to catch up on things like Agnes's arrest."

I could tell he'd heard about my activities on behalf of the jailed librarian. Only I wasn't interested in that. I was busy doing the girl thing of mentally scrolling through yesterday's conversation. There was a lot of yelling about Anthony and freaking out over Neil, but no mention of poker. "You never told me about tonight's game."

He shrugged. "It must have slipped my mind. Well, you're here, right? No damage done."

Wrong. I was wearing a tight, slinky top with a plunging neckline. Perfect for an evening with Lionel, but there was no way I was sitting across from Tom in this outfit.

Lionel waited for me to spill my guts about Agnes. When it didn't happen he let out an exasperated sigh. "Don't tell me. This is one of those woman things about communication or something. Okay, I'm sorry for not telling you about the poker game." He gave me a smile. "Now will you tell me about Agnes? Maybe afterward you'll let me kiss you."

Lionel's hair was windblown, and his mouth was spread into a smile that made my toes curl up with anticipation. God, I wanted to give in. The Agnes/Tom story was a really good one, even if I couldn't link Tom to the health food note. Words ached to leap from my mouth, but I bit my tongue and said, "Later. I have to go home and change before the game."

"Why?"

I rolled my eyes. "I can't play poker with Tom Owens looking down my shirt." Besides, I had a few loose ends I needed to tie up before being able to concentrate on playing poker.

I climbed back in my car and made it to the rink in nine minutes flat. The lack of traffic was one thing I would miss when I went back to Chicago.

I changed into a pair of loose-fitting jeans, a modestly cut T-shirt, and a pair of red tennis shoes. I looked about as provocative as a marshmallow, and the transformation had only taken five minutes. That meant I had at least an hour before the game started.

Hopping back in my car, I tooled past Shear Highlights. The light was on, so I parked in front of the salon and knocked on the door. A frowning Annette appeared and unlocked the door.

"What are you doing here, Rebecca?"

Not the most friendly of welcomes, but I smiled anyway. "I saw the light and thought I'd ask you a few more questions about that psychiatrist you referred me to."

"I'm glad you're thinking about talking to someone. It can really help."

While she seemed genuinely pleased, she didn't invite me in. "I was surprised when you said your psychiatrist prescribed medication. What kind are you taking?"

Annette's eyes darted toward the back of the store. "You know, I can't really talk about this right now. Call me tomorrow, okay?"

Without waiting for my answer she closed the door, turned the lock, and disappeared into the salon. I stood on the sidewalk fluctuating between bursts of irritation and concern. Annette had been acting strange ever since I questioned her about the note she wrote to Mack—like she had something to hide. Annette loved all foods greasy and fattening, so I was pretty sure she wasn't Mack's killer. Still, her behavior made me wonder what secret she was protecting.

Mind whirling, I got back in the car and pulled around the block. My foot hit the brakes as I watched Danielle Martinez cross from the sidewalk through the front doors of St. Mark's Church. I glanced at the clock. Questioning Danielle would only take a few minutes. If I was late to the poker game, Lionel and the guys would just start without me. No big deal.

I parked next to the church and walked inside. The place was deserted. Clearly God wasn't as big a draw as the Cineplex on a Wednesday night. I checked out the statue. Aside from the nail in my purse, Jesus was intact. My car was safe . . . for now.

Following the discreet signs hung near the front and side doors, I entered a linoleum-tiled hallway. That led me to the church's set of offices and Danielle Martinez. She was seated behind a small reception desk, her eyes riveted on the compact in her hand. Smiling, she closed the compact. The smile disappeared and her eyes widened when she spotted me.

I gave her a smile. "Hi, Danielle. I had no idea church receptionists work so late."

Danielle's lips thinned into a single line. "I'm not actually working right now. I have a date."

I raised an eyebrow. "With Pastor Rich?" She gave me a sharp look, so I explained, "I heard from someone here in town that the two of you were dating."

"Is that a problem?" Danielle's chin rose. Her tone was defiant. Why? Did she actually think I cared who she dated? I had more important things to worry about, like staying alive.

"No problem. I was just making conversation." I walked to the side of the desk and smiled. "You know, I was at the market talking to Felix about starting a gourmet food club. He mentioned you liked health foods." Danielle's head tilted to the side as her eyes filled with a wary confusion.

I leaned forward. "You wouldn't by any chance eat wheat germ, bean sprouts, and tofu, would you?"

Danielle stood up and hastily began shoveling makeup from the desk into her purse. This woman no longer looked confused. She looked terrified. "I really should go before we're late. Richard must have lost track of time. We have reservations."

She slung her purse over her shoulder. The strap broke, sending the purse and its contents crashing to the ground. Danielle scurried to collect her makeup. In an effort to be helpful, I got on my hands and knees and rummaged under the desk. My fingers tightened around a plastic tube. Triumphant, I got to my feet, opened my hand, and stared down at a tube of lipstick.

A dim lightbulb began to flicker in the back of my brain.

"Can I have that back?" Danielle held out her hand as she shifted her weight from foot to foot.

I took a step back so Danielle couldn't take the tube of lipstick and began digging through my purse. "This color is really unique," I said. "Give me a minute to write down the name of it. I want to look for it in the store."

"Here, I'll write it down for you. Just give me my lipstick back." Danielle reached for a notepad on her desk as my fingers found the item I'd been looking for. I pulled a lipstick-coated paper napkin out of my purse, and surprise—Danielle's lipstick was a perfect match.

Twenty

"You know, Danielle"—I set the tube of lipstick on the desk—"I don't want this lipstick after all. The color isn't right for me. It wasn't right for the rink's front door, either."

All color drained out of Danielle's face. Unlikely as it seemed, my verbal thrust scored a direct hit. Danielle, the pastor's girlfriend, had scribbled on the rink's front door. She was the maniac I was looking for. That also meant she was Mack's killer.

Only now that I'd found her, I didn't know what to do with her. The woman was whacked. For all I knew she had a knife or a gun stashed somewhere. I took a step backward as Danielle's hand moved toward a letter opener lying on her desk. For once, calling Deputy Sean sounded like a good idea.

Slowly, my hand reached into my purse. I pulled out the phone and began pressing buttons.

"Who are you calling?"

I looked up at the sound of Danielle's trembling voice. She looked scared. Pissed off, I'd understand—but scared? Something didn't feel right. My finger paused over the last number. "The sheriff," I answered her.

Danielle sank into her chair as tears welled up in her dark brown eyes. She shot a look toward the pastor's office door. Whispering, she begged, "Please don't call the sheriff. Calling the cops will ruin my life."

Sounded fair to me. Keeping Danielle's life on track wasn't high on my priority list. I shook my head. "Sorry, but you've been busy destroying mine for the past two weeks, not to mention the fact that you killed Mack Murphy. I'd say your concern for other people's lives is flexible at best."

"Mack Murphy?" Danielle blinked, and her head cocked to one side. "What are you talking about?"

"What do you mean what am I talking about?" I demanded. "You killed Mack."

"No, I didn't," she said, shrinking back in her chair. "I liked Mack. Why would I kill him?"

Good question. Too bad I didn't have an answer. I studied Danielle carefully. She didn't look like she was lying. She also didn't look like a person who'd set fire to an innocent scarecrow, but her reaction to the revealing lipstick said she had. She had to be the person who killed Mack; otherwise, why would she have bothered trying to scare me into leaving town? None of this made sense.

I clutched my phone. "You killed him for the same reason you've been terrorizing me—you're nuts."

Danielle's eyes met mine, and tears leaked down her face. "I'm sorry I did those things to you, but I didn't kill Mack. I swear."

My heart sank. I believed her. The woman looked scared and unhappy. She didn't look like she was plotting how to off me.

I lowered the phone. "Why did you threaten me and flatten my tire? What did I ever do to you?"

"Nothing, yet," she sniffled, "but it was only a matter of time. You'd tell someone in town that you knew me, and then my life would be ruined. I had no choice. I had to scare you into leaving town. It was the only way."

I took a long look at Danielle. She seemed to think I knew something incriminating about her, but I didn't. I didn't know her, period. The woman really needed to get a grip. "Danielle," I said, "I don't know you."

Disbelief sparkled in her eyes, and her body began to tremble. "I did it all for nothing? I thought you recognized me from a Christmas party I worked. It was two years ago, but I remember you. You were there."

I mentally rewound my life. Two years ago Neil threw a Christmas party. The guest list included everyone he'd ever met, including the entire office staff. That night Jasmine's date consumed too much holiday cheer. In his liquor-induced haze, he decided I was a Christmas present. Before he got too forceful about unwrapping me, the entertainment arrived. The creep's attention was diverted when he spotted the sexy Ms. Claus and her elflike girls that Neil had hired to take pictures, sing songs, and jingle their bells. After that all I remembered was doing my best to keep Jasmine from clawing her soon-to-be-ex's eyes out as he ogled the entertainment. I had no clue how Danielle fit into the whole mess, but apparently she did.

Wait. Maybe it was the tilt of her head or the fall of her hair, but suddenly I remembered. Danielle Martinez, Lutheran church receptionist and Pastor Rich's girlfriend, was a stripper.

Holy shit, I thought. "You were Ms. Claus."

"You really didn't remember me?"

"Not until just now."

"Figures." Danielle gave a dejected shrug. "I was certain you'd remember since you were right up front with your friend."

"I wasn't really paying attention to you. No offense."

"I wish more people had your ability to forget. Not long after the party, I got my degree and gave it up. I hoped to meet a nice guy and have a couple of kids, but strippers don't have those kinds of lives, at least not where people know them. So last year I moved here."

"Then you started dating Pastor Rich." I was beginning to understand her motives even if I didn't agree with her method.

"I couldn't believe it when I saw you driving around town. I knew I had to get you to leave before my life was ruined." Danielle wiped at her eyes. "So I tried to scare you into leaving, but you wouldn't go away."

"Trust me, I wanted to."

She sniffled. "Really?"

"Really." I must've been the only person on earth who would find it necessary to bolster the ego of my would-be stalker. Funny, but I could actually forgive Danielle's antics now that I knew her reasons. There was only one thing that still bothered me. "Danielle, did you mean to hurt Neil?"

Her eyes welled up again. "I didn't plan to. Someone told me you moved into the rink, so I decided to see if it was true. Only he opened the door. I remembered him from the Christmas party. He wanted way more than just a dance. When I saw him standing there I freaked. I didn't even think. I just hit him with my flashlight.

Once he was on the floor I didn't know what else to do, so I tied him up."

I couldn't fault Danielle for her instincts. Neil could come on a little strong. More than once I myself had had the urge to crack him over the head. In a strange way, Danielle did me a favor. Maybe the woman wasn't so bad after all.

Danielle wiped her eyes with a tissue and gave me a watery smile. "Don't worry about calling the cops. I'll turn myself in. I deserve to go to jail for everything I've done."

"No, you don't," I said firmly. Okay, I know that after all the problems Danielle had caused, she really should be in jail, but I didn't want to be the one to send her there. Danielle came to Indian Falls to turn her life around, and she had until I showed up. Besides, I thought, no permanent damage was done. I was fine. Pop was fine. Neil had a bump, but he'd be back to normal in no time. Well, as close as he could get. The world wouldn't be a safer place with Danielle locked up.

"Look," I said, "maybe we can work something out."

Danielle's tears stopped. Her mouth turned up in a tentative smile. "Why? I tried to destroy your life."

"Well, you didn't," I said. "Besides, we have something in common."

"Like what?"

I started to explain about my experiences with Neil and stopped. That conversation needed more time than we had right now. I said, "Why don't we get together sometime for coffee and talk about it?"

I left a smiling Danielle convinced I'd made the right choice about calling the cops. With Mack's killer still at large, what was one more crazy person loose on the streets of Indian Falls?

. . .

I parked in Lionel's driveway next to a row of cars. The gang was here and ready to play poker. I strolled toward the barn, and Elwood trotted with me through the dimly lit building to the back room.

Doc Truman spotted me and smiled, causing Lionel to turn and cross the room toward me. Before I could say hello, Lionel's mouth was on mine. I scooted back out of Lionel's embrace with an apologetic smile. Having three other guys in the room and a camel behind me made me feel funny about the public display.

"Feeling frisky?" I asked Lionel.

"I missed you." He grinned. "You were gone a long time."

I smiled up at Lionel. "Sorry for the wait, but I had a couple of stops to make." I glanced over to the table, where the guys were waiting for the game to start. Doc and Zach were chatting. Tom was glowering—at Lionel.

I asked, "Did something happen while I was gone?"

"Not much." Lionel leaned close. I gave him a stern look, and he admitted, "Tom and I had a few words about having his aunt locked up. Everyone knows Agnes couldn't hurt a fly."

"I don't like you sticking your nose in my business," Tom blustered from his seat next to Doc. I couldn't help feeling a stab of satisfaction when I realized his eyes were watering and still a little puffy. Way to go, Precious!

Lionel ignored Tom's surliness. "Let's play poker." He took his seat at the poker table while I took mine, bewildered by the lack of conflict resolution. Tom shuffled the cards. Lionel passed him some chips. I thought the whole thing said worlds about the male psyche.

Two hours later, I'd played very few hands. I wasn't in the mood for cards. My mind was on other things. I hoped Agnes was sprung by now, and I was thrilled to know my grandfather's lawn ornaments were safe from Danielle. Too bad I didn't know who killed Mack. Plus I couldn't get past Annette's strange behavior. It haunted me.

Trying to think about something else, I asked Doc, "How's Neil doing?"

Doc folded with a harrumph. He finished off his beer and popped the top on another. "Checked on him just before I came over here. Don't worry, Rebecca, the boy's doing just fine." The last was said with a dazed kind of smile. Chugging beers had done a number on Doc's head.

I folded my hand as Lionel took another pot. "Is he still being held for observation?" I asked Doc with a quizzical smile.

"Nope." Doc gave a drunken shrug. "Neil planned on heading out of town as soon as he could. He said that no woman's worth risking his life over." Doc winked and swayed in his chair. "Guess he was talking about you, although I don't agree with him. I'm pretty sure Lionel doesn't either, since the whole town is talking about the two of you. Eleanor's running a pool about when you'll be getting engaged." He leaned close. "I took the first two weeks of September."

"Really?" I looked at Lionel, who was staring intently at his cards. Clearly, Doc's comment hadn't bothered him, but it bothered me.

Not that I wasn't fond of Lionel. I was. He was sexy, sweet, and smart. I'd have to be dead not to feel something for him, but we weren't serious. Lionel knew that. Right?

Doc sucked down the rest of his beer. "I told Neil he should stick around. I thought he'd want to catch the person who walloped him, but he said no. Can you believe that?"

I shrugged. No Neil meant one less problem to deal with. "Maybe this is for the best," I said. "Now all the sheriff's resources will be focused on finding Mack's murderer." I raised an eyebrow in Tom's direction. "His real murderer."

Tom's head swung in my direction. His eyes narrowed. "Aunt Agnes is sitting behind bars. Did you forget?"

"No," I shot back, "but the sheriff decided to release your aunt. I guess senility wasn't a good enough motive for murder."

I leaned my elbows on the table and stared straight into Tom's eyes. "The sheriff is not real happy about you turning on your aunt and then moving into her house. You might want to watch your step." Acting bitchy lifted my spirits. Suspecting Annette was a murderess had made me edgy.

Tom didn't appreciate my cathartic release. He shot out of his seat, sending his chair crashing to the ground behind him. "What the hell does that mean?" he yelled.

My heart jumped as Tom's face turned a deep shade of magenta. I watched with a combination of fascination and fear as his hands balled into tight fists. "Tell me what you meant by that." The threat in his voice was unmistakable. I shrank back in my chair, hoping Tom wouldn't leap across the table. The self-defense class I took a year ago didn't give pointers on how to outmaneuver a pissed-off drunk.

Tom kicked his chair out of the way and started to stalk around the table. Lionel stood up and blocked his path. "I think we've all had enough for one night. Why doesn't everyone pack it in and head home?"

Tom looked like he wanted to complain, but Zach cut him off.

"I need to get to work early tomorrow anyway. Come on, Tom. I'll drop you at home." A still red-faced Tom followed Zach out the door. As they disappeared around the corner, Doc began singing a rousing rendition of "He's a Jolly Good Fellow." Doc was wasted.

Lionel waited for the men's footsteps to disappear before saying, "You shouldn't push Tom. He's got a mean streak. You don't want to mess with him."

I'd already figured that one out for myself. "Why are you friends with him?" I asked.

"Mack introduced him to all of us. He was the one who asked Tom to join the game. Guess it's time to uninvite him—which will thrill Zach. He hates the guy."

"Really?"

"He was Mack's best friend until Tom showed up. The first couple of poker games we had a few tense moments, then things settled down." He gave me one of his toe-curling smiles. "Until you came along."

Lionel's fingers massaged the back of my neck. I leaned into his touch as my neck muscles relaxed. The rest of my body started tingling. I contemplated what those fingers could do if we were alone. If nothing else, he'd make me forget about the icky feelings I'd had since visiting Annette.

I smiled at him, and his mouth crushed against mine. My lower abdominal muscles clenched as his tongue slipped between my teeth and did a little dance. When his fingers skimmed under my waistband, I felt tiny explosions in the pit of my stomach. Then they headed southward.

A loud voice bellowed, "Happy birthday!" in my ear. We broke apart and looked over to see Doc tilting dangerously to one side. Meanwhile he was happily singing birthday tidings to himself.

"Is it Doc's birthday?" I asked Lionel.

He shook his head and sat down. "His wife throws him a birthday party every year. It's in October."

For some reason this struck me as funny. I started to laugh. Maybe I could order a Louise-style scarecrow for Doc's birthday. That thought made me laugh even harder.

Doc must have taken my amusement as applause. He started the song again, this time dedicating it to Lionel. When he got to the end he flung out his arms and bowed, which promptly sent his body careening forward right into Lionel's fully aroused lap.

Lionel looked down at Doc, and a smile twitched at his lips. "I'd better drive Doc home. He's in no shape to do it himself. I'd let him sleep it off here, but his wife will come looking for him if he isn't home by twelve." Lionel helped Doc struggle to his feet and glanced over his shoulder at me. "Wait here. We have unfinished business."

I nodded, and Lionel disappeared through the door, half carrying an intoxicated Doc. I took a seat on the couch because Lionel was right, we did have unfinished business. Only my brain couldn't concentrate on it right now. My mind kept returning to Annette. Thinking that Annette might have had something to do with Mack's death was driving me nuts. As much as I wanted to stay and wait for Lionel, I needed to go see Annette and demand some answers. Lionel would understand.

I hurried down the hall into the main barn area. A sheep bleated from a stall. Hay crunched under my feet as I crossed to the front door.

The sound of a car pulling up the driveway made me quicken

my step. Lionel had gotten Doc home faster than I'd expected. I needed to get out of the barn before he could corner me in a stall and make me forget my investigation.

I was four steps from the entrance when I heard the sound of footsteps coming toward the barn. A figure filled the doorway, and I smiled. The person smiled back and leveled a gun right at my face.

Twenty-one

Tom Owens's face glared at me from behind the gun barrel.

The minute I saw the gun my mind shut down. "What are you doing with a gun?" I asked stupidly.

Tom's smile widened. "I brought it for you. Don't you like it?"

No. Not especially. In fact I was pretty certain I hated it, but I couldn't be sure. My body had gone numb.

Tom took a step into the barn and extended the gun toward my nose. His eyes narrowed into two angry slits. "You've caused me a lot of trouble. Everything would have been fine if you hadn't come to town."

I blinked. Except for evicting him today, I hadn't done anything to him. Could he be holding a grudge about that first poker game?

"I'm sorry?" I said, hoping it was what he wanted to hear.

It wasn't. Tom's nostrils flared as he tightened his grip on the gun. "You'd better be," he shouted. "If it weren't for you, Mack's death would have remained unsolved, and the sheriff would never have connected those pills with me." His mouth twisted into a sneer. "You should have left Mack's death alone. Then none of this would be happening."

Holy shit! "You killed Mack," I said, gaping at Tom.

"Don't pretend you're surprised," he screamed. The gun waved hypnotically in front of my eyes. "I knew what you were up to tonight. I knew the minute you told everyone the sheriff was re-leasing Aunt Agnes. You were taunting me, Rebecca, playing cat and mouse. Well, we're done playing. You missed your chance to expose me, and I won't give you another one."

Tom steadied the gun, and with his left hand he gave me a tiny, farewell wave. I searched my brain for something to say, anything that would stop Tom's itchy trigger finger. The best I could come up with was "You can't kill me yet."

Yet? Why did I say yet? Tom must have wondered the same thing, because he lowered the gun a few inches and asked, "Why not?"

"You have to tell me why you did it," I said, grasping at straws. "I know you're having financial problems. What I don't know is why you had to kill Mack. I thought he was your best friend."

"He was," Tom bellowed, the gun swinging wildly to the left before it settled back on me. "Don't you understand? Mack wasn't supposed to die. The pills were only supposed to make him dizzy. How was I supposed to know that he'd fall into a toilet and drown? Who does that?"

In the dim light I thought I saw tears glistening in Tom's eyes. A guy that cried over killing his friend might be talked out of killing an innocent woman. In the movies a talking villain got distracted. Sometimes he even forgot about shooting his victim. Real life was different, but Tom didn't strike me as a multitasker. I just needed to keep him talking long enough to come up with a better plan or until Lionel showed up.

I asked, "Why did you do it, Tom? Why give Mack drugs if you didn't intend to kill him?"

Tom gave me a "boy, are you dense" look and lowered the gun an inch. "Don't you understand? I wanted to make it look like my aunt drugged Mack. The whole town knew she didn't like him. The cat took those pills. It was perfect. I was going to have her committed so I could get her bank account and the house. I couldn't wait for the old lady to kick the bucket. Mack understood. He knew I needed the money now."

A lightbulb in my brain clicked on as the phone number in Mack's CD case made sense. Mack wasn't looking for an investment company. He was checking in on his friend Tom. "You made some bad investments?" I guessed.

The gun lowered another inch. Tom nodded and started to pace. "The guy said these investments would pay off big. The first one did, so I sank more money in. I wanted to earn enough money to stop teaching." Tom's hand began to shake. I prayed the gun wouldn't go off in a moment of hysteria. That would be depressing.

"You don't like teaching?" I asked, my eyes following the gun in Tom's zigzagging hand.

"I hate it." Tom raked his free hand through his hair. He took a deep breath and let out a loud burst of air. "Have you ever taught high school kids? Well, it sucks. The kids don't give you any respect. The football part is good, but it isn't enough to make me want to do it for the rest of my life. My broker said I'd make enough money to ditch my job. I don't know what went wrong. All of a sudden he called and told me I owed him money. A lot of money."

Tom must never have heard the expression "If it sounds too good to be true, it probably is." Since he had a gun, I wasn't about to educate him. "Why didn't you just ask your aunt for a loan?" I remembered the nine thousand dollars under Mack's mattress and added, "Or Mack. One of them could have helped you."

"My aunt hates me, and Mack tried to get me some fast cash. He took a lot of jobs and offered me the deposits, but he couldn't get his hands on the kind of money I needed. There was only one option."

"To drug Mack and hope your aunt got committed. Only Mack died."

Tom nodded. He used the back of his gun hand to wipe his runny nose. "Mack promised to help me make my aunt look unstable. I got him the job next door to Aunt Agnes. He purposely picked on her cats and reported her responses to the cops. Only Mack got uncomfortable with the whole thing and tried to pull out of our deal. He said he'd find another way to get the cash." Tom squeezed his eyes tight, and I took a tentative step toward the door. Hay crunched under my heel. Tom's eyes snapped open, and the gun swung back toward me. "Where do you think you're going?"

My body went completely still. "Nowhere," I answered, although Tahiti sounded like a good idea. Anywhere I didn't feel this cold, numbing fear sounded good. Trying to keep the terror out of my voice, I prompted, "So Mack didn't know you slipped him Precious's drugs?"

"No. He would never have taken the pills. He only took the

ones Doc gave him because he had to," Tom grumbled. "The pills were supposed to make Mack sick. He wasn't supposed to drown. The cops would've suspected my aunt. Once she was out of the way, I was going to pay off my debts and start fresh. I never wanted to kill Mack. If he hadn't backed out of helping me, I wouldn't have had to drug him, and none of this would have happened. He would have been playing poker tonight. Instead . . ." Tom raised the gun. My stomach lurched and I sucked air as the thing pointed right between my eyes. "I had to sit across from you."

My heart pounded. There were no more questions to ask. Tom's face was stone cold. Conversation was over. My mouth went dry as fear raced through my body. My stomach clenched and unclenched. This was it. Lionel wasn't coming back in time to save me. He was going to find me dead, never knowing how much I really liked him.

And poor Pop. He'd have a heart attack after hearing I'd been shot here in Indian Falls. Chicago wouldn't have surprised him. Come to think of it, getting shot there wouldn't have surprised me either. I guess that said something about my choice of residence. If I survived this I'd have to rethink that. I'd probably rethink the Lionel thing, too. Right now, the thought of avoiding a relationship with a wonderful guy seemed really stupid.

Tom's finger twitched on the trigger. Hay shuffled somewhere nearby, causing Tom to glance to the side. His eyes grew wide as his gun swung widely to the right. My eyes followed the movement in time to see Elwood and his poker visor barreling out of his barn stall. Right at Tom.

I felt like someone switched everything to slow motion. Elwood charged toward Tom. Tom's mouth dropped in surprise.

The whole thing would have been funny if I hadn't been para-lyzed by terror. Elwood galloped closer, and Tom's finger squeezed the trigger.

"No!" The horrified scream flew from my mouth as Elwood stumbled, let out a hair-raising whine, and slumped down to the ground. Tom had killed Elwood.

Seeing Elwood shot made something snap inside me. I launched myself at Tom. My tackle caught him off guard, and we both tumbled hard to the ground. The gun flew out of Tom's hand. We both turned our heads and watched it slide across the barn's hay-covered cement floor and come to rest about ten feet away from us.

I scrambled over Tom's body toward his gun. His strong fin-gers dug into my ankle, and I felt him pulling me backward. I reached out my hand and urged my body forward. My fingers brushed the handle. A wave of triumph swept through my entire body as my hand closed around cool metal. Then Tom's foot made contact with my knee. A crunching sound echoed in the barn as a blinding pain traveled up my leg. I bit my lip. Tears stung behind my eyes. Steeling myself, I flipped over and aimed. Tom blinked. Now I was the one with the gun, and it was pointed right at him.

Tom scrambled to his feet. "There's no way you're going to shoot me," he said, looming above. I tightened my grip on the gun. The pain in my knee was bad. I wasn't going to win any races on my leg.

I glanced over at Elwood. He was lying on the ground, not moving. Tears blurred my vision. Elwood had saved my life. He couldn't die. I wanted both of us to live.

"Come on, Rebecca." Tom's deep voice taunted, and I looked away from the lifeless camel. Tom took another step closer. "We both know you don't have the killer instinct. You saved my aunt's crazy cats, so there's no way you'll kill me in cold blood. We both know it. It's time to put down the gun before you do something you'll regret." Tom held out his hand and waited for me to hand him the gun.

Right, I thought. Even I wasn't that stupid. Sure, I wasn't bright enough to figure out who killed Mack without being held at gunpoint, but I wasn't dumb enough to drop the gun. Problem was, Tom was probably right about my ability to pull the trigger.

Tom took another step toward me. I leaned backward to get a better angle, all the while praying I didn't have to shoot him. I didn't want to kill anyone, not even a cat-stealing, camel-shooting creep like Tom.

"Come on, Rebecca." He took another step, and my pulse hit the accelerator. The gun began to shake in my hands. Seeing that made Tom smile. "See. You're more afraid of that gun than of me. Why don't you put the gun away and end all this right now?"

He was almost on top of me. I willed my finger to press the trigger, but I couldn't. Tom leaned down. Out of the corner of my eye I noticed Elwood's eyes open, and my heart exploded with joy. Elwood was alive. He wasn't dead. My eyes narrowed at Tom. Elwood had saved me; now it was my job to defend us both. A flood of adrenaline coursed through my body as I leaned back on my elbows and took aim.

Direct hit.

My foot connected with its intended target. Tom's eyes rolled back into his head. His hand cupped his privates, and he crumpled to the ground mewing in pain. I kicked him again, feeling a jolt of satisfaction as I watched him roll face-first into the hay.

Pocketing the gun, I pushed myself to my feet, and my knee

burst into white-hot agony. I saw stars and grabbed a barn stall for support.

"What the hell is going on in here?"

I spun toward the angry voice, and relief flooded through me. Lionel was standing in the barn doorway, his eyes shifting from a moaning Tom to a crippled Elwood. He then looked at me. I actually smiled as my knee started to give way. "Tom killed Mack, and he tried to kill me. Could you please tie him up?" I asked. "I'd do it myself, but I think I'm going to faint."

Twenty-two

My knee still hurt two days after my brush with Tom the maniac. According to Doc Truman, Tom dislocated it. Doc put a brace on it, then sent me home with a large bottle of codeine and a prescription for rest. The codeine I took. The rest lasted for twenty-four hours. Then I got bored and started planning two dinner parties, one for tonight to talk about Mack. Tomorrow, the Indian Falls Gourmet Club would meet for the first time. Reginald was so excited he'd already called to confirm the time, twice.

I uncorked a bottle of wine while waiting for my friends to arrive. Indian Falls was buzzing with the news about the killer high school football coach. My answering machine was filled with inquiries for gossip, none of which I'd answered. I didn't have all the answers yet. Tonight, I hoped, my friends could tie up the loose end that had been bothering me. Turns out I don't like loose ends.

The first to arrive was my grandfather. He didn't wait for me to let him in but instead sauntered inside, holding a bottle of tequila in one hand and Marjorie Buckingham's hand in the other. Marjorie was wearing a triumphant smile as she clung to my grandfather. Her expression reminded me of an Academy Award winner. I guess to a female senior citizen of Indian Falls, dating Pop was akin to winning an Oscar. This was why I wanted to die young. Pop would make a great game show host, but the idea of dating a guy like him made me queasy.

Marjorie took a seat on the couch while Pop walked with me into the kitchen. He put the bottle of tequila on the counter with a clank.

"What's with the tequila?" I asked my grandfather. Tonight Pop was decked out in a big-collared white satin shirt and shiny black pants. A purple scarf completed the outfit. Elvis was in the building.

Pop grinned with a full set of teeth. "Marjorie said all entertainers have to have a signature drink. Dean Martin always had a martini, which is why he was so popular. You got to have a gimmick."

The doorbell rang, saving me from coming up with a reply. Lionel, Zach, and Doc Truman had arrived. I put out some cheese and crackers while Pop handed out beers and wine. He then poured a glass of tequila for himself and stared warily at it as everyone settled into chairs.

While my guests chatted, I pulled Lionel into the kitchen. "How's Elwood doing?" I asked, then held my breath for the answer. The bullet hadn't hit any major organs, but Elwood had lost a lot of blood. Lionel had removed the bullet from the camel's right shoulder and stitched him up. Ever since then we'd been waiting for Elwood to improve.

Lionel's smile made me feel like dancing. "Turns out Elwood's going to be just fine," he said. "He won't be giving any rides for a while, but give him a few weeks and he'll be good as new."

Lionel ruffled my hair and planted a quick kiss on my lips. Between my knee, Elwood's gunshot wound, and interviews with the cops, we hadn't spent much time together. Now that the danger was over, I wasn't sure what I would do when we got the chance. I'd think about that tomorrow, I decided.

The doorbell rang again, announcing the final two guests, Annette and Agnes Piraino. Agnes was smiling and carrying a Bundt cake. She helped herself to a shot of tequila and took a seat next to Pop, who hadn't touched his drink. Maybe he wasn't so set on the entertainment field after all.

Grabbing two glasses of wine, I passed one to Annette and said loudly, "After what happened, I wanted to say thank you. You all helped put Mack's murderer behind bars where the jerk belongs." I caught Agnes looking down into her glass and quickly added, "Sorry, Agnes."

She waved off my concern. "Don't be. He deserves to be in jail, but I don't understand why he didn't come to me with his problems. I had no idea he needed money that badly. Sure, he didn't get along with me and my cats, but he's family. I would have helped him because that's what you do for family."

Agnes took a sip of her tequila while Pop patted her on the arm.

"Don't feel bad, Agnes." Doc leaned forward in his chair. "I stopped by the sheriff's office before coming over here. Turns out, Tom owes more money than you could have given him. The sheriff said your nephew wasn't going to pay off his debt with your money anyway. He was going to sell your house and start a new life in Mexico. They searched his apartment and found a plane ticket to Cancún along with some of your jewelry."

We all contemplated Tom's deceit while a wide-eyed Agnes threw back the rest of her drink and looked around for more. Pop handed her his. She downed that without blinking, and Pop headed to the kitchen for the bottle. Tom was definitely a schmuck. Too bad for Agnes.

"Doc?" I asked, scratching my head. "Did the cops find any money in Tom's stuff?" Like nine thousand dollars?

Doc shook his head. "Not that I heard, but they did look into how Tom purchased the plane ticket. He used Agnes's credit card."

"Then who stole the nine thousand dollars?" I asked. Everyone turned and looked at me with various degrees of shock. I explained, "I searched Mack's house before the cops did. He had nine thousand dollars in his mattress, but when the cops arrived the money was gone."

"It was me."

Every head swung toward the corner of the room where Zach stood with his head bowed.

"You?" I blurted. That made no sense. Mack was Zach's friend. There was no way Zach would steal Mack's money. "I don't believe it."

"It really was me," Zach said. "I knew where Mack hid his money. When he died, I took it. He had no one who cared about giving him a good funeral, and I didn't have the money to do it myself. Mack's money was the only answer."

The pieces clicked. "You bought the headstone." Zach nodded. "And paid for lunch at the diner?" Another nod. I cocked my head to one side. With a soft smile I said, "Mack was lucky to have you as his friend."

Zach blushed, and everyone began talking. I took the opportunity to pull Annette to the side.

"Okay," I said. "You've been acting really weird, and I want you to tell me the truth. What was really up with you and Mack? Why did you threaten him?"

It was Annette's turn to blush. She glanced around the room to make sure no one was listening and whispered, "Mack and I slept together. Once, before he ripped me and half the town off. I didn't want anyone to know."

"But why were you trying to get me to leave town? I thought you wanted to get rid of me."

Annette sighed. "Never, honey. I just want you to live your own life. I'd love to have you stay here, but it has to be your choice. Not your grandfather's or your mother's or even mine. Otherwise you'll never be happy."

My eyes grew misty, and my throat tightened. I tried to respond, but nothing came out. For the first time, surrounded in this room by friends and family, I felt welcomed in my hometown. More than that, I felt wanted. It was a feeling I couldn't put into words.

The timer sounding on the oven rescued me from the emotional moment, and I directed everyone into the dining room before heading off for the kitchen. Opening the oven door, I bent over to retrieve the lasagna. As I stood up, a masculine body cozied up behind me.

I smiled at Lionel.

He didn't smile back. "Well, Rebecca," he said while watching me set the pan down. "You've solved Mack's murder. Does that mean you're leaving town soon?"

The heat of the kitchen combined with Lionel's presence made my neck start to sweat. I didn't know what to say. Doreen had already called to say she'd put the rink back on the market. Funny, but the announcement hadn't made me feel deliriously happy. My brush with death must have left me in shock.

Lionel leaned forward and pressed a soft, heart-stopping kiss to my lips. His eyes met mine as his hand brushed my waist.

A horribly off-key rendition of "Teddy Bear" from the dining room made us both jump, and I began to giggle. A moment later, several other voices joined Pop's, and Lionel shook his head even as he started to chuckle.

Still smiling, he asked, "Are you going to give me an answer before we go in there, or do I have to wait until later?"

I looked into Lionel's green eyes as the sounds of my friends' laughter echoed through the apartment. The combination of the two made my life in the city seem very far away.

Shaking away the uncomfortable feelings, I grabbed the lasagna pan and headed for the dining room. "I'm staying here at least until the rink sells."

After all, I thought, how long could selling one rink possibly take?